Limited

Partnerships

A NOVEL BY

Lisa Zeidner

This is a special advance reading copy of a novel to be published in hardcover by North Point Press.

Since this was prepared using uncorrected page-proof copy, please check any quotations or attributions against the bound copy of this book. We urge this for the sake of editorial accuracy as well as for your legal protection and ours.

North Point Press
850 Talbot Avenue
Berkeley, California 94706
(415) 527-6260

For publicity information on this title, please contact:
Lisa Levine, (415) 527-6260.

North Point books are distributed to the trade by
Farrar, Straus & Giroux.

Lyrics from "Nice Work If You Can Get It," by
George and Ira Gershwin, © 1937 Chappell &
Co. (renewed), all rights reserved. Used by
permission.

The author would like to thank the Rutgers
University Research Council for its assistance.
Thanks as well to Ross Feld, Denise Gess, and
Susan Going Willhouse.

Author's note: This is a work of fiction. The
characters are invented. Any unfaithful lover,
corrupt bureaucrat, tax evader, or drug dealer,
living or dead, who thinks he recognizes himself herein should know that the resemblance
is *purely coincidental* and try not to take it too
personally. All of us, alas, are types.

For John

Also by Lisa Zeidner

NOVELS
Customs
Alexandra Freed

NOVELS
Talking Cure
Pocket Sundial

The man who only lives for making money
Lives a life that isn't necessarily sunny.
Likewise the man who works for fame;
There's no guarantee that time won't erase his name.
The fact is, the only work that really brings enjoyment
Is the kind that is for girl-and-boyment,
Fall in love, you won't regret it,
That's the best work of all if you can get it.
Ira Gershwin, "Nice Work If You Can Get It"

Liberty is always threatened by those who do not
own property.   Thomas Jefferson

Limited

Partnerships

One

MALCOLM DEWITT LIVED exactly two miles from the house where he grew up. His great-grandparents bought the house with cash in 1886, and it had been downhill for the DeWitts ever since. A century later, Malcolm wasn't treading water so much as frantically dog-paddling. The upward spiral of his fortune was supposed to begin with a client named Benjamin Stone, but now Stone was going to jail.

1

The first time Malcolm got a ride in Stone's chauffeured black Jaguar, he had asked for a tour of all the car toys: bar, phone, compact disc player, videocassette recorder. The design of the backseat console was tight as a Swiss army knife. One button brought forth a writing desk in bird's-eye maple. Another button controlled a television that Stone had commissioned from an electronics firm in Japan. When not in use, the television screen was flush against the console; but the push of a button levered out a thin screen on a swiveling arm, so you could relax and watch a movie from any angle you chose. This slick bit of engineering had clearly required some thought, and at the time, Malcolm was impressed.

Malcolm was slow-talking, slow-moving, tall and lean, with the kind of explosive temper that gentle men often have. He had played center in high school basketball and, though half a foot shorter than most of the other players, had been known for ruthless elbows.

Stone, short and fleshy, walked fast and talked fast. He asked a lot of questions. As you answered he fixed his dark, hypnotic, pulsing eyes on you—he made you feel like you were hiding something. The energy level, Malcolm later discovered, was not entirely a natural high.

Malcolm and Stone were not a promising match, but then who would work happily with Stone? A jury of the deaf, blind, and brain-dead could have fingered Stone as trouble. At least he's not cheap, Malcolm had thought. A rich man who appreciates quality is not the worst possible boss. Besides, it was Malcolm's experience that *all* rich people were crazy.

Not that Malcolm had had much choice when it came to designing Stone's new company office in downtown Philadelphia. No designer refuses the renovation of a big old brownstone as wonderful as this one—especially not an unemployed designer. So Malcolm hadn't mentioned third-world children when Stone said he wanted a wine cellar, library, screening room, and gym in his office, even though he already had all these things at home. According to Malcolm's college friend Lucy (who was Stone's assistant and had recommended Malcolm for the job), Stone paid someone to come to his house once a week to press his underwear (French linen). Although Stone was married and had teen-age children, his sexual tastes were known to be not predominantly heterosexual; he'd need a second, private sauna. If you can afford two of everything without spending any money, not a cent of actual cash, your entire empire built on imaginary assets, then you're not crazy at all—at least not until the FBI catches you.

When Malcolm showed up at Stone's office a couple of minutes late, breathless and laden with plans, he found Lucy waiting on the steps to tell him everything she had been able to piece together—the FBI men wouldn't let her inside.

Stone's company was completing a high rise in Florida. The Florida bank that held the construction loan had called to confirm some detail about Stone's assets at his local brokerage house. They must not have liked what they found out, because by the end of the day the Florida bank had declared the construction loan due, and Stone's lawyer had resigned. By Monday, when Lucy and Malcolm showed up for work, the FBI men, black-suited and grim as undertakers, were already confiscating Stone's records for the grand jury investigation.

The FBI had frozen Stone's assets. No one would get paid until everything was straightened out, which would be months—if Stone didn't go bankrupt first, in which case no one would get paid at all.

The minute Malcolm heard that, he couldn't do anything but laugh.

Malcolm DeWitt had a finely honed sense of absurdity, and that was good, because it was clear to him that his whole life was a joke. If there was a god, He had clearly chosen Malcolm to chase around the ant farm with a twig.

Malcolm's first job was as a social worker for the city's Youth Conservation Field Operations. From 1969 to 1971 Malcolm counseled delinquents from housing projects who raped seventh-graders and knifed clerks in grocery stores. This period challenged his knee-jerk liberalism and started him on a career as an experimental filmmaker. If his films were bleak and humorless, Malcolm said, it was partly the fault of having been a social worker and partly the fault of the Vietnam War.

Malcolm blamed a great deal on the Vietnam War, having drawn twenty-one as his lottery number after his college graduation ("the only thing I ever won," he liked to say—"a free trip to Saigon") and gotten an exemption when he actually convinced the draft board that he was insane. This was not an easy thing to do by 1969. Malcolm's psychiatric letters remarked that he did not want to fight in a war and that he got surly when asked to do things he didn't want to do. "No one wants to fight in a war," the examiner said. But Malcolm coughed a great deal in the examiner's face, stared lethargically at the floor, and when asked what he was doing for a living, Malcolm shrugged, "Nothing." He told the examiner that he liked to walk around the city, alone, at night. "Go and make something of your life," the examiner commanded, madly stamping a series of papers.

Malcolm preceded for examination the regulation Black Panther and a man wearing a mohawk and loincloth whose entire body was painted purple. "Bye, fellas," Malcolm had said, breezing out with his 1-F. But for the next several years he was very worried. He thought perhaps the examining doctor was right: at the very least, he was having trouble focusing.

He spent the next three years rushing home from his job to make films that even he couldn't watch now. They were "non-narrative," as people said then; by the time Malcolm realized that he wanted to make films with more mass appeal, he had already quit the job and depleted the $11,000 he had earned by auctioning off a nineteenth-century painting he'd picked up for $40 at a flea market.

That was the thing about the seventies. Eleven thousand dollars still seemed like a lot of money, and money always materialized somehow. With the funny money from the painting Malcolm had lived for almost two years, obsessed about his filmmaking, and bought a house. He had partially renovated the house and stocked his basement wine cellar with 1966 Bordeaux.

By the time the money ran out Malcolm was already disenchanted with film.

He went back to work for the city in 1974, this time as a police photographer. He was still on the rosters from his last city job and years ago had listed photography as an interest. Police photography was a tangent that he fumbled onto in a season when he was desperately broke, and it changed his life, since he got to see as much—maybe more—bloodshed than he might have seen if he'd actually gone to Vietnam, and since it got him involved once again with still photography.

Just months after learning to gulp down his revulsion when confronted with a corpse, or his fear when positioned in an upstairs window across from an Italian funeral home to take telephoto shots of the arriving guests, Malcolm was staying long hours in the police lab, making extra prints, and calling his photographs art. Soon thereafter he began to enjoy an enormous amount of success as an avant-garde photographer.

He got a state artists' grant, then a national one. He was included in group shows at the Whitney, the Guggenheim. All this happened during a three-year period, in the kind of rush that old movies represent by fast-flipping calendar pages and montages of newspapers with inch-high, dense black headlines. Then his work simply fell apart.

Evidently it was Malcolm's fate to take artistic escalators in the wrong direction. As realism made its comeback in the galleries, Malcolm's work got more and more abstract, until he would photograph the hand of a prostitute waiting to be arraigned rather than her whole face and body in the police setting—or not even her hand, but a cuticle through a weird filter. He was shooting wounds so close up that they looked completely inhuman.

I used to shoot cuticles was the kind of line that, accompanied by ironic eyebrows at a party, could make Malcolm seem dapper and art-smart. But in truth, the end of his inspiration had hurt. It hurt still, when he let it—a rift much worse than his adolescent break with the church.

Malcolm's Keuder Vocational Preference Test in high school had told him to become a clerk. He was a list maker, a clipper and filer of newspaper articles; a collector of wine, single-malt Scotches, records, Fiestaware. Nora Worth, the woman with whom he lived, often claimed that his anality (Malcolm called it "love of detail") was what kept him from becoming a great artist. She claimed he couldn't focus on the big picture, and it was a shame, because his instincts were so . . . well, hardly visionary, but eighteen months ahead of their time, which is enough lead time to allow someone to become famous for *something*. He'd bought that painting, hadn't he, a good two years before anyone but museum curators had once more glommed onto Americana?

Similarly, he'd bought a run-down house in a run-down neighborhood and learned how to renovate Victorian buildings, hooking up with a developer (Beth, an ex-girlfriend) about two years before "gentrification" was an urban catchword. His idea was to learn a practical art, one that would guarantee a modest income without his having to go anywhere too early in the morning. Architecture, Malcolm thought, was a nice compromise between his artistic impulses and his organizational side. He was right. He loved interior design enough to have stayed with it for almost a decade now, through various financial crises.

So now he spent large portions of his year as an unemployed designer rather than an unemployed filmmaker, and he got to deal with criminals who wore ironed underwear.

After Lucy left, with a promise of flash bulletins, Malcolm sat on the steps of Stone's erstwhile offices for a while, his chin in his palms, trying to assimilate the news, and watching a bus attempt to turn a tight corner, its radius blocked by an illegally parked car. Most of the passengers on the bus were suddenly alert. Annoyance at the delay inflated their usually passive posture into a slight jauntiness. When a policeman arrived to ticket the illegally parked car, the bus passengers' heads reared back some on their necks—a righteous satisfaction—as the policeman leaned toward his walkie-talkie, ordering a tow truck. On the eighth or ninth attempt, the bus cleared the corner.

The car had out-of-town plates, and Malcolm felt the way he imagined the driver would feel when he got back to his car and it wasn't there. The suspicion that the car has been towed is never as terrifying as your first thought: that you have forgotten, entirely and permanently, where you parked.

He went to his own car, put the plans in the trunk, then decided to walk around town awhile to calm himself. For focus, he shopped for a brand of crew-necked Shetland sweater he collected. Good Shetland sweaters had a smell he loved, the fresh clean smell of new wool, and though Nora told him he was crazy, he was sure the different colors—the heather and cool gray, the charcoal gray and camel—had slightly different smells, just as different-colored jelly beans had had different tastes when he was a child.

He'd been searching for a hunter green Shetland. Most of the greens were kelly, most of the hunter greens too blue or too yellow. As a matter of course, whatever item he wanted was never available in the right color, size, or style. Most of his purchases were the result of quests. There were some items he should have bought and didn't, which he still mourned, still wanted as deeply as he wanted certain women who had never returned his interest.

Malcolm DeWitt was not falling apart. Not yet. Ever since he was a child—an infant even—Malcolm had had a very strong sense of where he wanted to go and that he hadn't gotten there yet, so why feel lost now?

He claimed to remember being five or six months old, in his stroller and crying passionately because his mother took a different path to the park than the one he had imagined taking. He didn't talk yet. He couldn't say, "Go that way." He just knew that something was wrong. As an adult, things were much the same, but he didn't cry anymore because he knew that you can't always control the directions things take. If Stone had been caught four months later, it wouldn't have touched Malcolm's life at all.

Now, with the mortgage already two months overdue, a sherriff's sale of his house was not the only problem. The letters from the IRS were not encouraging either: he hadn't filed for quite a while and the IRS felt out of touch. So did a series of creditors who had left frantic messages on the answering machine until it broke.

Malcolm totaled the money he had lost, the money he owed. The mortgage, the gas bill, the electric, the phone, the jammed Mastercard undulated down mental runways like beauty pageant contestants. The rest of his brain (the parts that weren't savoring details of the buildings he passed) recited Shakespeare: *There is a tide in the affairs of men that, taken at the flood, leads on to fortune*; except he couldn't remember the rest, except for *all the (something) of their lives are bound in and (something)*. He wanted to remember the quote.

He also wanted to think of a way to protect himself against one inevitable aspect of Stone's ruin, one he had been evading as he poked through men's departments, his coat thrown over his arm.

Nora was going to kill him.

The bright side: given his present financial state, she might lay off asking when they were going to get married.

2 NORA WORTH AND Malcolm DeWitt lived in a big old house they had never quite finished renovating. The house was in a marginal neighborhood just minutes from the center of Philadelphia—a city that, despite its relatively large size, never managed to become a real city. Rather, it achieved a real city's crime, trash, noise, and expense without a real city's diversity or animation.

Periodically they discussed moving. The last time was on the Fourth of July, the night Nora lost a contact lens at a party, on a dark roof where she'd climbed to watch fireworks. Now it was November, and half a year had evaporated like the soft contact lens, not even a mica glint on the black roof.

Time, she felt, was running out. Days, weeks, months seeped away like heat through their poorly insulated windows.

At the breakfast table on the morning Malcolm was to find out about Benjamin Stone's fall from grace, Nora attempted to tame her self-pity with the newspaper. A five-year-old child had been wounded at a bowling alley by a loony tune with a semiautomatic. Condition critical. Nora imagined the child's room—the flowered wallpaper and, through the lacy curtains, a full moon, sweet and round, harmless as baby fat.

Wanton urban violence was a more serious problem than a broken answering machine that would take forever to fix and had to be fetched in a car that spluttered and died at every light, a car bought moments before the Japanese started building cars to run. So technology roared ahead while Nora and Malcolm couldn't wake up mornings, and when they did, they couldn't get anything done. So her free day was already half-over. What is life on earth but aging and irritation unto death?

The cheapest property on the Luxury Homes and Estates page was $360,000.

Across the table Malcolm played with his hair, as usual. He had newsprint all over his forehead. No matter how much Malcolm had to do, he spent exactly one hour every morning with the newspaper and three mugs of coffee. He slept naked until ten or eleven, woke up, put on his pajamas, then had his juice, his granola, and three mugs of coffee. Nora thought: *I don't love him at all*. The thought was quite loud and perfectly distinct, and it terrified her, as did the next thought: *Who will get the clock?*

The living-room wall clock was a life-sized, bright yellow cat looking back over its slumpy spine. The numerals were on the cat's back, the cat's red tail was a pendulum, and its black eyes shifted back and forth as the pendulum swang. A meow-gong used to signal the hour, but once that broke there was just a muffled clunk you had to really concentrate to hear, though it still produced a vibration that, on the hour, made the cat's red whiskers shiver. They'd found the clock in an antique store in Vermont, and the memory of that vacation—not a memory so much as a quick shaft of mental light on the elms and the grass, the eaves of the stately gray houses—made Nora's heart ache so much she might have cried, had she not gotten up abruptly and walked to the windows.

"Christ!" Malcolm said, grabbing his mug as she bumped into the table.

Nora had not been graceful lately. She kept dropping glasses, banging her shins on chair legs. Her timing was bad. Everything was seconds too soon or too late. The sensation was of missing the connecting flight, of garments left dangling in the back of hotel room closets.

"Mal," she said. "I feel terrible."

"What's wrong?"

"Brain tumor, probably."

"Maybe the weather?" Malcolm suggested, giving her a sympathetic look before turning back to the paper.

As a couple, they were like cat and dolphin. Nora was the cat. She was too talkative to be properly feline, but she certainly had a cat's jumpiness, its taste for getting scratched behind the ears, and its abhorrence of water, especially on the face. Malcolm, on the other hand, "splashed off" every time he saw a sink. In restaurants he often returned from the bathroom with his shirt wet. He had a dolphin's kindly expression, a dolphin's look of subterranean intelligence. Their differences were elemental, and on good days it was fun to be intimately linked to someone so distant on the personality spectrum—as far as you can cross-mate, between mammals. But sometimes (more and more, lately) they were like a wet cat and a beached fish, and their alliance felt unnatural.

They looked somewhat alike, with their slightly wild eyebrows and grayish-greenish, hazel-blue eyes. Nora was flushed and lightly freckled. She walked with the slow roll from the hip that saves a tall, slim woman from seeming too boyish. As a teen boyishness had been her curse, although it had landed her the part of Rosalind in her high school's production of *As You Like It* (a part she still identified with in self-approving moments). Now her look was fashionable: her once-blonde, now only blondish hair chopped close to show off the shape of her skull and her soulful eyes.

Outside, the city went about its dirty business. Speeding cars without mufflers took the curve onto Springfield fast enough to kill the pedestrians who for five minutes now had been cowering in the median strip waiting to cross. A shrimpy, foul-tempered brown mutt did its unchaperoned circuit of the block, lifting its nose from the ground only to bark at black men and the handicapped. The dog appeared to detest blacks and anyone with a goofy walk, inconvenient tastes given that their neighborhood was integrated and housed the Home of the Merciful Saviour for Crippled Children.

The tiny old man who managed an apartment building down the block was out cleaning trash from his lawn, as he did every morning. Every morning he arrived wheeling his fat old bulldog in a red wagon, picked up all the trash from the lawn, then threw the trash in the street and kicked it downwind. At first Nora thought that only the concentration camps could have so distorted a man as to make him this fanatical about personal cleanliness at the expense of his environment, but she had subsequently decided that he was an unapprehended Nazi war criminal, this lawn his last dominion.

Across the street a man with a disorganized walk and plaid pants, striped shirt—the standard outpatient costume—was going somewhere in a hurry. The vicious mutt crossed the street to bark at the outpatient.

"Malcolm?" Nora said. "If a dog came at you really fast ready to bite, why couldn't you grab its snout and twist, or go for its eyes? Shouldn't you be able to outsmart a dog?"

"The problem is, your arm is usually in the dog's mouth," Malcolm smiled. "Dogs, unlike you, have pretty good reflexes. May I read now?"

Self-defense was something that Nora found herself thinking about lately, as part of her vigilante fantasies. Nora's glamorous mental alter ego did not merely bemoan the injustices and indignities of city life: the erratic trash pickups and reliable traffic jams, the overcooked burgers at overpriced restaurants, the teen-agers with blasting radios the size of infants' coffins. She did something about it. A baby-boom Rambo, hip and well educated, she practiced Aikido on muggers and wrote letters that congressmen never forgot.

"I was just wondering," Nora said. "Could you talk sternly? Point and say, '*Bad dog*'?"

"Once," Malcolm sighed, "I was inspecting an abandoned property and saw a pack of dogs. Instinctively I knew it was bad news and picked up a brick. One of the dogs came charging toward me full speed. I turned with the brick raised and made like I was going to go for the dog's head. The dog snarled and backed off. It surged forward again and again I raised the brick. This happened three, four times until it gave up and retreated. They're real big on eye contact."

"If you didn't have the brick, and it went for your leg, couldn't you attack back?"

"If you didn't mind the fact that your leg was getting ripped apart. It would depend on the dog, too. Shepherds tend to clamp down and hold on, whereas Dobermans keep clamping and opening. Yip yip yip, rip rip rip. That's why they're so good."

"How about a mutt?"

Malcolm stared at her, bemused.

"Make love to me," Nora said, climbing onto his lap.

She especially liked kissing Malcolm before he had brushed his teeth or showered. She enjoyed the brisk feel of his unshaven chin and all his morning mixed impressions: the bitterness of the coffee against the sweetness of the granola, a whiff of the sachet from the closet where he hung his pajamas against another whiff that told her she should *wash* his pajamas, then the Malcolm-smell that after five years with him she still couldn't identify, though it always seemed familiar in a shadowy way, like a dream almost remembered.

As they disengaged from the kiss, Nora felt a panic: a warning bell clamoring in a frequency she couldn't quite hear, and when she strained toward it, all she could make out was her own heart.

This intangible awareness of loss was becoming common for her lately. A week ago, in her car on the way to lunch with a friend, before the temperature had gotten preposterously warm for November, she'd found herself craning her neck to look in the rearview mirror at what she was almost sure was a man with no nose. Most of the people at the bus stop were bundled against the cold, their movements slow. Only the noseless man had his coat open, his neck bare, as grimly he watched for the bus. Nora had been haunted for weeks by the glimpse of triangular absence on the man's face.

They weren't going to make love. Malcolm would be late for a meeting with Stone ("Have you billed him yet?" Nora scolded, and Mal rolled his eyes), and she had to get to the bank, as well as do errands which Malcolm didn't have time for.

Workaholic or unemployed. For months he had been cranky and distracted because he had no work, and now he was cranky and distracted because he had too much. He was like one of those sinks where the hot and cold water gushed from separate faucets.

Relationships, Nora thought, were like cars. There were only so many models. You got domestic or imported, family sedan or sporty. Older and Wiser Mate or Opposites Attract. Still, looking around during traffic jams, she was amazed that anyone managed to choose. She was amazed—and touched—that in a parking lot someone could recognize at once his own sky-blue Honda Civic.

Lately Nora had been beginning to think, not for the first time, that she'd gotten a lemon.

She was sick of her liberated relationship in which she was free to be a whole person who supported her man. *Man*, when she said this, came out *my-yun*, like in a country-western song. For a while she had been bringing home the bacon. True, Malcolm cooked it, and took out the trash; but despite being perennially poor, he was always busy, so as well as being the breadwinner and having to work all day, Nora, more organized, got to pick up the dry cleaning and vegetables, while Malcolm slept late, read the paper, and yakked on the phone with his friend Tobias Maxwell. When was Nora supposed to attend to her *own* professional life?

How about now, Malcolm would suggest, *instead of giving me this crap?*

The question was to what, exactly, Nora was supposed to attend.

For almost a decade after she graduated from art school, Nora Worth had been dedicated to the creation of big, whimsical collage-sculptures like the one occupying most of the floor space in their bedroom. The canvas propped on a magenta easel was star-shaped. One of the star's prongs ended in a brass hook from which dangled a garment, partly spray-painted, partly embroidered, and—at the sleeve, which was tacked across the painting—transparent. The painting was of a bathing nude, fragmented because of the star cutouts. Jutting out from behind the canvas was a shelf with a basket of papier-mâché fruit and a wine bottle in the manner of an old master's arrangement, except that the wine bottle had two straws, like a fifties malted, and the fruits were the wrong colors—fuchsias and midnight blues.

Mal called Nora's art "Kitchen Sink," as in "everything but." The pieces at her local shows had sold well. She had also been in group shows at a New York gallery, and those pieces had been singled out for praise in several reviews. She sporadically taught drawing at a local college.

So things had gone as swimmingly as a thirty-ish female artist who does not live in New York can expect.

Although Nora and Malcolm didn't yet know each other, their disenchantment with art was parallel. As Malcolm's photographs had become myopic in 1978, Nora's pieces had begun to grow. The larger they got, the more small objects, carefully pinned or soldered or watercolored, had to be completed before she could move on to the next square foot. Toward the end she was spending a week gluing dewdrops on glass, which meant it would take a while to finish a thirteen-foot piece. In nine months of the last year she finished one.

Part of the problem was that by then she had begun to earn a living making similar objects for commercials. Partly as a joke, a New York friend had recommended Nora for a job making a glass of diet soda look frosty for long enough to be filmed. Most food stylists began as caterers or home economists. Nora bypassed that segment of training, thanks to a childhood of helping her mother cook Middle American (macaroni and cheese, meat loaf) for a big family and thanks to the social skills which big families bestow. Nora apprenticed for a year and became friendly with the well-known food photographers; in less than two years she was relatively established as a food stylist.

For TV she primped fast-food hamburgers until they looked towering and virile, not smashed and soggy. She mopped pools of oil from the pepperoni on fast-food pizza, made steam rise sinuous as a charmed boa from TV dinners that she kept from seeming stale and skimpy, and made the strawberries in frozen desserts shine like wet nail polish.

At the period when Nora fumbled into food styling, photorealism was being extolled in the art magazines whose suffocating pomposity represented everything she hated about self-declared "serious" art, and she spent a great deal of time in her dusty studio—by now a room in Malcolm's house—looking at the papier-mâché or plastic items she had made to attach to her collages (things that were intentionally not quite the color or texture of the real things) and considering what she had begun to do for a living, which was close to what she called her art (closer, in fact, by current definitions) but not, of course, art at all, since the aim was simply to make people buy diet soda.

Like Malcolm, she never officially stopped making art. Whenever she squeezed past the piece in the bedroom, she felt an almost domestic pleasure and trust. There were mornings when she'd wake up sure that she was going to paint again, when she'd feel the pull of an almost primordial excitement and drive. Sometimes she'd even act on that drive—go to her studio and do something to her last canvas, or simply stare at it and think.

But that was as far as she got. Other things simply intervened—errands, house maintenance, work that earned money.

Money had become more important to her, as it had to everyone. In New York she billed at $400 a day for print ads, $600 for commercial work. With overtime, she sometimes earned $1,000 a day. But the commute was trying, local work paid far less, her work was highly irregular and seasonal, she had huge equipment bills, and she never managed to save. The ways of becoming more "ambitious" in this field were ludicrous. Even if she could work every day at the highest end of the business and bring in $300,000 a year (unlikely given the competition, even assuming she could afford to live in Manhattan and devote her spare time to client seduction), the whole point of the job had been to leave time for worthier pursuits. The more she felt trapped in a dead-end branch of a dumb profession—as peripheral to real life as their neighborhood was to center city Philadelphia, as Philadelphia was to New York—the more she felt guilty for not loving her work more. There were housewives with Nikons and degrees from cooking schools in France who would kill for her job.

Malcolm was sympathetic to her dilemma. Why shouldn't he be? He was no stranger to career crises. Meanwhile, she was keeping him in triple-crème cheese and obscure Handel operas.

They should just simplify. Pack one suitcase and take off for Paris, or live as they had the summer they met, before inflation made them needy and greedy, before cohabitation reduced their frequency of intercourse to way below the reported national average.

Nora had two conflicting explanations for her ugly mood as she drove to the bank. One was that she was closer than she could confront to leaving Malcolm DeWitt. The other was that she loved Malcolm, and they didn't have a single problem that $25,000 or $30,000—make it $35,000, accounting for inflation—couldn't cure.

The traffic was bad. It took almost ten minutes to make a merge. When she finally did squeeze in, the car in front of her stopped with no warning and Nora came within inches of ploughing into it. Her Toyota's failing brakes squealed, then the car stalled out. Once she got her car moving, no one would let her pass the stopped car in front of her. One car missed her bumper, speeding up to prevent her from changing lanes. She shot that driver the finger, but since he was already long gone she wound up giving the finger to a Ford Tempo full of nuns.

An even voice in her head, similar to the kind her car would have if her car were advanced enough to talk, said: *None of this is worth dying for. If you drive this way you will soon be dead*, and it was true, she was driving viciously, but she couldn't stop, except to wonder if all the city's drivers were always as angry as she was now, venting their frustrations on the road. If only someone would bring the truckers their slippers, give them back rubs, melt the hate in their hearts—but it wasn't going to be her. Not today.

Philadelphia was the kind of city that offered neither public transportation nor parking facilities. Instead it had an aggressive troop of meter maids and men who were right there when your meter expired, and sometimes a few minutes before. Almost a decade in this city, and Nora had never managed to befriend a single one of the Parking Authority bureaucrats who were regularly busted for ticket-fixing. Today she was determined to block a driveway or hydrant if necessary, but in a stroke of luck an actual unmetered space opened up on Mortimer Street, a short walk from the bank.

Usually Nora loved to walk on Mortimer. It was one of the last bastions of elegance in her decaying metropolis.

The steps leading to the houses here were marble, the huge doors carved mahogany. There was no traffic noise—the street is one-way, linked to another one-way street, making vehicular traffic forbidding— and in the quiet Nora could hear actual birds. A maid in starched white polished a fist-sized door knocker shaped like a ram's head. Through leaded glass bright as rhinestones she could see seductive flashes of old volumes, original oils in gilt frames—the deep reds and blues of old money and good blood.

Someday, Nora thought, *all of this will be yours*.

It's what she always thought walking here—or rather felt, as she felt the sun on her shoulders.

But that day she caught herself, and another voice in her head—a man's voice this time, authoritative and vaguely upper-crust, like a public television announcer—enunciated: *No it won't*.

You will never be rich, the voice said. *You will never be famous.*

You will never live on Mortimer Street.

Let's say Nora started earning $100,000 a year (unlikely). Let's say Malcolm did too (even more unlikely). Let's say their income was gloriously sheltered, and let's say they unloaded their present house for the best possible price.

They still couldn't afford it.

They were smart, capable, ambitious. But no matter how well they did, everyone else—the people who already had racehorses in Florida,

Manhattan condos, cottages in Italy, all the Benjamin Stones of the world—would always do better.

The pleasures of middle-class life which Nora had assumed were her birthright would always dangle just out of reach, like those wallets on strings that children plant to tease pedestrians.

This depressing certainty froze her for long enough that a woman at the other end of the block, walking two whippets on leashes, turned to stare.

Nora walked on grimly.

Who cared, anyway? For how long had their predominant topic of conversation been real estate? Why did she think her life would be better in a bigger house? Why weren't they happy to live cheaply, as they did in the old days and have abundant free time, which is the truest currency?

Nora waited in line at the bank to withdraw fifty dollars in cash. She also asked the teller for her balance. Money was tight. They'd been living off her money for months. And that didn't count the money she'd loaned Malcolm for his own debts—by now a sizable sum. She wouldn't be surprised, in fact, if those loans had reached $10,000.

Her friends all thought she was crazy.

The teller's red fingernails were so long they turned under. Later, Nora would recall that the teller was polite, even deferential, as she handed Nora the piece of paper on which she'd written, in slightly curly, Catholic-school printing, the balance in Nora's checking account.

According to the bank, Nora's balance was $32,354.04.

That was exactly $30,000 more than Nora thought she had in her checking account, not to mention about $30,000 more than she had ever had in a checking account at one time in her life.

$32,354.04. Exactly $30,000 of this sum had been mysteriously deposited into her account.

If Nora had been paying attention, her on-the-spot surprise might have ruined everything. But she didn't even read the amount. She wouldn't see the slip until later the next day when, fumbling for a tissue in her jacket pocket, she would find it shoved down in there and recognize the writing as the teller's. By then she would decide that the windfall couldn't have befallen a more deserving person. She didn't react at the bank because someone was calling her name: David Martella, smiling and waving frantically from the end of the line.

THE NIGHT THEY met almost three years before, David and Nora had gone to Nora's apartment to talk and spent five or six hours twisted toward each other on a couch, their eyes full of liquid heat.

They were exactly the same height and were both almost thirty, born three days apart in the same year. They had the same stubby fingers, the same circles under their eyes when they were tired. Both of them were cynics whose eyes welled with pity at the sight of anyone with a physical handicap. They took the same commuter train to New York a couple of days a week (on different days or surely they would have noticed each other before). They had graduated from similar first-class universities. Both had slept with upward of forty people in college, and both were presently involved with someone else.

3

As they talked, Nora had watched David's mouth. Their goodnight kiss was the cinematic kind you get only a couple of in a lifetime, no matter how many people you sleep with. Nora could still feel how everything had narrowed to that kiss; David's mouth was the vortex she tunneled into, as when on laughing gas your whole brain constricts to the tunnel-rush of the high.

The next morning Nora told Malcolm she had fallen in love with someone else and wrote Ken Worth, who had been her favorite of four brothers until he married, to announce that she had met the man she herself would marry.

At the time, after two years of steady dating (the verb has yet to be coined for what unwed grown-ups do), Malcolm was still insisting that marriage was a petty-bourgeois institution. If Nora was so conventional, narrow-minded, weak, and unimaginative as to think a relationship needed to escalate in the direction of marriage—or even cohabitation, which interfered with solitude and with deep, true feeling for the other—she should look elsewhere. So she had.

Before David, Nora's image of a plausible relationship had been something like a men's shirt ad. Her future mate wore an expression of beneficent strength and a white shirt that was completely smooth against his chest. The chest was trim, with a shadow of pectorals: the kind of chest a modern girl could bury herself in to pout, if her hard day at the office required that, but what would she pout about, given this fellow? He turns, face lit at the sight of Nora, strips off his shirt, throws it down (who cares where—she isn't going to iron it) and—wooliness! Irony! Talk so good they almost forget to make love, though the three times yesterday ought to compensate.

David Martella was the man who had come closest to Nora's fantasies. He was ambitious—in fact, he had fingers in so many pies that he often seemed like one of those many-limbed Hindu deities updated for our troubled times: God of the Résumé. He was a scholar, a journalist, and an actor, a combination that he would be the first to tell you was inspired. Of course, if you scratched any line on his résumé you found the "but." Yes, he had published a book, but it was a slim volume from a university press entitled something like *Early Hitchcock: A Deconstructionist Romp*. As for acting, his only role so far was as a sufferer from overeating in a sour-stomach commercial. Still, the hip New York magazine for which he wrote nasty film reviews sent him to L.A. and Cannes, and he had tenure. For watching movies twice a week nine months a year he got a retirement plan and an audience of wild-haired, leggy girls. Not that he needed the salary. David claimed to be independently wealthy. He was circumspect about the details, telling Nora that she wasn't entitled to a full accounting of his assets until she married him. Though Nora imagined that his financial portfolio was rather like his résumé, there were hints of a house on the Cape, an ancestral villa in Tuscany.

By their third or fourth date, David, very late, had brought his laundry. He didn't exactly ask Nora to wash his clothes. It was just that her apartment building had laundry facilities, he could put in a load before their quickie, and afterward, he had some errands—maybe Nora could shift the loads around? Within three months, Nora had reunited with Malcolm and moved into his house, proclaiming that David had taught her to appreciate Malcolm's trustworthiness, depth, patience, and sincerity.

David had been mystified by Nora's decision. He claimed that she hadn't given him a chance. That was probably true, even if more time would only have confirmed what she knew from the start. He would never be faithful; whatever woman he chose, no matter how accomplished, should be prepared to be wifely, providing clean clothes and praise. Not that the dedicated service would keep David at home—you could treat him like the infant Jesus in the manger and he'd still feel neglected.

Malcolm was a homebody, and Nora liked that. Cleaning up the kitchen together, they'd share a kind of low-grade, ongoing tenderness that's sometimes better than sex, so when Malcolm emerged from a long bath with water still beaded on his legs and arms, Nora would feel her heart wink or shiver with affection—*Hello my dolphin*; Malcolm depressed, or distracted, or talking animatedly, out of nowhere, about city planning.

When Nora got nostalgic for living alone, it wasn't solitude she missed: she had solitude enough with quirky Malcolm in the big house. What she missed was that sense of infinite possibility that singlehood allows, the sense of the outlines not already having been drawn, as they are around the splayed figure of a corpse, in thick chalk. That first night, Nora had glommed onto David's mouth like a lamprey to rock. Maybe all lust was lust for change. David's mouth was the mouth of a lion: Nora had pulled the jaw apart and stuck her head in, fearless; inside, she expected to see a livelier world with more exotic foliage, as in the shoebox panoramas she'd built in the fifth grade.

Still, over the years of their testy friendship—David, a sore loser and an Italian (his stereotype, not hers), didn't quite see the point of women he couldn't screw—there was a sense of unfinished business.

Across the bank, David waved. Nora waved back. Their eyes locked. It was the look of two people who after decades apart find themselves staying at the same *pensione* in Venice, in winter, in the year 2000, both graying but still slender, widowed by their respective spouses and simultaneously longing for each other as they meet against a backdrop of snowy rooftops. Although they had chatted on the phone only weeks before, they hadn't seen each other in the flesh for a couple of months.

"Nice haircut," David said, performing a quick, approving, David-style toe-to-head as she approached.

Nora smiled. Her hair was growing out, a mess, no cut at all. "You know what?" she said. "I think you were in my dream last night."

"Was I sweet?" David asked.

"Probably not."

Nora stepped over the velvet cord channeling the line to stand shoulder-to-shoulder with David, facing forward, waiting for his turn. After a moment he reached out to pat her shoulder.

David Martella looked like Franz Kafka without the big ears. His head was a little too big for his body, and he liked to wear a slightly pained expression: the expression of someone who is dying of tuberculosis but is determined not to inflict his pain on you. Though he was six years younger than Malcolm, he looked six years older. David was the only adult Nora knew who still did regular all-nighters to finish work on deadline, and since his diet consisted mainly of Twinkies gulped down in train stations (when he did eat meals, he ate only pasta—Nora guessed he hadn't swallowed a vegetable since junior high, except maybe a couple of peas on tortellini), he had a washed-out look. The pastiness was oddly attractive. He was like a child with the flu, home from school, whose forehead you wanted to stroke.

"Big weekend plans?" David asked.

"It's Monday, David."

"Really? What happened to the weekend?"

"You missed it?"

"Seems that way."

They stood, smiling at each other and waiting for David's turn in line. Then David asked, "You married yet?"

"Nope."

"I think you're making a big mistake," David said.

"Not marrying Malcolm?"

"Not running off with me."

"I was worried. You haven't asked me to run off with you for at least half a year."

"I asked you telepathically."

Nora sighed. There was a time when the fact that their money inter-mingled in the same bank would have produced in them a romantic shiver, a conviction of destiny.

They had reached the head of the line and moved toward a teller, the same teller who had given Nora her cash and her balance. "I'm sorry, sir," the teller said, "but I can't deposit this check as cash. This is an out-of-town check. It will take a week to ten days to clear."

"If you look at my file," David said, smiling patiently, "you'll see I have two jobs, one local, one in New York. This is a payroll check."

"It doesn't say payroll," the teller said.

Nora studied the other people in line while David displayed his driv-er's license, his work identification, and his passport.

"You carry your passport around?" Nora asked.

"It expired. I have to renew it. I may go to Rome next week. Want to come?"

"Sure."

"My treat."

"Right," Nora said.

The teller went to consult with another teller. They studied David in a huddle. The original teller returned to report that neither of them had ever seen David before in their lives.

"Then why have I never had this problem before?" David asked, still attempting a tolerant smile.

"It's got to say *pay*roll on the check," the teller said, enunciating each syllable, deadpan, "or else you got to know a *tell*er who *knows* it's a pay-roll check."

The people behind them in line had begun to glare. Nora, however, was only recently attentive to what was going on, having turned away from the teller to survey the bank, with its museum-height ceilings and self-important hush, until David demanded to speak with a supervisor, who now approached. The supervisor was his kind of woman—at least she had enough hair. David leaned slightly forward over the counter and fixed his big black eyes on her to indicate that only gentlemanliness re-strained him from sweeping her into his arms for an afternoon of pas-sion. Poor David, Nora thought. If he didn't light a fire in every female breast, his ego got frail and limp as a damp paper match. But even as she mocked him, she could recall the excitement she'd felt when he zoomed in on *her* across the multitudes at the party where they met.

The supervisor studied the check. She seemed to be assessing the amount, approvingly. Then she said the name of the magazine. "You work there?"

"Film critic," David offered.

"I read it all the time," she said.

"And you don't recognize my name?" David mimed a cleaver through his heart, then did a little geisha bow of supplication. The supervisor smiled, initialed the check, and left with a bounce. The teller, narrowing her eyes, began to punch numbers into the phone, at a slowdown-strike pace.

"Someone needs to break our teller's legs," David said to Nora under his breath, moving a little closer to her as if to inhale her. "Someone needs to drop our teller from a helicopter into an ocean full of sharks."

"How much do they pay you, anyway?" Nora asked, reaching for David's face-down paycheck. But David reached for it too, to prevent her from seeing the amount, and they wound up with her hand on the check, his hand on hers.

For a second he stroked the webby part of her hand between thumb and forefinger. It was the most physical contact they'd had in years, and sparks were flying along their old loose wire. David leaned close enough for her to see the pointillist blue-black hairs on his not-too-closely-shaven chin, like the dots that make up a cartoon.

The teller had to clear her throat to get their attention, to get their hands off the check. Nora felt herself jump, then was surprised to hear herself think, relieved, that Malcolm used a different bank. *Young love, true love*, the teller's caustic smile implied, except that Nora Worth wasn't so young anymore, and as she and David left the bank the shadowy panic came back: there wasn't much time left. Whatever she was going to do with her life, she had better do it fast.

MALCOLM DIDN'T TELL Nora about Stone that night. At dinner, every time he looked up, she was staring at him. The look didn't mean anything he could determine; it was mostly blank, with a blurred edge of distaste. "Do I have something between my teeth?" Malcolm asked (Nora was forever noticing things between his teeth), and she didn't even answer.

Malcolm feared that her silence meant she was brewing some new theory. A devoted Freudian, Nora had many explanations for Malcolm's personality. When she talked about his passive-aggressiveness, how he needed a pushy woman to compensate for this and that in his family, a heavy velvet curtain closed across his mind. He hated that kind of theorizing, especially when Nora turned her powers on his career—as she was bound to do when she found out about Stone.

There was, for instance, her Fear of Failure theory: the minute Malcolm was confronted with the next step in any career, whether social work or film or photography or architecture, he ducked out. The Fear of Failure theory dovetailed with the Catholic theory: his mother and the church had taught him to be a good little boy, and good little boys don't do too well. "Humility," Nora would say, "can be a form of arrogance. You try to act like you don't care how the world judges you, but in fact you're so needy of people's good opinion that you won't risk asking for it. You'll never get anywhere until you learn to stand confrontation, rejection."

Passivity. Confrontation. Rejection. Tension. She had a whole wardrobe of terms, and there was no jumble in her mental drawer. Malcolm had already escaped one religion; if forced to take on another one he would certainly not choose a monotheism with Freud ruling the roost. Benjamin Stone's FBI investigation was as arbitrary as the weather—the gods hurled a thunderbolt at Stone, and now Malcolm DeWitt, along with many other people, had to brush the fallout off his coat. But Nora Worth was going to think that Malcolm had brought his fate upon himself: he'd done or said the wrong thing, neglected some obvious form of self-protection.

I'll tell her later, Malcolm thought, *after we make love*. Making love often seemed to put her in a better frame of mind—or at least it used to. But tonight there was a long, anti-aphrodisiac discussion about the logistics of her diaphragm. Then the phone rang: Nora's mother, with an update on the plans for Nora's brother's wedding. Nora sat up in bed, naked, and stroked Malcolm's knee while discussing whether or not it was necessary to get floral bouquets for the bathrooms. Needless to say, by the time the conversation ended, both of them felt more like watching television.

"How old are we again?" Nora asked. "Have we retired yet?"

Malcolm didn't tell her that he was once more unemployed; that the $9,000 or so he already owed her was unlikely to be paid back in the near future; that he was unlikely to take her to Venice this winter (a nice way, she'd suggested, to repay some of the interest); that in fact he was already two months behind on his mortgage and might lose the house. Nora claimed to hate the house anyway—the rough neighborhood, the noisy street, their neighbor's television laugh tracks and disco blaring through the party wall (for this was a city twin, not a suburban single-family like the house in which Nora had grown up, where she had never once looked out the window to see a stranger urinating against a tree). But the equity in this house was the only thing that might keep Malcolm from becoming a street person.

When he finally told Nora about Stone the following morning, she manifested all of the appropriate shock and sympathy. It took her a full ten minutes of condolences before, with widened eyes, she said what he'd predicted she'd say first thing: "I *told* you to bill earlier."

"I wish I had," Malcolm said. "But it'd still leave me unemployed. I'm sorry," he added, patting Nora's arm across the tangle of newspapers, which in the strong sun gave off an acrid hot-newspaper smell, like ammoniated Brie.

He *was* sorry, especially watching her stunned face as she reread the two column-inches on Stone at the bottom of a back page of the business section, buried between ads for photocopying machines and mutual funds.

"Doesn't say much," Malcolm said.

Nor had the almost-identical inches in the *Wall Street Journal*. Lucy had called in the morning to read him the plug on Stone in that revered periodical and to tell him the latest, which Malcolm now passed on to Nora. Stone's lawyer, who resigned as soon as the FBI arrived, had checked himself into a local institution for acute depression. His wife was eight months pregnant. And Stone's new chauffeur had arrived from Paris the very day of the bust. He didn't speak much English. His luggage was lost. When no one was there to meet the plane, he'd called the office. The FBI men told him to call back in a couple of months.

"How does Lucy know all this?" Nora asked.

"Because the guy made his way to the office and was so suicidal that the FBI gave him Lucy's home number. Seems she and Jack are putting him up for a couple of days."

"Why would Stone hire a chauffeur from Paris?"

"So he could have a real French chauffeur. The guy was a lover, of course."

"But think how long it'd take for him to learn his way around the city."

Malcolm smiled. How like Nora to focus in on the big picture. Smiling back dolefully, Nora thought how like Malcolm it was to manage to smile in the storm. "I'm sorry," he said again.

She made him repeat the story of Benjamin Stone several times, dwelling on the fate of the new chauffeur, stranded at the airport with no luggage.

"You should have known," Nora said.

"I did know things were strange. Why did Stone hire me to begin with? He could have afforded anyone. I assumed he's like all rich people—he wanted to squeeze the most out of the least. He knew I was good, and I'm certainly cheap."

"You're free," Nora corrected.

"Now it's clear. He wasn't really a millionaire, he was only posing as a millionaire, so he would naturally be drawn to an architect who wasn't really an architect. He was always hiring people who weren't officially qualified but whose potential he recognized. Look who he hired as a secretary. Lucy types forty words a minute, but he said, 'You're smart. We'll hire a typist.' He wanted to be the first kid on his block. He wanted to be visionary."

"What's so visionary about a Wang and a black Jaguar? And the thousand-dollar socks. He sounded like an asshole to me. He sounded worse than Beth."

Beth was the woman with whom Malcolm had lived for three years during the last decade. They went into real estate together with $10,000 fronted by Beth's parents. They'd done a great deal of shady fiddling with FHA loans until they had accumulated about thirty properties. They had no legal agreements between them, so when they split up, Beth, whose parents had after all made the initial investment, got everything except three houses, two of which Malcolm had subsequently sold to survive during later periods of unemployment. He'd continued to work for Beth, under the assumption that she would soon start earning big money, but once she did she stiffed him. She squandered all of her money on high living and finally married a businessman from Buenos Aires who could keep her in cocaine, sequined outfits, and restaurants expensive enough to wear sequins to. Malcolm sometimes dreamed about killing her.

"He wasn't like Beth," Malcolm said. "Beth nickel-and-dimed. She was way too cheap to ever get anywhere in business. Stone would really spend. Quality got him hot. He *liked* spending."

"Why shouldn't he? It wasn't his money."

"That's how you make money, by spending money you don't have. The emperor's new clothes. You also have to be able to delay gratification. That's the part Beth never got. A million dollars in real estate assets is garbage unless you sit on it for nine, ten years."

"Sounds like Stone didn't understand that part either."

"Stone was playing for much higher stakes. Four months and he would have successfully completed a fifty-million-dollar construction job. Then his assets wouldn't be overstated anymore."

"Four months and you pass go. Four months and you collect zillions of dollars."

"Does have a game-board feel," Malcolm agreed. "But why would the bank close down a fifty-million-dollar project that's under construction and going well? Is it the scale of the lie, or was there some other crooked business involved?"

In his pajamas, Malcolm was slumped in one of the living room chairs, an art deco number in maroon and gray mohair bought for ten dollars from a local fraternity, one of the fraternities that had snatched up all of the best Victorian mansions in the neighborhood after the buildings had finished their incarnations as funeral parlors. In the future—the future that got dimmer and dimmer, farther and farther down the tunnel—they would have this chair reconstructed, reupholstered. Meanwhile it listed a bit to the left, as did the house itself, from settlement. Stuffing and springs were visible.

Nora felt seasick. She had gotten up from the dining room table (their dining room and their living room were really one, except semantically) to pace. For the last couple of minutes she had been tracing the mandala in the center of the rug with her feet, placing one foot before the other as if measuring. She stopped.

"What are we going to do?" she asked.

Malcolm looked at her across the expanse of the carpet in a way he often did when he sat in his armchair: as if remembering her dimly from his past, as if she were someone who wheeled a cart by him in the grocery store whom he thought he might have shared a bunk with in summer camp.

"I haven't the foggiest," he said.

"We could sell that," she suggested, pointing to a ragged chunk of wall salvaged from the wrecker, now displayed on top of one of their apothecary bookcases. Almost entirely intact in thirties-style lettering was the message ASBESTOS: THE MAGIC MINERAL, illustrated by a muscle man who partly held up, partly pushed an orb (the earth, presumably). One of Malcolm's prize finds, this was a panel from the GM Futurama Pavilion at the 1939 World's Fair. There were pieces of cast iron and plaster from demolished buildings all over their house, and every one evoked nostalgic reveries in Malcolm, but he was especially fond of his piece of the 1939 World's Fair. He and his buddy Tobias Maxwell knew a great deal about the fair, which occurred at perhaps the last time in history—pre-Hiroshima and Three Mile Island—when anyone could unironically believe in progress.

"It's not worth anything," Malcolm said.

"I bet it is."

"It's nice," Malcolm said, "and we like it. But it's not worth anything."

"Like everything else in our life," Nora said, plopping down in the other armchair. "What will happen?"

"I don't know."

"What are you going to do?"

"I don't know."

"You don't *know*?"

"No."

"Don't tell me you're going to take a wait-and-see attitude."

"What choice do I have?"

"Malcolm, they're about to take you away."

"Well, not quite."

"So you're going to sit in your armchair, drink milk, eat cookies, blast music, and wait for them to beat your door down?"

"I guess I have to look for a lawyer."

Nora burst into tears.

Malcolm could never help grinning when Nora cried, since her tears were so wet and fast, shooting out centrifugally, like banking racecars. Crying, she looked like Betty Boop. Her mouth formed the mask of tragedy's downward spiral and her eyes became two slitty pumps. Tears ricocheted off her cheekbones.

"Very funny," she wept.

Malcolm knelt before her and tried to soothe her with knee pats, waist strokes. "There, there," he smiled, reaching up to take a breast in each hand. "There, there." Teardrops fell on his head. Their perverse Pieta amused him so much that he laughed.

Nora stopped the faucet and glared. "You're a crazy man," she said.

Malcolm lifted her bathrobe to suggest, with a tongue on her inner thigh and much movie-villain movement of eyebrow, that some of the best things in life are free to the public.

"Forget it," Nora said. "I've got to go to work. *Someone* works around here. Though God knows you didn't choose the right season to make me pay all the bills."

She left the house an hour later, still somewhat teary, carrying the six-foot, lifelike cloth pig costume she had designed for the owner of a local sausage factory. This was a job she'd fought for, though the pay was lousy. She needed to build her portfolio; if she could get ad costume work like this in New York, she'd be in a whole different financial ball-park. What a thrilling advance for Nora and humanity. It was not an afternoon she felt like using to watch a grown man prance around in a pig costume, but she had promised to be on location as the commercial was shot to make sure the oinker's tail and snout moved properly.

Malcolm lifted weights to Renaissance lute music while waiting for the hot water to replenish itself from Nora's shower. He thought, all things considered, that the news-breaking had gone rather well. He lifted weights with a vengeance, trying to remain calm.

Later, having delivered herself of the pig costume, coached the pork merchant on how to move in a porcine way, and stayed to watch the filming of the commercial with the merchant's wife (who looked on with mock but really not-so-mock attention, as though watching a Little League game), Nora was walking toward her car by way of Mortimer Street, as usual.

But today, the fact that she was on the very block of Mortimer where Benjamin Stone kept his wife and children while he took off to fall in love with French boys and import them as chauffeurs brought on a fresh wave of tears.

Nora reached into her jacket pocket for a tissue and found, instead, a small slip of paper with a figure printed on it in writing that wasn't hers.

$32,354.04. Her balance.

NATURALLY, NORA'S FIRST thought was to give the money to Malcolm.

The timing couldn't be better. Thirty thousand would pay the overdue mortgage, not to mention credit card debts and the accountant, with some left over for a champagne celebration.

5 Nora's second thought was, *If the slug doesn't shape up, I'll keep it all*—but she suppressed that idea, ashamed of herself.

She backtracked to the branch where she had opened her bank account. Now the branch was staffed entirely by money machines and by an exuberantly gesturing street person who smelled like a foot that has been in a cast for a couple of months, in summer. Nora waited in line to ask for her balance. *Me-meep, me-meep*. The machine confirmed: $32,354.04.

As an indication of how far Nora had already slipped under financial duress, it took her a while to remember that this money wasn't quite hers at all.

Unlike Malcolm, she had always been a lucky person. She was the kind of person who found things on the street: a rabbit's foot dyed magenta, a latchkey, a huge Greek coin, a tarnished button from a Nazi uniform. She wore an old ring of pearls and tiny diamonds that she had rescued split seconds from the wheel of a tractor-trailer.

Sometimes she found money. Usually it was only the change that flies from pockets. But once a crisp ten-dollar bill had appeared beneath her feet, and once, unlocking her car door on the passenger's side where the groceries were, she'd seen, among a pile of dirty leaves, corn chip bags, and beer bottles, a fifty. Then, almost under the wheel, another fifty. As she walked with the groceries she'd stooped every couple of feet to pick up the bills that had been scattered like bread crumbs to mark her path.

Finding money brings a particularly intense rush of satisfaction. It isn't just the rush of getting something for nothing—not two-for-one drinks or complimentary tickets, a mismarked item in a discount shop—but a feeling so deep it seemed to Nora primal, archetypal.

She withdrew $200 in cash, the limit you could get from the machine. Her stub now reported a balance of $32,154.04.

There was a flower stand next to the bank. Nora bought an armload of hot pink gladiolas and stood there like a prom queen, wondering what to buy next.

In the past, when she'd played "What would I do with a million dollars," she'd always said she would buy some clear, unencumbered time to make art. Like the moneyed Monet, she'd pursue her leisurely vision, parking her bright children with a warm, wise nanny. But in her more honest self-appraisals, she recognized that poverty was not what had cut short her artistic career. She had simply run out of steam. Now that she was only making commercials, maybe she'd settle for a cruise around the world. Europe in late fall.

She'd always imagined that if she ever made a killing, she'd give the money to Malcolm to invest in real estate. Then he wouldn't have to tolerate any more insane, cheap, or power-hungry developers. Except this wasn't 1970, and you couldn't go very far on $30,000.

Only when Nora found herself wishing that the bank had given her $300,000 did she remember that this wasn't quite like playing finders keepers with $158 in cash on a curb. She was playing with a bank, and the banks in her city were *mean*.

If you're going to steal, people always say, steal big. Rich people understand that. Even Malcolm understood that. But a measly $30,000 was enough to tempt Nora Worth, who had always been boringly moral and dependable—who always remembered to send birthday cards and mailed a pittance to every Democratic charity that had her on its mailing list.

From a phone booth nearby she phoned Malcolm and was irritated to find that his line was busy. So was her best friend Julie's (on the other line, said the secretary). Her next-to-best friend Jessica wasn't in. Unavailable as well was a cast of other friends and acquaintances, all of whom were busy making management decisions or entertaining toddlers in the park, or out of town.

She would have called her brothers, her parents, but it would be at least a month before anyone in her family could sit still long enough to concentrate on her news. Her brother Richard was getting married over the weekend, the theory being that people didn't really want to spend Thanksgiving with their families anyway, and even if they did they'd be thoroughly sick of turkey and relatives by Saturday night. Once Richard was married, Nora and Alan would be the only remaining single Worths. Meanwhile, Ken's second child was due any minute, and Mark's wife was pregnant too. Marriage destroyed the attention span of the participants for anything but flatware and seating plans for up to a year. Children, from what Nora could make out, destroyed the attention span permanently. As the oldest of five children, and the only girl, she had spent most of her own childhood playing den mother to four boisterous brats, one of whom always had a cold, a baseball game, or trouble with a teacher. She imagined her legal defense when she was caught with the bank money, the psychiatrist testifying—*The woman never put a penny in a piggybank that was hers alone*—but she caught the self-pity, scolded herself.

Other people managed picnics, eggnog with friends around the fire, lunch-hour racquetball dates. Malcolm and Nora had the worst of both worlds: artistic work with none of art's integrity and no control over the finished product; self-employment without fun or profit. They were running in place, but whose heart would bleed for them? After all, they ate long, late dinners of the world's most rarefied foodstuffs, during which they discussed how much they loved Buñuel, current foreign policy, what people could possibly find appealing about Johnny Carson fingering his nose like a thumb-sucking child, or how Soviet citizens might react to Stupid Pet Tricks if smuggled a contraband tape of "The David Letterman Show." *How smug, how superficial*, Nora thought, but she wasn't sure what they were supposed to do instead: run for office? Volunteer as candy stripers? Keep a kitty jar in the kitchen, so that every time they bought a sun-dried tomato they'd bestow a matching grant to the Committee to Aid the Homeless?

David Martella was in New York, Nora remembered, until Monday, when they'd scheduled lunch. She left a message on his machine that she had amusing news.

She had made seven calls. After each call she redialed Malcolm, and each time the line was still busy her rage at him increased. By the time she was done, her gloveless hands were numb. Nora Worth had reached no one, and suddenly she felt panic-stricken.

What was she doing in a phone booth in the cold with her coat unbuttoned and $200 in her pants pocket, inventing madcap ways to announce her sudden wealth? She was like a stand-up comic at a noisy club where no one even listened to her jokes.

On automatic pilot she started walking back to the machines to redeposit the money. Three blocks later she realized that it wasn't too smart to deposit $200 in cash.

She also realized that she had forgotten the gladiolas.

She sprinted back to the phone booth. Miraculously, the flowers were right where she'd left them, propped against the back wall of the booth, their pink even more shocking against the gray steel and dirty glass. This urban tableau was odd enough that Nora had to stare for a couple of minutes.

It was exactly the kind of still life she would have transformed into art, back when she had such ambitions, and for a minute her breathlessness felt like inspiration.

Nora Worth, manic to match the weather, was suddenly elated.

When her car threatened not to start, then did, it was a windfall. When she got home she'd offer to make Malcolm lunch and tell him about the money, her bare feet in his lap. He would wear the ironic smile he'd used that morning to report on Stone. The thought of Malcolm in his too-short, two-decades-old black chinos and a black T-shirt that made him look like a fifties punk, except for his scholarly expression, brought a rush of fondness. All of the limitations of monogamy were counterbalanced by the pleasure of having someone at home to worry if you were dead on the highway.

Malcolm DeWitt, meanwhile, had balanced his checkbook and was trying to order his bills by degree of delinquency and danger.

The bottom line: he had $486.92, no money forthcoming, and owed money to everyone in America.

"All of us overlook a bill now and again," one of the reminder notices commiserated, but the rest were less sympathetic. "Your debt, referenced above, is SERIOUSLY DELINQUENT in the amount indicated," some said; or "You have ignored our previous request for voluntary payment of this seriously delinquent account. Most states provide for the garnishment of wages to enforce payment of outstanding and overdue accounts. In accordance with existing statutes, it is our intention to recommend the use of *every* tool available to enforce the collection of this account without regard for expense."

Malcolm smiled, imagining the National Guard on his front lawn to collect the last $24 on his color TV from Penney's. The fact was that, even this close to the brink, his ruin would mosey along. Bill collectors could no longer blow your door down. It would take the bank at least half a year to foreclose on the house on the house. The stay of execution should have comforted him. Instead, he saw himself as Sisyphus pushing not a rock, but a bag of money up the mountain—a penny for every cent of debt.

On top of this slow torture, there was Nora. A woman who lived life by the stopwatch, who was always itchy to get somewhere and, the minute she arrived, itchy to leave. She would have millions of suggestions for him in these troubled times, like a deranged camp counselor.

In the mail, friendly letters from both the gas and water companies, warning him about shutoff in English and Spanish.

He called the gas company. While on hold he read a piece of the obscure product information he was always sending for. Today he had received a brochure from a company that specialized in "security accessories": soap dishes, tissue holders, and clothes hooks for penal institutions and detention facilities, "designed to minimize the concealment of contraband and to reduce the possibility of suicide."

People spent their whole lives making soap dishes for prisoners, or talking on the phone with people who wouldn't pay their gas bills.

The woman at the gas company refused to make a payment agreement with him, because he already had a payment agreement. If he couldn't pay, he would be sent a shutoff notice; only then could he make a new payment agreement. At that point his monthly rate would go up, because he didn't pay. Malcolm, cosmically bored, argued with her for a half-hour. "This is absurd!" he said finally.

"Don't you be abusive with *me*," the gas company woman said, and hung up on him.

Malcolm had a glass of milk and a cookie and called the gas company back.

The woman who answered the phone this time said fine, no problem, and made a new payment agreement.

If at first you don't succeed, try, try again.

The Water Department, however, would not talk to delinquent customers over the phone. He would have to go there and spend several hours in the plastic chairs waiting his turn, making exasperated expressions along with people who at least looked like they had more reason to neglect their bills. By the time Nora returned with her gladiolas, Malcolm had already left to deal with that exigency.

The phone was ringing when Nora got home, and it kept on ringing, with people returning the calls she'd made that afternoon from the phone booth.

It was good to be reminded that she was not the only person with problems, financial, physical, or spiritual. One friend was presently investigating nursing homes for his ailing mother. Nightly the mother awoke before dawn, moseyed naked to the nurses' station of the hospital, and demanded a margarita, or else said, "Excuse me, miss. What time does this store close?" There were writer's blocks, difficult stepchildren, dead-end jobs, and stubborn flus.

Each friend was a swirl of disaffections, divorces and debts, alike as snowflakes. Nora and Malcolm were in touch—singly and collectively, locally and afar—with enough eccentric, complicated, active people to write a casebook on the modern middle-class condition. They were poised on a brink of century and sensibility. Amid space shuttles and artificial hearts, they still didn't know how sound came from a stereo; if they survived a plane crash, they might not be able to produce a fire. Everyone talked about their tiny strivings—for raises, bigger houses in better neighborhoods, or, among the parents, just a babysitter. Nora didn't feel superior, but she didn't feel connected either. She didn't mention the money to anyone, or her troubles with Malcolm. "What's up?"

her friends asked, implying that a midday call required some tragedy or glory. "Not much. Just checking in," she responded. And then the doorbell rang.

She bounded down the stairs, expecting a UPS truck or flowers. A sign of her dumb faith and hope: she always expected interesting mail, never got it. If Malcolm were home, he'd exhort her not to answer at all—it would only be a meter reader, a workman, or a Jehovah's Witness. He didn't even have his name on the doorbell; it just said "Worth." The other two doorbells, relics from the pre-Nora days when Malcolm rented out the first two floors of the house, were blank.

At the door was a business-suited woman with a briefcase and clipboard who wanted to know if Malcolm DeWitt was home.

"No," Nora said.

"He does live here, doesn't he?" the woman asked. "I don't see his name on the doorbell."

"Yes," Nora said, then got nervous and added, "sort of."

"'Sort of'?" the woman asked.

"Is there something I can help you with?" Nora asked.

"Who are you?" the woman asked.

"A tenant," Nora said—which was true, for tax purposes at least: Nora was officially renting the second floor of Malcolm's house.

"How many tenants are in the building?" the woman asked.

"Who are *you*?" Nora asked back.

"Ann Marie Lewis," the woman said. Now that Nora stopped to notice, Ann Marie was young, and attractive. "Do you have the second and third floors?" she asked.

"Maybe you ought to talk to Mr. DeWitt yourself."

Ann Marie Lewis smiled what Nora imagined was the smile of people who were used to being despised in the line of duty—dentists, bill collectors. She held her clipboard toward her chest so she could write out of Nora's view. She folded what she had written, put it in an envelope, licked the envelope, and handed it to Nora.

The return address said "INTERNAL REVENUE SERVICE."

"Could you see that Mr. DeWitt gets that?" the woman asked.

"I'll try," Nora said, "but I can't promise anything."

Nora raced back upstairs with the envelope, pausing at the second-floor landing to see if the IRS spy was watching to see which apartment door she entered, but Ann Marie was gone.

I will die young, Nora thought, and sat down at the dining room table to read the letter:

> We have been unable to resolve your account (see attachment) by correspondence and our attempts to reach you by telephone have not been successful.
>
> We have therefore sent an investigator to your residence or place of business on [and here Ann Marie had inserted the date].
>
> Please call the above number to arrange for another visit with [Ann Marie had inserted her name] immediately, or send payment in full and all delinquent tax returns. . . .

Nora put her head down on the table and waited for her heart to cut the marimbas.

When she looked up and out the window, she could see Ann Marie across the street, straddling her briefcase and staring up at the building, taking notes on the clipboard she'd balanced against her hip. With her other hand she held a candy bar from which she took occasional nibbles. Even from that height Nora could tell that the candy bar was a rare treat; she could also tell that Ann Marie was glad to be away from her desk on such a nice day.

Nora ducked out of the IRS agent's line of sight.

When the phone rang some minutes later, she didn't answer. In fact, she was so startled by the sound of the ring that she tucked her head between her knees, air-raid fashion.

"It's serious," Malcolm admitted, when he got home and read the letter from the IRS, with Nora watching him as if her dog had just gotten run over.

An accountant had completed the forms, but Malcolm couldn't pay what he owed, not because he had earned so much but because clients had been so late in paying him that his loss carried forward was totally screwed up. He had little choice but to attempt to launder the forms using the accountant's return as a model—and pray he wasn't audited.

"She wanted to know how many people lived here," Nora said.

"What did you say?"

"I said I wasn't sure."

"Oh, God," Malcolm said.

"She asked if *you* lived here, because your name wasn't on the doorbell, and I said 'sometimes.'"

"*Sometimes?*"

"Then I said I wasn't sure."

"Good work." Malcolm sank in the chair and rubbed his eyes.

"So what happens now?" Nora asked.

"Now," Malcolm said quietly, "I think we may have to think about selling the house."

"You know I'd love to move," Nora said, angling into his lap, "but I wish it were under happier circumstances."

"Me too."

"You know, Malcolm, I have to tell you, today—"

"I tried to call you from downtown," Malcolm said. "I was walking by the auction house on the way from the Water Department—"

"They're not about to shut us off, are they?"

"Not now. There was an Empire dressing table there, in this really amazing shade of honey-colored bird's-eye maple and in very good condition. I've never seen anything like it. You may want to take a look."

"Singin' in the rain, huh, DeWitt?"

"Something like that," he said.

"Mal, there's something I have to tell you."

"No."

"Today, at the bank, I—"

"No. Later, okay?"

When Nora started to talk again, molding her face into the comically grave expression she always used for discussing money, Malcolm cut her off with a kiss. She could have gotten indignant, but apparently the idea of passion amidst financial ruin pleased her enough that they wound up in bed.

The phone rang and rang. Nora resisted answering. The noise of the phone got incorporated into the rhythm of their lovemaking, as did the rain that began to drum the window, distracting Malcolm: he couldn't remember if the bucket was positioned under the skylight. They made love with their eyes open. For some reason, Malcolm found himself thinking about the time they'd made love after deciding to break up in 1982. Both of them had cried the whole time. They'd come crying.

He had to bury his face in Nora's neck as he was surprised by another memory, a disturbing one. Right before Beth left him, when he had no idea that he would shortly be plunged into renewed bachelorhood or that she was already seeing someone else, he'd had a premonition: beside her at a dinner party, he'd suffered a momentary collapse of heart and gut accompanied by the line *It's over*, the recognition intense as a stroke. He'd written the insight off as stress and forgotten about it until after the fact, when he swore to attend to his instincts. But what *were* his instincts? Nora murmured, shifted, grinded back. And why was he thinking, mid-act, about a trivial exchange they'd had a week or so ago, when Nora had awoken indignant to announce that she'd dreamed he was having an affair with a freckled strawberry blonde, and he'd shot back, *That's funny. I think I dreamed the same thing. Was she English?*

Nora worked hard to suppress the thought of David Martella stroking her hand. The most sensation for the least movement—very Oriental, very minimalist. A touch like a Frank Lloyd Wright house, all evergreen and waterfall.

This is it, Malcolm heard himself think, trying premonition on for size. *This is the last time*, and just as he caught the thought enough to ask, *What am I talking about?* his own pleasure streaked right by him.

6 IF NORA AND Malcolm had been contestants on a game show called "Can This Non-Marriage Be Saved?" the studio audience would have prescribed relaxation as an antidote to the stress of financial collapse. Making love was a good start. Next step: have a nice dinner. See a movie—a romantic comedy, no gangsters. But do not discuss money, success, or the nature of life on earth, which is exactly what they did after dinner.

The conversation started innocently enough, with Malcolm telling Nora about a building underway downtown. He'd passed the site that day and read the construction permit made out to someone he knew, an architect who wasn't very good—but made an impressive sales pitch. Eight years ago the architect and Malcolm had been in the same position, but while Malcolm poured years down the drain with go-nowhere Beth, this fellow had courted all of the city's most ambitious developers.

"It's not too late," Nora reassured him, but he feared it was. Those developers all did new construction now, and Philadelphia might be a depleted market for renovation, especially under the proposed tax laws. If only Malcolm had moved to Boston or San Francisco before his last financial crisis—their house would be worth a fortune there. Those cities grew and grew, attracting people who spend money on the kinds of things that make a city inviting—restaurants, repertory movie houses, kinky kitchen-gadget shops, avant-garde theater and dance—while Philadelphia got poorer, grayer, and grittier.

"What was Rizzo doing while Baltimore got federal funding to renovate the harbor?" Malcolm demanded, more loudly than necessary. "Putting the cops in leather jackets, painting the cop cars fascist blue, making midnight raids on hippies!"

Nora called this routine the Regretter's Club. Malcolm and his friend Tobias Maxwell were always saying, If only we'd invested in X neighborhood in 1979 when it was dirt cheap. If only we'd bought that wine by the case, or followed up on that idea in college and patented Trivial Pursuit. And what about Reebok stock? Malcolm had spent a decade searching for black leather sneakers. He was mournful about women, too, or at least she thought he was—he denied it, denied as well that there was anything defeatist about his business attitude. She knew from previous discussions which had dissolved into arguments that Malcolm did not want marketing tips for DeWitt Associates or analyses of his neurosis about asking for money. He did not want to be reminded that the time when they came of age was an oasis, deluding them into believing they could swim forever in ease and prosperity. He just wanted what, in the Worth family, was called an "Ah Baby."

Nora set her face into soft sympathy, the face of Donna Reed in *It's a Wonderful Life* comforting Jimmy Stewart that it isn't such an awful fate to be a local boy, stuck in Bedford Falls. "Don't be so hard on yourself," she said. "At least your time's your own. You haven't been on a narrow track, you've tried lots of things—"

"And failed at all of them."

"Just not gotten rich. And who knows, maybe this Stone thing will turn out to be a blessing."

"True," Malcolm agreed, "though it's perverse. I'd love to hear you explain to your parents how we can afford to move because I'm being foreclosed upon."

"Explain it to me."

"Hypothetically—well, wait." He went to his office to fetch an amortization table and a calculator, pushed aside the plates, and demonstrated how, assuming their house had appreciated by X amount, which they'd use as downpayment along with his equity, and assuming (a big if) they could find a fire-damaged place or shell for cheap which he could use his expertise to renovate for rock-bottom price, they could have a place downtown for, say, $1,400 a month.

"That's great," Nora said. "Can we have a deep-green marble bath?"

"We can have anything we pay for. But I have no guarantee of work, and you can't cover that kind of mortgage."

"Sure I can," Nora said. Despite herself, she was getting excited. The whole scenario had a starting-from-scratch, first-day-of-school texture: she imagined the double sink in the kitchen, the glass block of the shower wall, the housewarming.

"This way," she said, "we'll own the house jointly, and everything will be fair. I'll have a tax shelter, too. We can put the $9,000 you owe me toward the new place—"

"We can't put it toward anything," Malcolm observed, "if I don't have it."

Nora was about to mention her bank windfall when Malcolm made his next statement. He pointed out that such an arrangement wouldn't be exactly "fair" if she put in only $9,000 and he put in all of the equity and appreciation profit on his present house. Officially his share of the monthly mortgage should be lower—not even mentioning the fact that she'd get an architect and construction manager for free.

"You'd *charge* me?"

"Of course not. But it wouldn't be 'fair'; you'd be getting a deal."

Nora was incredulous. For the last three years, she reminded him, she had lived in his house as a tenant, paying rent. "Why should I both pay the rent and lend you money interest-free to pay the mortgage?"

Malcolm explained, for maybe the twentieth time, that only a *percentage* of that monthly sum went toward equity. And it was hardly fair for Nora to come in at the finish line, without having contributed to the original cash and sweat, and reap the benefits. If she was so anxious to "share," was she also willing to contribute to the building's expenses? The heat, hot water, and public electric which Malcolm paid as her landlord? Did she want to split the cost of a new roof?

"This is why people get married," Nora said. "People get married because it doesn't make sense to haggle like this."

As far as Malcolm could make out, Nora's main attitude toward money was that she deserved more of it. She saved in an old-fashioned way, like a kid in a Christmas club. No matter how many times they discussed real estate, he could never get her to understand the simplest thing. Like property tax: every time he added property tax to an estimated monthly cost, she'd always say "Tax?" in the same disbelieving tone, as if this was something Malcolm had made up, to trick her.

Nora grabbed the calculator and punched angry figures.

She presented him with the sum he owed her in interest on the money he had borrowed over the last three years.

Malcolm laughed. "You're charging me the yearly interest rate per month. I'd get better rates from the Mafia."

Nora started to cry.

"Poor baby," Malcolm said, patting her head. "Such a money moron."

"Yeah?" Nora wept. "Then how come I can pay my bills and you can't?"

"Because you don't own anything."

"Maybe I would, if you didn't keep taking all my money. If I'd moved in with a normal person, then paying my share would get me something."

"Like what?"

"Annual two-weekers abroad. Cars that aren't junkheaps."

He was sorry to have borrowed so much, Malcolm responded in his underwater voice, but he would pay it back, and she shouldn't exaggerate how badly he was doing. After all, debt was the American way. He felt tense enough about his situation without having to deal with how crushed she was.

Nora blew her nose and once more started hitting keys on the calculator. Feeling very heavy, Malcolm went into the kitchen for milk and a cookie.

"You and your milk," Nora said, following him. "That's why you get so many colds. You could at least drink low-fat milk."

He glared.

"I'm sorry," she said. "These are rough times. But Mal, you've got to acknowledge that it's rough for me now too."

"Everything's always rough for you."

"That's not fair."

"I'm sick of you blowing everything up."

"Well, I'm sick of you being passive and withdrawn in every area of your life except your willingness to lose money."

"Stop."

"Hey, *I* didn't start this."

Nora thought Malcolm was a passive-aggressive. Malcolm disagreed; further, he thought Nora was meta-aggressive—a storm trooper. Whatever the meat of the discussion, this basic disagreement always lurked underneath, hard as bone. What was the marrow? That night, Nora could have sworn the marrow was that there was no marrow. Malcolm DeWitt was a hollow man. She watched him eat the cookie: four neat bites, the chaser of milk calibrated to last until the next-to-last bite, whereupon he reopened the refrigerator, took out the gallon of milk, and poured another splash into the glass. His face closed in, avian. He wouldn't return her look. No doubt he thought his ability to filter her out was a Zen accomplishment, but to her there was something pathetic, primitive about him: a camouflaged animal holding still as the net swoops down.

"You never start anything," Nora said. "I have to—"

"Here we go," Malcolm said.

"What do you want from me? I've loaned you ten thousand dollars and we're not even married."

"You've let me know how grateful I'm supposed to be about it, too. But I've got a house you're living in for less than half of what you could rent an equivalent space for. Are you grateful for that?"

"I hate his house," Nora said. "I hate this neighborhood. If I weren't with you, I'd—"

"What? What would you do? I'm sick of you acting like I'm holding you back. Back from what? You're a fucking *food stylist*."

"Fuck you," Nora said.

The phone rang. It was for Malcolm. The voice sounded so official that Nora handed him the phone without asking who it was, her hand over the mouthpiece. Malcolm, however, was frantically shaking his head and waving his arms to indicate he didn't want the call.

"He's on the other line," Nora told the mouthpiece. "Can I have him return the call?"

It was the FBI. Someone named Tally or Tarry said he could call back until midnight. Nora scribbled the phone number on a legal pad.

"You asshole," Malcolm said when she hung up, before she could give him the message. "How many times do I have to tell you that *I'm not fucking home* when someone calls?"

"That was—"

"I don't care. *I'm not here.* Got that? I'm not *here!*"

Nora wrote "Federal Bureau of Investigation" before the name and phone number and handed the paper to Malcolm with a defeated expression.

"Now you're going to make a big deal about this, aren't you?" Malcolm said. "They probably just found my bill on Stone's desk. But I'm sure you'll find a way to make this the end of the fucking world."

"At ten at night?"

"So they work late."

Nora had had enough.

In her studio, she felt the time-lag sensation she'd experienced so strongly all week. A sudden lunge of the biological clock, some kind of emotional jet lag. The feeling when you pop awake on a Sunday morning at eight o'clock and think you've overslept, are late for work. Or as a child, sick, home from school, when you sleep through dinner and come downstairs to find the plates being cleared away. The clang of dishes in the sink startling, almost extraterrestrial.

She had to leave him. And she'd get no house, no alimony, having contributed $10,000 for the pleasure of his company.

To think she'd had to beg to move in with the foul-tempered sea slug, who disapproved of cohabitation as he disapproved of most things widely held to be endearing: dogs, children, vacation snapshots featuring loved ones standing in front of landmarks.

"Once we move in together," Malcolm had said, "you'll want to get married. Once we get married, you'll want a baby."

"What's wrong with that?" Nora had asked.

"Nothing if you want to do it. I don't."

"What do you want to do?"

"Just about everything else."

"Like what?" Nora demanded, and Malcolm had produced lists: he wanted to see Venice and Vienna, Prague and Peking. He wanted to make films again, spend some time with friends he never got to see.

Malcolm's objections to marriage, Nora said, were holdovers from the sixties, when the predominant demographic group was teen-agers and the predominant sensibility teen-age romanticism. Malcolm agreed that the sixties were an abberation, but then, the ruling forces throughout the history of mankind have been enslavement, torture, and tyranny—the same forces that Nora called maturity. And the sad fact was, she might be right.

On the way to her first brother's wedding in the summer of 1984, Nora had asked Malcolm what he saw as the future of their relationship. "I see it going on," he had said, "until it stops, or doesn't."

Soon thereafter she had started seeing David, and Malcolm claimed that it made him realize he wasn't going to be able to have the kind of life he wanted—which included the company of a female—unless he was willing to let her move in. "Compromise" was Nora's word for that decision. Malcolm called it blackmail. As he liked to point out he'd predicted, scant months after heated negotiations about closet space and picture placement, Nora began to speak about marriage. Last summer, during a tranquil period, he had finally agreed that they could begin to broach the subject in the fall.

And now this. Now Stone. Nora could spend another small fortune to keep Malcolm alive—and still not know if they were going to stay together. Why should she *want* him, anyway?

So this was it. Twenty-two years and forty-odd boyfriends after her first kiss, Nora would still have eyes swollen shut from crying and insides like overripe melon, and who would care? *I gave at the office*, everyone would say, slamming the door in her face and returning to spouses, children, careers. She couldn't say she blamed them.

Malcolm watched her mount the stairs with the high-headed posture of the wronged wife going home to mother. But she'd be back, probably in ten minutes, to demand, *Did you call yet?* All of her energy would now be focused on the FBI. His failure to return the call that minute would be representative of his whole slugabed life. Or else he'd be accused of not calling just to spite her. The woman simply did not know how to back off. Every worry was the paramount worry. She could patent her own neurosis: the Parking Ticket School of Anxiety. Heap a bunch of low-grade worries together until you're looking at a pile that makes you gasp, *The horror! The horror!* If you're a minute late on your meter, they'll boot your car, and before you know it you'll be in solitary confinement as a scofflaw. She never worried about anything important—like the fact that they might have wasted half a decade together. Just plenty of nothing, lots of hurry-up-and-wait, and meanwhile she credited herself with the honesty and emotional depth, called herself "the one who worked on their relationship." This meant that in a couple of days she'd demand credit for their reconciliation, which would entail her presenting herself and suggesting that Malcolm apologize. "You first," she'd say. This was supposed to be cute. *I don't need this*, Malcolm thought—even said out loud—as he put aggressively atonal music on the stereo and turned it up to top volume.

ON WEDNESDAY NORA stifled her misery and finished shooting a commercial for a supermarket chain. She cut carrots into careful sprigs like miniature chef's hats. She matched mushrooms for size and shape, painting them with lemon juice to prevent discoloration. Then she worked on the turkeys. She had to cook three: two as stand-ins, the same size and only slightly inferior to the chosen bird. The photographer would use them to set up lighting and exposure while Nora prepared what in food-styling parlance is called "the hero": the ad's pièce de résistance. The timing had to be precise, so the photographer was set up before the hero's fat congealed, the drumsticks separated from the breast.

As she worked she thought about David. She had been thinking about him since the bank—given her dream, even before that, even before the fight with Malcolm; not thinking so much as feeling his energy and humor like wind on skin. She kept getting subliminal flashcards of kissing him, and their lips met mentally now as she spread the turkey with Vaseline and sewed skin from one of the stand-ins onto the hero in a place where the hero's own skin had peeled off. David was a hard kisser, a lip biter, but his hands would be light along the back of her neck, a place Malcolm never touched. She knew exactly how David Martella's shoulders would feel against hers. The heft of him, the hunger.

She left the shoot carrying an immense uncooked turkey, too misshapen even to serve as a stand-in. She had to act grateful as the supermarket owner bestowed it upon her, making a crack about broken lollipops tasting just as good. Fashion models get to keep their clothes; Nora got a turkey that would never fit in their apartment-size kitchen's freezer. So they'd have to eat it at once—but when? They had Richard's wedding.

Outside it was snowing.

She wasn't even wearing her heavy coat. It had been so mild. But as she left the shoot, it was clear that the warmth had been a false, calm-before-the-storm warmth, because it was indeed snowing now.

This is the point, Nora would later say, when she lost what of her critical faculties remained.

People walked with their faces uplifted, with the slightly artificial awe reserved for weird weather conditions. In all the office buildings bodies were grouped around windows to stare. It was the first snow of the season, and some people looked joyful, but many of the faces were dismayed. Millions of holiday plans were about to be ruined.

Snow stuck to Nora's eyelashes. She put the turkey in her car trunk and marched to the same phone booth where she had abandoned and rescued the gladiolas. Not much of a coincidence, but in her weakened state it felt like a sign that what she was about to do was destiny.

She called David Martella at work locally, then in New York. She still knew both numbers by heart. He wasn't at either job. She called him at home and got his answering machine.

"I hope you're enjoying the snow," Nora said, giving her voice an edge of the plaintive, shy tone she and David had used as lovers. "We need to talk. Call, okay?"

The thought that she didn't even know where David would be for Thanksgiving depressed her.

The snow was getting heavier. Leaving the phone booth, Nora realized that her brother's wedding could be snowed out.

The snow was falling now in a glitzy avalanche, as from a slot machine—nickels (with inflation) from heaven.

It was almost a quarter to three before Nora got to her bank, which closed in fifteen minutes. The bank was always mobbed right before closing time, and would have been even more mobbed before a long holiday weekend, but the snow had created a run of people trying to get home before the snow-related traffic jams, so the bank was seriously congested.

The tellers were anxious to get their own battles with the weather finished. But beneath the impatience on all their faces was a sardonic touch of good cheer—the camaraderie city dwellers always get for power blackouts, water shortages, and World Series revelry. On top of all that goodwill it was someone's birthday. For some reason the cake caught

Nora's attention right away. It was the usual birthday cake iced in baby pink and blue; several sliced squares of cake remained on napkins on one of the desks. Most of the tellers, Nora now realized, were tipsy. They had probably taken the birthday girl out to lunch and had a couple. Everyone was glazed and happy. The bank had an expectant hush, as if the snow were muffling all sound. A softly whistling janitor had already begun to attack the pools of water and mud that had collected on the bank's cool marble floors.

It was obviously the perfect time for a bank robbery.

Nora didn't exactly think this. In fact, she later wouldn't remember having decided to take the mystery money at all. She did it under some kind of snow blindness that allowed her to wait in line and panic only once, right before the beeper went off and the light saying "Next teller please" flashed. But she found herself before the teller with the long, curly fingernails who had helped her on Monday.

"Hi, there," the teller said.

"Enjoying the snow?" Nora asked, handing her the check made out for $100 in cash.

"Oh, sure," the teller said, rolling her eyes.

"You have a long way home today?"

"Luckily I took the train," the teller said, handing Nora the cash without even checking her balance.

"That *is* lucky," Nora said. "Would it be hard for you to check my balance?"

"Not at all," the teller said, and after a minute on the phone handed Nora another slip of paper. "This is a balance before what you just withdrew," the teller explained, and Nora said, "Thanks so much." She held her breath and read the slip: $32,054.04.

Nora said, "I also need a bank check for—"

"That window," the teller said, directing Nora to a pudgy-faced woman across the bank.

"Have a nice holiday," Nora said.

"Same to you."

The bank-check lady was unoccupied. When she got to this teller's cage, Nora realized she was the birthday girl.

"Happy birthday," Nora said through the bars.

The teller laughed. "Do I look older?"

"You've got the corsage."

The teller and Nora both studied the corsage for a second, smiling.

"I'd like a bank check for—" Nora paused—"twenty seven thousand, nine hundred dollars."

Why $27,900? A stupid amount. If the idea was to remove the money from the account so the bank maybe didn't notice it, wasn't it more sensible to remove the whole $30,000? And what was she going to do with it, anyway?

"Want to make it twenty seven nine oh two," the teller asked, "or want to give me two dollars in cash?"

"Pardon?" Nora said.

"The bank check is two dollars."

"Make it for the even amount," Nora said, "and I'll give you the cash," and Nora wrote out a check, fast, made out to the bank, for $27,900.

"Who's it to?" the teller asked, examining the check.

"Excuse me?"

"Should I make it out to you?"

"Oh," Nora said. "Sure. Yes, thanks."

"Just a minute, please," the teller said, and as she brisked off toward the computer with a glance at the bank's huge clock—only minutes now before closing time—Nora thought, *Now they come back with the handcuffs.* When the teller called over a male manager, and he looked at the computer too, and then both of them turned to look at Nora, she almost screamed across the room, *Stupid me! I meant twenty seven dollars!* But the teller came back, smiled, and typed the check on the antique check-typing machine, holding her hands gingerly as women do when they're being careful not to damage their nail polish. Handed the check to Nora. Said "Two dollars, please." Nora got the bills from her wallet, trying to complete the task mostly inside her purse so the teller couldn't see her shaking hands. "Have a good holiday," the teller said most pleasantly, and Nora said, "You too, and happy birthday." The teller said, "Thanks again," looking not at Nora as the bank check exchanged hands but at the clock, the big hand of which was moving—slowly, as slowly as it used to do at the end of a school day—to three o'clock.

At three o'clock exactly the guard locked the door. He opened it to let Nora out.

My God, Nora thought, *they just want to go home before they're snowed in. They just gave me the money. They didn't even ask to see my driver's license.*

WHEN MALCOLM WOKE that day, Nora was gone.

Down the street a truck braked. The house whirred with the housely sounds of pipes and tanks, wind and traffic rattling windows. The roof and walls expanded, contracted like a body's breath in sleep. Not one of these soothing sounds, Malcolm knew without getting out of bed, was Nora Worth.

Malcolm didn't feel too well. Taking inventory of his body parts, he realized he had that heavy, overcast feeling in his limbs that prefigures a cold and is sometimes worse than the cold it-self. Weighing himself, as he did every morning, he saw that he had gained two pounds, which could only be explained as water weight—it had been so humid. It was humid and he was foggy, having stayed up until 4 A.M. fooling with plans.

The planet only seemed fresh to Malcolm, alive, when he was on his own counterschedule. His father too, after he retired, had liked to stay up all night to assemble some item in his basement workshop or just enjoy the almost holy sound of the city when all the phones have stopped ringing and all the dogs have been walked. But if Nora were home, she'd inform Malcolm that you can't stay up until four in the morning, even if you do get eight hours' sleep. The body clock gets overwound. His mother used to give him the same advice, then Beth. When was this idiotic bit of folk wisdom imparted to women?

Without Nora there he could drink coffee, read the paper, shower, and dress without being asked what he planned to do and when. At least that was the hope. But their argument the night before had made him feel like someone had tossed a grenade of molten rock into his lungs; and when Lucy called, the rock began a menacing pulse.

Lucy had spent the morning paying her little visit to the FBI.

"They did full fingerprints on me," she told Malcolm. "Tips of fingers, sides of fingers. Whole palm, side of hand. Messy. Then they made me sign my name about a hundred times on this split form. Then Stone's name. Then Stone's broker's name. They asked a lot of questions. What did I know about the relationship between Stone and his broker? How about Stone and his banker?"

"Did you get any information about Stone?"

"They were very circumspect. They said I could call in three or four months and inquire about the progress of the case."

"Does André know anything?"

André was the French chauffeur. "If he does," Lucy said, "he's not letting on to us. He's been making the rounds of the gay clubs. I think he already knows more people in town than we do. Talking about knowing people, I applied to you for a job. If Unemployment calls you, say DeWitt Associates couldn't use me, okay?"

Lucy was looking forward to spending time with her kids. She had cleaned house and gone on a reading spree. Though Lucy was (or had been) a secretary and her husband, Jack, was a high school principal, these old friends of Malcolm's were better read and more intellectually lively than most college professors. They were not particularly "ambitious"—just vibrantly alive. Maybe, Malcolm thought, he should follow their lead. It was too late to marry his college sweetheart, but he could return to social work, devote his evenings and weekends to motiveless personal enrichment. But the very thought of social work made him so weary that he had to remove his bathrobe and lie down, his brain buzzing from the caffeine.

He couldn't bring himself to return the FBI's call yet. Instead, he went downtown to shop for food at the Reading Terminal, a restored Victorian train station now used as a farmer's market. Inside, Orientals sold the city's freshest produce. The seriousness with which Orientals treated their vegetables always gave him a flush of patriotism, as did the fact that someone in the city had had the vision to keep the station from becoming a parking garage.

Malcolm loved how alike those grand old train-station markets were in Philadelphia, Baltimore, St. Louis. He loved the similar look of garment districts, Chinatowns. How the red-light districts always develop near bus stations; how the harbors, the first areas to be renovated, are the first to be overrun by gaping suburbanites and gangs of bored teen-agers.

Often, absorbed in the city's eaves, Malcolm would forget the side-walk and fall off, howling and clutching his bad back, or simply get side-tracked—which is what happened that day. He found himself outside the auction house where he'd seen the table the day before.

From the street the auctioneer's voice rose and fell like something from nature, like wind or waves. Malcolm went inside. The table was right where it had been, the celestial gold of the bird's-eye maple glim-mering.

Since Malcolm's childhood, the same auctioneer had been perched above the bidders in a box that could be wheeled around the huge room. As the staff pushed his box from piece to piece he adopted the world-weary, proud posture of a minor, aging raja being carted around atop an elephant.

Malcolm had arrived just in time. The china lots and less valuable pieces had been sold, and now they were working on the clocks and rugs. The table Malcolm wanted was one of the last pieces to be auc-tioned that day, and obviously a hot item. People kept going to stand be-side it or looking over their shoulders at it proprietarily. Malcolm sus-pected he didn't have a chance.

He put his bags of groceries on the floor between his legs, positioning himself slightly away from the cluster of people so he could study the bidding styles of the professionals. Most of the people here were dealers. The tone of the proceedings was one of strained jocularity with an un-dertow of pure self-interest.

Malcolm was ready to wait, as the professionals did, until the right moment. Yesterday an auction staff member had told him that the table would go for somewhere between two hundred and how badly some-one else wanted it—which was, obviously, at least two hundred more than Malcolm should be paying right now for anything except a lawyer.

By the time they arrived at the table, the crowd seemed to have dou-bled although maybe that was just an echo from Malcolm's pounding heart. He had been standing beside the table all along; as they got to the table the auctioneer and the crowd of dealers pressed toward him.

"Unusual piece here," the auctioneer said. "What do I hear?"

He didn't hear anything. Malcolm waited. No one bid.

"*Three* hundred," the auctioneer offered. "Three hundred. Do I hear three hundred? Two fifty? Two fifty. Two fifty."

There was the millisecond when no one said anything, when everyone seemed poised to burst into speech, and Malcolm raised his hand. Before he had recovered from the shock of his own voice saying "Two fifty," someone else had offered more and the auctioneer had raised the bid to three hundred. Knowing it was crazy, Malcolm said "Three hundred." He meant to say it loudly, but he had lost his voice. Before he could tell what had happened, he was on the edge of the group, the rest of the dealers having begun to defect to the next piece to be auctioned.

He had lost the table.

That was all right; he couldn't afford it anyway.

But then he realized that the auctioneer was looking right at him saying, "Name? *Name*, sir."

"DeWitt."

"*What?*"

"De*Witt*," Malcolm said, and the auctioneer said, "*Sold* for two hundred fifty to De*Witt*."

The dealers, now positioned by the next piece, were looking at him, mildly curious, but not for long: the auctioneer's box had been wheeled, the stream of numbers had recommenced, and a man beside Malcolm, taking his name and address and asking for one-third payment as deposit on the table, which had to be picked up by five o'clock today rather than tomorrow because of the holiday, and would Malcolm sign here, please?

Malcolm had now recovered enough self-possession to realize that no one else had even bid. Malcolm's offer of two fifty must have been the last offer the auctioneer heard, and then Malcolm's offer of three hundred—he had bid, apparently, against himself—had mercifully gotten lost in the scuffle.

He signed, and wrote a check.

All of this had taken a little over a minute.

It took considerably longer to fetch the car, wrap the table, strap it into the trunk, and ride carefully home. Whatever pleasure he might have felt in the spontaneity of his purchase was mitigated by the enigma of how he was going to get the table out of the trunk, up the steps, and into the vestibule without destroying his back—and how he would explain the purchase to Nora.

Once the table was in place, Malcolm lay down on a heating pad with the mail and the morning paper.

His foreclosure notice had arrived, or rather notice of his foreclosure notice: the final big boot would arrive soon by registered mail. He didn't open the envelope.

In the paper what caught his eye was an article in the business section, which he normally didn't read, but for some reason—maybe because he was reading with more than usual languor, to avoid the foreclosure notice—he saw the headline: MONEY LAUNDERING: THE BANKS AREN'T ALONE. The subtitle added, *Federal strike forces are cracking down on brokerage houses and casinos for their roles in an estimated $100 billion annually of dirty money.* Malcolm skimmed the article, hoping for a hint about Stone and his brokerage house, but of course found none—only an amusing explanation of "check kiting," the strategy by which E. F. Hutton had moved money from one checking account to another just ahead of bouncing checks, thereby getting interest-free use of four billion dollars at a time when interest rates were almost twenty percent. Malcolm had certainly engaged in the practice himself, on a smaller scale. He called it "riding the thirty-day wave": the process by which, graceful as a surfer, he skirted payments until the crest. If E. F. Hutton could do it on such a grand scale—and the federal government, for that matter—why not Malcolm DeWitt? Nora could lend him money to pay the mortgage, which he'd lend back to her to pay her bills, which she'd lend back to pay his bills.

"Most fraud," the article said, "starts small. An employee in the bookkeeping department discovers that he can create fictitious checking accounts, or replace original invoices in a file with photocopies, change the amounts, and collect the difference. As the perpetrators of such fraud move up in the organization, the scope of the fraud also increases."

Smiling to himself, Malcolm turned to the classifieds; his smile widened as he read:

> The Internal Revenue Service in downtown Philadelphia has an opportunity for an Interior Designer to apply state-of-the-arts skills to assist in planning our office space. Major responsibilities include designing, drafting, and presenting proposals for new or revised office and architectural plans.

The ad stressed that "good communication skills are essential" and also insisted on "superior skills in the use of computer-assisted design systems." And for these talents the IRS was willing to bestow all of $18,326. On that salary a young adult could afford a nice efficiency apartment, maybe even payments on a college loan.

Automatically he clipped the ad for his dumb-ad file. Only as he imagined showing it to Nora (she'd like the synchronicity, and anyway, she never seemed to believe how bad things were for employed architects) did his stomach flipflop. What was funny? Why was he imagining a cartoon of himself doing plans for the IRS to pay his back taxes, as if washing dishes at a restaurant as payment for his dinner? Very likely, very soon, he would be working for that salary himself—if he could even find a job, with no architectural degree, no office experience. It would not be easy. *But with your talents*, Nora would retort, believing against all evidence that you could have anything if you wanted it badly enough. To Malcolm, the knowledge was as sharp as the pain in his back. You couldn't. "Go for it" was Hollywood—just as it was, at this point, to think that Nora would be around for long.

ONCE NORA WORTH had gotten hit by a car. The driver made a right on red without looking. Nora had not been paying attention and noticed the car only when she found herself pushing against its hood to keep her balance. The driver rushed to her. They both studied Nora's body for damage. None was visible. Nora assured the driver she was fine and walked another five or six blocks before she doubled over, dizzy, nauseous.

9

That's how it was with the bank. At three o'clock she put the certified check in her wallet, walked out into the snow, and walked to her car without an umbrella, snow crystals in her hair.

She was dizzy then, and nauseous.

Somewhere in America, a machine that made Big Brother look easygoing had an up-to-the-minute account of what she spent, what she owed. Another computer knew that she subscribed to *Vogue* and belonged to the ACLU. The computers of marketing firms had no doubt analyzed this data, knew what strange lingerie or outdoor equipment catalogues to send to an urban woman with her financial and personal profile. Sublime credit rating aside, it was not going to be easy to back-date a deposit slip for $30,000, keep the pink copy, and claim she fed it to the money machine but lost the receipt. Nor was it going to be easy, if caught, to claim that so much money went in and out of her account for business that being far too rich and busy to balance her checkbook, she hadn't even noticed. They had her average daily balance—how could she run from that?

Getting into her Toyota, which reminded her of a geriatric with emphysema because of its phlegmy-sounding acceleration and sniffling idle, Nora remembered *Psycho*. She'd wind up stuffed in a car trunk, her pile of cash pristine and unspent beside her, still not having learned the lesson that the pharaohs learned centuries ago: you can take it with you, but it doesn't do much good there.

Her car wouldn't turn over.

She sat in the car for a long time, periodically turning the key in the ignition and bending her head to the steering wheel to listen, as if the car would say something more revealing than *What? In this weather?* Finally it said, *Pfft*, almost a mocking noise. And then, like Malcolm, it decided it had repeated itself too often, and wouldn't say anything at all.

Malcolm had a turkey too—a tiny turkey. He was fixated on miniature food: tiny new potatoes, tiny brussels sprouts, anorectic asparagus. The turkey was already stuffed with chestnuts and wild mushrooms and in the oven. The Empire dressing table was already in position in what passed for their vestibule.

Malcolm had spent the last couple of hours struggling up from the heating pad to look at the table and the snow, or to answer frantic, despondent phone calls from Nora's relatives. The thought of Nora's brother's wedding being canceled because of inclement weather pleased him as deeply as the thought of a snow day from school had when he was a child.

He had prepared this dinner knowing that he might eat it alone. He didn't remember whether Nora's shoot that day was local or in New York. The snow would foul her up in either case, even if she chose to come home. But he found himself waiting for her at the windows. She finally appeared, walking up the path to the house in the fashion of defeated soldiers with bloody rags on their feet. Malcolm and the aroma of the dinner met her at the door.

"Did you have trouble without snow tires?" he asked, taking her coat.

"No, because my car wouldn't start. I'm parked downtown. I took a cab. Why are you walking so funny?"

"Because of that," he said, pointing to the table.

"It's gorgeous. How much?"

"You don't want to know."

"Yes I do."

"Two fifty, but it's worth a lot more. Or it would be, if it wasn't chipped. See? The veneer's messed up here, but I can have it patched. Either that, or Empire just doesn't sell here yet. It was the only Empire there. People seemed, unless I imagined this, real attentive to who was going to bid, and when it was clearly not a dealer—"

"You spent your last pennies on antique furniture?" Nora asked. "I suppose I'm going to pay the electric bill. You moved it up here by yourself? Are you going to wear a corset to the wedding?"

"May have to," Malcolm said.

"Smells good."

"Early Thanksgiving dinner."

"They gave me an eight-hundred-pound turkey at the shoot, but I left it in the trunk."

"I doubt it'll defrost."

"How many relatives have called?"

"Your mother. Alan. Ken. Mark."

"Same general message—'Oh no there's snow'?"

Malcolm nodded.

"No one else?" she asked.

The call she was waiting for was David Martella's. He called at the end of the meal, which they had passed in the usual small talk about logistics—broken cars, travel plans, turkeys in car trunks. Nora didn't tell him about the money. She didn't ask how he'd spent the day, and he didn't ask her who called that made her jump up so fast from the table.

"Can I call you back?" Nora asked David. Malcolm had gotten up to clear the dishes, but he was still within earshot.

"I'm at a phone booth at the station," David said. "I only have a minute. I wanted to let you know Monday lunch is no good unless you're going to be in New York. How about Monday dinner? Because otherwise I won't see you until after Rome."

"Why are you going to Rome?"

"If I tell you, promise you won't make me miss the train proving to you that it's true. I'm going to be in a movie."

"Uh-huh."

"I knew you'd say that. I knew in just what tone. How come I always know exactly what you're going to say and I'm still not bored?"

"What movie?"

"We can discuss it at dinner. Dinner's much better than lunch anyway. Let's go somewhere nice. Have you been thinking of me since the bank?"

"Yes."

"How often?"

"Lots."

"You can't talk?"

"No." Malcolm had returned for the wine glasses.

"Shit," David said. "Doesn't he *ever* go out?"

Nora was about to tell David that Malcolm had already left the room, but David was already talking: "The train's boarding. I've got to go. I'll call you later. Ten minutes in broad daylight and I was ready to—it doesn't make any sense. I was looking at your legs."

"I was wearing—"

"You can still tell the shape. Your legs make me just want to pummel them. Entirely metabolic. There's something old-fashioned about it— we could be the last people in America to marry for sex. Do you feel the same way? Just answer yes or no."

"Sort of."

"You're so contentious. Nora?"

"Yes?"

"I'm so glad. It's just like the old days. I could just stand here feeding the phone quarters so I could listen to you breathe."

Through the phone, a cavernous voice announced the final boarding call. Nora was familiar enough with this commute to imagine the sounds of the herding passengers, the grind and squeal of the arriving train. "David?" she said.

"I'll miss the train," David said quietly.

"I'll miss *you*."

"I'm glad."

"So what have we decided? Monday dinner?"

"Yes. But I'll call you before that."

"I won't be here. I'll—"

"So call me," David said. "*Call me*, okay?"

She had to sit for a long time after they hung up to wait for her heart to stop.

It was still snowing. Nora went to her studio, called back various family members, and managed to discuss how the weather would affect the wedding—rather than her imminent split from Malcolm, or David, or the fact that she'd just stolen $30,000, for that was the truth: *I am a thief*, she thought, several times, but the Hunchback of Nora Dame—the creature in her brain who offered spiteful criticism through a megaphone—could only say this blithely.

Everything with David had been, still was, like a rush to catch a train. A matter of timing, dangerous but also exhilarating. Whereas everything with Malcolm was like a train stopped in the middle of nowhere, in another century. You just sat there with your head in your hands and your steamer trunk by your feet and waited and waited and waited.

In the kitchen, Malcolm was washing dishes in his own obsessive way, with hot water first, then cold to kill the spots, then shaking water from each dish before putting it in the drying rack so the water didn't run past the cracking grout into the compartment under their sink. When Nora approached to suggest that they had to talk, Malcolm pointed out that they couldn't. That was the problem.

"We've got to try."

"Don't act like you're aiming for heartfelt exchange," Malcolm warned, "and I'm holding back."

"Did I say that?"

"You've said it in the past. Now you'll tell me I'm merely 'holding a grudge,' because I'm not so retarded as to not remember what you said. You hurt me, then decide to forgive me for it. Thanks."

"Give me a second," Nora said, "to process the double negative."

"Typical," Malcolm sighed, turning away to dry a plate.

"I know," Nora said. "If you call me retarded, *I* can't be hurt. I provoked *you*, right?"

"Let's just not play who-cast-the-first-stone, okay?"

"My point exactly. We have to just—"

"Yes. When you say so."

"Do you want to play who-goes-first," Nora demanded, "or not? Make up your mind. Can't we have a conversation that's about something other than how we're having a conversation?"

"See? You fight to the death. Whatever I say, you just snake out of it."

"What *are* you trying to say?"

"You don't know who I am," Malcolm said. "You have no idea."

Nora made a patient face that meant she would control herself from saying, *Pray tell.*

"According to *you*," Malcolm said, "I'm this asshole that hides behind thinking of myself as a big, tragic secret because I don't know how to 'express myself.' Like that time after we'd first met and you were so angry because I wasn't more 'lively' at dinner with your friend Jessica, as if she was the most fascinating—"

"You can't still be angry about that. That was over five years ago."

"You still do it. You treat me badly, then get angry because I don't want to get married. How am I supposed to trust you? You don't listen to me. Everything I say you distort. Like that 'Regretter's Club' routine. It totally oversimplifies everything I've gone through, makes me into this bumbling idiot—"

"Stop screaming at me, Malcolm."

"I'm not screaming. And then when I *do* tell you how I feel, about work or whatever—"

"If you don't stop screaming—"

"Hey. This is *emotion*. You're supposed to like it. I'm 'expressing myself,' right?"

"By emotion I meant—"

"I hate to break this to you. Anger is emotion."

"Your only one, apparently."

"Screaming's the only way to talk to you because you don't fucking listen. So now you're crying, and *I'm* going to wind up having to comfort *you*, and we're back to—"

"No," Nora said, "because I've had enough."

"Oh. *You've* had enough."

"Are you happy?" Nora asked. Are you happy now?"

She made a gesture to indicate her face, the eyes already puffy from crying, and the galley kitchen, which had grown narrower and tinier. Malcolm looked at her coldly. As usual, she hadn't heard a thing he said. Now she would do her mistreated female routine. It was almost enough to make a misogynist of him. There were four brothers and about fifteen women she could call now for commiseration. They would all agree that Malcolm was a dull cad and demand, *Why do you stay with him, then?*

In the spare bedroom, Nora dreamed not about David or the money or the wedding that she and Malcolm had decided the next morning to attend together, despite the fact that their relationship seemed to be ending. All she dreamed about was the turkey in the car trunk. They wouldn't have time to stop for it before they left for the wedding, and by the time they got back the turkey would be a creature from a deep lagoon. Over and over in the dream she had to open the car trunk and be attacked by the foul smell of the rotten turkey oozing mold. Her friend Julie, a psychologist, would probably claim the dream meant Nora was about to get her period. She *wanted* to get her period, because otherwise what was she going to give birth to? A turkey. Nora didn't buy it. Even in the dream Nora recognized that the dream was trying to tell her something, that the turkey symbolized something. She just didn't know what.

10 ALMOST NO EXPERIENCE put Malcolm DeWitt in a worse mood than a wedding.

He didn't like arranged flowers, he didn't like posing for symmetrical photographs under police-interrogation floodlights, and he didn't like churches. Staying conscious for church weddings was even more difficult because everyone seemed to want to get married in the morning. Eleven o'clock on a Saturday morning, so far as Malcolm was concerned, was a barbaric hour to expect anyone to dress up, drink Bloody Marys, and smile like Howdy Doody.

Twice already, for two of Nora's brothers, Malcolm had driven to the suburbs of Northeastern corridor cities to endure this. At least it wasn't hot this time. The weather had gotten worse, icing over the roads. Malcolm liked the note of panic the snow had added to the proceedings, and of course the erratic weather provided a topic of conversation other than *What do you do? Is there money in that?* And the unspoken question (accompanied in Malcolm's head by the plaintive crescendo of a lone violin): *When are you going to marry Nora?*

Nora came from the kind of big, chaotic family in which no one ever got sick or arrived at the airport at the same time. Everyone assumed that someone else had pocketed the house key, fed the slobbering golden retriever. On top of the standard number of parents (Nora's thankfully had not divorced and remarried) and almost a hundred aunts, uncles, and cousins, the Worth tribe had been further augmented by her brother's wives and children. They occupied a full two floors of the hotel for Richard's wedding, and there was a great deal of travel in pajamas between the rooms. Since Ken's room was directly below Nora's the brother and sister even continued a childhood tradition of passing notes to each other on strings.

After today, Nora would be the next-to-last unmarried person in her family after Alan. She felt like the next-to-last single person in the galaxy, but she was determined to be good-natured today, so she consoled herself by remembering that the back pages of any city magazine carried personals from thousands of other singles. *Sweet-and-sour ex-tomboy*, her ad would read, *seeks passionate, practical man to resolve her love-hate relationship with the bourgeoisie.*

Because she partly agreed with Malcolm. Something about marriage was like the invasion of the body snatchers or the night of the living dead. It was hard to explain to anyone the pleasure she'd felt hanging out with her brothers in the old days. Their freckled faces and wire-rimmed glasses, their sharp shoulders, gauntness, and baggy pants: "Nora and the Thin Men," Malcolm called them. Five tall, wry kids with "creative" jobs. Alan, a video artist, worked part-time in a gallery; Ken was a partner in a company that produced trailers for Hollywood films; and Mark dealt in "concepts" (he'd recently earned $50,000 selling a promotional giveaway scheme to a gas station). Between them, they were a WASP Mafia, a good-old-boy-and-girl network. She would never know anyone, nor would anyone ever know her, that totally. And each brother who married, Nora lost. Much as she liked her brothers' women (all but one of them, anyway), there were new emotional rules in each household, as subtle and arbitrary as which piece of silverware to use for what at a formal dinner—rules she was always breaking. All of the wives were surprisingly down-to-earth and emotionally stable, so Nora simply did not have as much fun with her brothers as she used to. Somebody's wife always had to be up at dawn.

When Ken got engaged, the rest of her cohabitating brothers spent hours mocking the engraved invitations that spelled "honour" with a *u* and wrote out the year in words. They'd outdone themselves thinking up the kind of invitations they'd send out. Mark wanted a postcard rubber-stamped WEDDING, and Richard wanted to make a wedding ransom note on a lined yellow legal pad—WedD*in*G in newspaper cut-outs.

"Not me," Nora had said. "I want the most tasteful, simple, elegant invitation in the universe."

Her brothers had stared at her, amused. She had only just started dating Malcolm. Her bounteous ex-boyfriends had been mostly worms and jerks. She had done time with a married college professor, a hard-drinking Southern poet, and a golf-playing workaholic lawyer who cheated on her. If she wanted the happy couple welded atop the cake, she certainly wasn't hanging with the right crowd.

So Mark had married, and now Richard, and both of their invitations were exactly the kind they had mocked.

Then Ken had a baby, and her other brothers had wagged their heads because Ken and Annie would never again get a good night's sleep, engage in a spontaneous act, or have a prolonged, challenging, uninterrupted conversation.

"You know what they say," Nora had reminded them. "You never know how you'll feel about a kid until it's your own."

Her brothers replied that was exactly what they were afraid of.

But now Ken's wife was hugely pregnant again, and Mark's wife had just gotten pregnant too, and all the life preceding the pregnancy was warm-up, kid's stuff.

"Every day," Annie said at the wedding feast, "you wonder why you're putting yourself through having a kid, but every day you wonder how you lived before it. It's just an incredibly intense, incredibly fragile feeling."

Annie's daughter, Emily, sat in Nora's lap. Nora stroked her legs, which were cool and smooth enough to make Nora think she'd missed the boat entirely: she should have married years ago, so this could be her own critter she was fondling. As if reading her mind, Laurie, Mark's wife and Nora's least favorite sister-in-law, got a holy expression as she fingered her conspicuously empty champagne flute. Since marrying Laurie, Mark had become opinionated. If they bought a Honda, Datsuns were a crime.

"Children make you so nostalgic for your own childhood," Annie continued. "You think about riding a bike and playing in the mud and catching grasshoppers."

"Malcolm hated his childhood," Nora said, trying to draw him into the discussion, but he was across the table, commiserating with Mark about the black comedy of New York real estate prices.

Malcolm had been born to his parents late in their lives. His sister was fifteen years older than he, almost Nora's parents' age. His father died right before Nora met him; he and his mother communicated mainly by birthday cards, despite living so close to each other. Malcolm's old-fashioned toy soldiers, which decorated a shelf in the TV nook of his ancestral home, made Nora's heart ache for him. Each tiny tin French soldier was hand-painted right down to the dot of blood on the tip of its sword. How could he understand what it's like to have a family like a small, stable, self-contained tribe?

At the next table, Nora's mother had put on Nora's father's jacket. There was always a point at a wedding where Sylvia Worth got cold, borrowed her husband's jacket, and took several drags of his cigar. In the huge jacket she looked like a little girl playing gangster. Nora's father, who acted a bit like a gangster in real life, got expansive when he was drunk, blurting out his love for everyone. Sylvia Worth twisted around in her chair to give Nora a hug.

"Do you think they'll be happy?" she asked.

"Yes," Nora said.

"Sarah's such a quiet girl," she whispered (Sarah's parents were seated right across from her). "Do you think she's too quiet for Richard?"

"How could anyone be too quiet for Richard?" Nora whispered back.

"That's what I mean," Mrs. Worth said. "All his other girlfriends were so boisterous."

"Look at you and Dad. You and Dad are both quiet."

"Do you realize your father and I have been married for thirty-six years next month?"

"That's wonderful."

"That's a long time. And let me tell you, Nora, I'm not bored."

Nora was not a weepy drunk except from champagne. Champagne made her see the bittersweet poignancy of everything, like the fact that she hardly ever confided in her mother anymore, and that the last time she used the evening bag she was presently opening for a tissue was also over a toast, the last time a brother of hers got married.

A hundred and twenty eight people raised glasses over melting sherbert and said, "Here, here."

Malcolm scowled, his brow furrowed.

His back was killing him.

He was disappointed that nothing outlandish ever happened at weddings. Not once had one of the waiters suffered a heart attack in the middle of collecting the soup bowls, to be revived by heroic cousin Tom, cardiopulmonary surgeon—a much better role for him than rattling on about investment tax credits. Not one bride and groom had decided that they'd made a mistake, or that maybe they had better wait.

The groom designed planetariums. The only sibling with any mathematical abilities, Richard had actually majored in physics, and now now traveled around the world to advise governments on how to paint and light their fake heavens. In India he'd spent five months designing a private planetarium for a guru, a birthday present from his followers. He recently returned from Mexico. "You wouldn't believe how corrupt things are down in Mexico," Richard had just finished telling Malcolm, and Malcolm had said, "Sure I would." Yet here Richard was, cutting a piece of cake as if, just because the bride and groom atop the cake were made of brightly painted cardboard, he were somehow immune from the cliché of shoving a piece of cake into the bride's mouth as the photographer fired a flash.

Across the room, Nora danced with her brother Mark. She hadn't even bothered to try to coerce Malcolm onto the dance floor, as she usually did after champagne.

Malcolm watched her with grudging admiration: nervous women have great bodies. Obsession just churns the calories off. Most of the women Malcolm had loved were tiny and taut as Balanchine dancers, with mangled nails and cuticles—he associated groomed fingernails with obesity. Nora was the tallest, with arms so chicken-thin he could circle them with his thumb and forefinger clear up to the elbows. Her legs, though, were perfect, genetically. Totally unjust: she didn't exercise, whereas Malcolm's own lean and hungry look had to be maintained with weights, the last exercise he could do—after screwing up his knees at basketball, he couldn't run, and with the present condition of his back, he might not be able to lift weights for long either. As Nora danced, all of Malcolm's energy flowed into the base of his spine and knotted. He couldn't will the pain away.

He thought of great athletes whose injuries robbed them of not only their livelihoods but also their whole senses of self. Arthritic pianists, sopranos with throat cancer. But he couldn't shake the feeling that such people knew, at least, what they had lost; they could paint a line, in bright yellow as on a highway, between then and now, start afresh; whereas he was chased, had been chased for years, by the mistakes of his past. With Nora and their fights more repetitive than weight lifting, with his back taxes, even with the kind of work he did (or failed to do). Why renovation? Why couldn't he do new construction? Why did he always have to be hemmed in by parameters he didn't set?

"Hey," Nora's present favorite brother, Alan, said to her. "Are you all right?"

They were leaning against a column in the hallway. Nora had taken off one shoe to rest her foot, the leg up behind her flamingo-style. Alan had his arm around her. "I'm fine," Nora said.

"Are you sure?"

"If I tell you something," Nora said—the older guests were dancing as older people do at weddings, acting more drunk than they really were—"will you promise not to tell anyone?"

"Sure."

"Not Jane? Not even Malcolm? And I mean *really* not tell?"

Alan said, "This better be good."

She told him about the $30,000 in her checking account, about getting the bank check.

"Are you nuts?" Alan said. "What are you going to do with it?"

"Put it in my money market. Leave it there for a while, in case they catch me."

"*In case?* Then what do you think you're going to do, act like you didn't notice?"

"Give it back."

"Maybe it's not an error," Alan said. "I've read that banks do some juggling of funds, especially end of the year. Stash money in various accounts so they can report the bank assets as low on their tax return, then switch the funds back after December 31st. Also, a lot of middle-management types 'misplace' money and take it out for themselves a bit at a time. In either case you can bet they know where they buried the bone."

"What about the simple computer-error version?"

"It's *criminal*, Nora. You know? Like you walked into a bank with a gun and a big bag?"

"Not the same."

"No? Remember Joey Coyle, in your own fair city? Are you going to plead temporary insanity? You know, I just read an article somewhere—some woman got a hunk of money that way, spent it, got caught, they sued her, she countersued—"

"Did she win?"

"Don't remember. Your attitude is weird. What gives? Why haven't you told Malcolm?"

"I thought I'd try to keep the money for a couple of days, before he spent it all in one place. Anyway, Malcolm and I are breaking up."

"Yeah, yeah," Alan said.

"Really. We're just being good, other-centered, and unmelodramatic today, that's all."

"I never know when to believe you about Malcolm," Alan said. "You're always breaking up with him."

"Doesn't that tell you something? Don't you think that after five years there ought to be some kind of basic trust?"

"I don't know," Alan said. "Maybe. But what if you *have* it and just don't know it? Or what if you never get it? What if no one does? What if that's the lie of marriage—that it settles anything?"

"That's not the problem. I mean, look at him over there, frowning, Look at how he's been acting today."

"So? I thought he said he hurt his back. Now you tell me you're breaking up, and he said he's having some financial problems—"

"Another charming DeWitt understatement."

"So how great a mood is he supposed to be in? Anyway, he hates weddings."

"Why? Because he's an unloving person. A block of ice, a stick-in-the-mud. A dud."

"Well, *I* like him. How much is he supposed to enjoy being cooped up with hundreds of Worths? Which isn't to say—I assume you know this—that I won't understand if you end it. He doesn't seem to ever get very far, work-wise. But Nora, many marriages end in divorce without the disappointed parties taking to crime. Is this the only way you can get his attention?"

"Here's the other part you're not supposed to tell anyone. I think I'm going to see David again."

"The film prof from a couple of years ago?" Alan said. "That's disgusting."

"What are you talking about? You never even met him."

"Look, why don't you come stay with us for a week or so? Maybe you and Malcolm just need a vacation. Let's say you *are* breaking up. No reason for you to—"

"What makes you so sure David's so bad?"

Alan sighed.

Jane, the woman Alan lived with, approached to give him a head-cocked glance in a private pig Latin which Nora couldn't read.

"They're about to throw the bouquet," Jane said.

"Shall we hide?" Nora asked.

"It's no use," Jane said. "They'll wait for us."

Soon thereafter, the bride threw flowers at Nora Worth. The bouquet bounced off Nora as she tried to flee, and landed at her feet. *Pick it up!* everyone said. *It's yours!* Nora said she didn't think so. She said it was Jane's. Everyone, including Jane, disagreed. Nora looked around for Malcolm, but he was in the men's room, taking a leak beside her father.

"Strange weather," Ted Worth observed.

"Certainly is," Malcolm said.

"They say that whenever the fall starts like it did this year, whenever it's that warm that late, you're in for a terrible, terrible winter."

"How about that," Malcolm said.

They shook themselves off, smiled at each other, and reentered the crowd.

When Malcolm approached, Nora handed him what she estimated to be her twentieth bouquet. If she had a hundred dollars for every photo album in which she appeared in pastel colors, her arms blurred as they caught a bouquet (or in this case, failed to catch it), she would have enough money to—well, at least to open an Individual Retirement Account.

"Why are you crying?" Nora's mother asked her, as they stood on the steps to see the bride and groom off.

"They're going to Europe," Nora said, "and I'm not."

"I bet that's not it," Sylvia Worth said softly, linking her arm through her daughter's. "You can tell me. What's wrong?"

"Nothing," Nora told her mother. "I couldn't be happier." And they shivered, coatless, as they waved to the car riding off in the snow, trailing TV dinner trays strung together with bright yarn. Alan eyed her through the crowd with an expression of deep fear and pity, as if he was the only person who knew she had just received the diagnosis, month left to live.

Both Nora and Malcolm loved the party-favor, grab-bag quality of hotel rooms: the wrapped soaps, the one-wash shampoo packets like servings of ketchup. This hotel room was an unusually tasteful one, with a huge bed and a restrained Japanese theme in jade green.

Nora's period, she announced from the bathroom, had just begun.

She took off her clothes and pulled down the bedspread to white sheets as smooth and cool as the skin on her niece's legs. The room was dark except for the glow from a streetlamp in the snow-covered parking lot outside, muted through the curtains, and the UFO glow of the television, which Malcolm had already turned on. Whenever he entered a hotel room he immediately found the classical music station on the radio and flipped the channels of the television with the sound off.

The radio was playing *The Rite of Spring*—hardly seductive music, but Malcolm danced a bit, hunched over the TV. Ba-pa *ba*-pa *ba*-pa: for a second the rhythm reminded Nora of the noise of her personal identification number, punched into the money machine.

"This is the transcription for two pianos," Malcolm said. "You know it? It's very nice."

The Stravinsky made an interesting score for a National Geographic rerun about a rain forest in Central America. The trees developed toxins against the insects, which in turn developed antibodies against the toxins, so that each insect could eat only one kind of tree. A preposterously colorful frog laid its eggs in tiny pools of leaf-water, so the eggs could be eaten by a preposterously colorful snake. Every time she saw these shows Nora regretted not having majored in biology.

"Aw, Mal," she said as he changed the channel.

"What have we here?" he asked.

He crouched, still fully dressed, in front of the soundless television and fiddled with the antenna. He had found a cable porn flick: a woman kneeling, hands kneading her own nipples, as a man produced a pleasurable sensation below with his tongue. Close-up of long tongue. Close-up of commensurately long male part grabbed by woman. Malcolm turned around to grin at Nora, who had knelt herself, to see over Malcolm's shoulder, as a close-up of the happy woman's face showed her whipping her head around to express sounds of what should have been pain, according to Stravinsky's strident rhythms.

Malcolm took off his pants, turned up the Stravinsky, turned up the TV sound, and knelt beside Nora.

They were fond of each other, even if they *were* breaking up, and her periods were always erotic times. Furthermore, something about the anonymity of hotel rooms always worked as an aphrodisiac for them.

"Mmm," Nora said, as the TV actress moaned.

He removed the tie, but left the television on. Why not? Maybe all of the wedding guests, including the bride and groom, including the pregnant women—maybe even including Nora's parents, married thirty-six years—were watching the same movie and doing just this in the privacy of identical hotel rooms, eyes closed to the moans of a partner who could leave at any moment; who could be any stranger in the world, but wasn't.

Two

THE MONTH BETWEEN Thanksgiving and Christmas always feels bloated and empty at once, like the aftereffect of Chinese food. No matter how much you get done, there's a hazy certitude that you've forgotten something crucial—like the coffee machine with an inch of liquid left in the pot that, two hours into the trip, you remember you didn't switch off. Soon, a new year. Each year takes less and less time. You don't need to be a time traveler to be stuck in time, nor does time have to move slowly to trip you up, viscous as quicksand.

11

During the car trip back from the wedding, Malcolm and Nora had engaged in a session of *You, no you*, speaking loudly over the heave of the engine. The rusted old gas-guzzler could barely do fifty, whereas Malcolm and Nora, like tires spinning on ice, covered the same ground, dug a deeper rut, and hoped for traction.

Malcolm argued that he could hardly attend to the relationship now, with his entire life collapsing. If good feeling were to grow between them again, it would happen on its own, over time. Nora countered that the watched-kettle-never-boils school of relationships was evasive and dangerous, which led them right back to his resentment about her whole conception of him as the little engine who couldn't.

Their only choice was to try to stay out of each other's hair for a while, until the tensions between them eased or until it became clear that they weren't going to ease. Nora couldn't afford a hotel, and if she got an apartment she'd have to sign a year's lease. So they would live with and without each other through Christmas and New Year's, in a state of suspended animation that, Nora pointed out, just about summed up cohabitation: neither married nor single, neither together nor apart, suffering all the pain of divorce without benefit of any of the emotional comfort of marriage.

"'The emotional comfort of marriage,'" Malcolm retorted, "isn't worth shit when you get to this point. The only difference if we were married is we'd get to pay lawyers."

"If we were married," Nora said, "we would never have gotten to this point to begin with."

"You think marriage is some kind of garlic you wear around your neck? You think Stone wouldn't have gone under?"

"It isn't the money, Malcolm. It's your refusal to deal with the feelings involved."

"Here we go. What do you call what I'm doing now?"

If Malcolm had reached across the car seat and patted her knee, Nora would have hoped. But he was snarly, self-enclosed.

Talking to Malcolm, Nora thought, was like trying to balance a checkbook when your version and the bank's version don't agree, and no matter how many times you retotal the numbers, retrace your steps, you just can't find an error; any second all your checks are going to bounce.

On Monday morning, Nora Worth deposited the bank check for $27,900 in a money market account that had been inactive for almost a year, since Malcolm, the termite, had clamped down his jaw on what was left of her savings: a couple of thousand, hardly a foundation, but at least a two-by-four of financial security. The snoozing $27,900 would accumulate interest at the modest rate of around $6 a day, which was enough to treat someone you loved to a drink every single day of the year or, once a year, to take an all-expenses-paid European vacation for two. You might even be able to fly first class: leg room, a flute of champagne, and a curtain to separate you from the throng of cretins lined up to use the toilets, one of which by mid-flight always gets clogged.

Or you could just put the whole $27,900 down on a big old house (mahogany staircase, servants' entrance) and stay inside, curled up in your Josef Hoffmann armchair by your marble fireplace.

Would you feel too distant from the real world, out of touch with the rough pulse of city life?

Not for a second.

Nora's money market was a box number downtown and a voice at the other end of a toll-free number. She borrowed Malcolm's car so she could drop the envelope containing the check in the box outside the main post office. She would call Tuesday morning to see if the check had been posted to her account yet. Of course it wouldn't be; it wouldn't even arrive until that day. The figure would appear on her monthly statement. What did she expect, a letter from the chairman of the board? *Dear Nora Ann. The minute we saw this sum in your pathetic no-account we called the police. How dumb do you think we are? We suggest you pack your pajamas.*

If they caught her, she would simply give the money back. It wasn't *her* mistake. Still, at her money machine on Monday her heartbeats were as high-pitched as the key's touchtone *meeps*. *Enter your personal identification number*, the machine instructed; Nora complied, and waited for the wrath of God. The gargoyle crouched behind the money machine would punch through the sheetrock and swoop for her neck, alert the cops, or at least refuse to give her a cent. But the machine said, *Press OK to verify*, asked her the nature of her transaction—(there was no button for grand larceny), then asked the amount. Behind her, the people waiting for their turn at the machine (one machine, like the airplane toilets, always appeared to be broken) shuffled, so perfect a picture of boredom that Nora suspected they were hired: each person in line— even the mother with the baby in a stroller—was in fact a bank dick with a black belt in karate and a magnum, or whatever the name was of Squintin' Clint's big gun.

Maybe, Nora thought, after surviving the chasm between *Transaction is being processed—please wait* and *Please remove cash or receipt*, I ought to just turn myself in.

And this was just Monday.

"You're the one who always demands complete itineraries of my every move," Malcolm had accused, "and all of a sudden you're talking about 'needing space.'"

"The good old 'you're the one who' construction," Nora sighed.

"Yeah. The one who comes into my office whenever you feel like it. But now *you* want privacy."

He was right: her sudden stress on privacy was uncharacteristic. She would usually share the more colorful details of her brother's wedding, no less an event as major as her bank windfall. She often told the same story many times to different people, as if—like the stand-in preparations before she began work on a food-shoot hero—the repetitions would help her get it right. But other than Alan, she'd told no one about the bank money, not even Julie. When her best friend Julie Peszko called on Tuesday, however, Nora found herself whispering on the phone, pausing to listen for Malcolm's breath.

"Speak up," Julie said. "You sound like you're in Yugoslavia."

The minute she heard Julie's voice, Nora was desperate to tell her everything, but it took a while to get around to it, because Julie was falling in love again.

Julie had almost become a nun, and now turned her spiritual intensity toward men. She liked in a man what Catholics like in a church: flash and filigree. Her relationships were gothic, oozing incense and long shadows.

Her last serious relationship had been with a man she'd faced for a silent toast at a crowded gallery opening. They'd gestured toward the exit and left without even asking who would drive, his place or hers. The car and place turned out to be Julie's, and their first time—the most astonishing sex Julie had ever experienced (not an insignificant sample)—was completely wordless. Their second and third encounters were beyond language as well. The lean, dark stranger with the thick eyelashes would appear at her door and ring the bell but not talk to the intercom, so it wasn't until their fourth encounter that Julie found out the man was a deaf-mute.

He was a deaf-mute lawyer specializing in the rights of the handicapped. He taught Julie sign language. For a while all Nora heard about was Ameslan. On top of being brilliant and a world-class lay, the lawyer was kind and independently wealthy.

Evidently there are hoards of brilliant, rich, sensual men, and Julie kept meeting them, despite AIDS and the new chastity. Of course most of them were married (the deaf-mute lawyer's wife, an ex-model, was also a lawyer—not deaf-mute—and they had a gorgeous daughter in tiny blue European shoes), but this didn't seem to bother Julie much.

Julie's new love was a patient, she told Nora on the phone, and Nora groaned. Julie was a psychologist in the schizophrenic teen-age ward of a ritzy suburban mental hospital.

Julie laughed. "No, he's an adult. I met him when he came to the teen ward to do adjunct art therapy with the kids. He's not crazy. Well, he's a *little* crazy. He's sort of drying out."

A mathematical genius, Julie's latest had been integral to the original microchip revolution in Silicon Valley, but he had had a crisis of faith over how commercial the business had become, how competitive his co-workers, and had a breakdown. Sporadically he suffered from clinical depression that could be medicated, but he liked to check in for a while during the really bad spells.

"How sweet," Nora said. "Same time, same padded cell in the loony bin. I assume he's a married, productive grown-up the rest of the year?"

"Separated," Julie said.

"I wonder why," Nora said.

"When you meet him you won't talk like this."

"Maybe I can stop by for a chat before his shock therapy," Nora suggested, regretting it at once: old friends were too easy to mock and take for granted. "I'm sorry," she said.

"That's okay. I'd say the same thing, if it were you."

But when Julie said that before he committed himself he had been working for a bank, Nora realized how useful the fellow might be.

"That's a wonderful coincidence," Nora said. "Incidentally, I'm having dinner with you tonight, in case anyone asks."

"Where are we going?"

"Nowhere. How about Wednesday?"

"Sure."

"Quiz question," Nora said. "What would you do if you found out you had a million dollars?"

"Get an investment counselor."

"Or not a million. Less. Say, thirty thousand."

"Let's see," Julie said. "I'd buy the building on the other side of the party wall and evict the punk rockers."

"Do you think if I met you at the hospital on Wednesday I could talk to your new boy about banks?"

"Why?"

"In utmost confidence, right? I appear to have taken $30,000. Well, $27,900. I didn't really steal it. It sort of fell into my lap. Or into my bank account. It showed up in my balance last week, and I took it."

"Are you serious?"

"I haven't told anyone but my brother Alan and you. I haven't told Malcolm, because we're breaking up."

"Breaking up like you usually are, or really breaking up?"

Sketching her present situation for Julie, Nora felt oddly defensive of Malcolm. Julie found him boring, though she was too tactful to say so. Malcolm did not make incisive eye contact with strangers or say romantic or enigmatic things over drinks. During the last near-breakup, Julie had rooted for David. Of course, David had courted Julie's approval. A careerist even in romance, he had handled his happy hour with Nora and Julie like a job interview. But Julie surprised her.

"Don't do anything too hasty," Julie said. "Things with Malcolm have been good."

"They have?"

"What do you mean, 'They have?' You said so. And if you're going to have an affair, why wouldn't you do it with someone new, someone you didn't already know the limitations of—like someone who could make you come?"

"Coming isn't everything."

"Neither is money. I'd hate to see you leave Malcolm just because he's not rich, because you don't really care about that."

"I don't?"

"Don't you know?"

"No. I don't feel sure of much, except I'm seeing David tonight, and you know what's weirdest? I can't really think about Malcolm. I can't think about the money either. All I keep thinking about is David."

"You don't need a computer expert. You need a psychiatrist."

"What are friends for?" Nora asked Julie.

Nora was welcome, Julie said, to stay with her. But Nora was weepy enough without the sneezing and itchy eyes that would result from sleeping on Julie's couch with its hundred thousand hairs from what Julie insisted was a hairless cat. Furthermore, the thought of their sobsister slumber party—bitching about boys and consoling each other that they were pretty, perky, and smart—bored her.

"You know what boredom's a sign of," Julie said. "Repressed rage."

"Phooey. Too much boy trouble—there's a whole world out there I'm not attending to."

"So attend," Julie said. "It'd probably be better than leaping into something with David."

Nora agreed, but at the same time felt that David—her affection for him, and the promise of its return—was the sweetest, surest thing in her life, despite the fact that "dependable" was not an adjective one could reasonably apply to David Martella.

You never knew whether David was going to keep an appointment until he was beside you, and even then he might have to leave the country after the first course. Since Nora was the kind of person who had to concentrate to arrive places on time rather than early, this had been one of their problems during Round One.

In David's presence, she always knew he was a jerk. Or not a jerk—just not for her. Too demanding, too unreliable. Away from him the longing set in. Don't fight me, he had always said. Don't rationalize; the longing is what's real. And Nora would roll her eyes, knowing—because she was nothing if not self-aware, or at least self-aware enough to know when she wasn't—that a longing wasn't worth much if the grass you wanted to roll in was on the other side of the fence.

For the rest of the day she sat by the phone, afraid to leave the house to run errands she wouldn't have time for later in the week for fear of missing David Martella's call. From the moment she'd hung up the phone before the wedding she'd longed for David, and when she woke up on Monday to the sleeping, open-mouthed form of her insignificant other, she could think only of David, as if the dinner would settle all accounts.

12 BENJAMIN STONE WAS not the only person who wanted to relocate. Many buildings near Stone's old office sported "For Sale" signs. Real estate values had plummeted here when a local church started a hospice for homeless women, a service that everyone agreed was essential, just not in their neighborhood. The church opened its doors to the women in the evenings; during the day they made themselves at home among the gentrifiers, lecturing pedestrians, defecating on doorsteps. The homeless women attracted homeless men, who were more aggressive in the amount of territory they staked, sprawled on heating vents with their scabbed feet and their essence of urine and beer—a brew so potent that it shocks no matter how familiar, like the smell of skunk or cat spray.

In Stone's office, the Federal Bureau of Investigation had emptied file drawers and stacked papers everywhere. A man at the computer terminal, drinking coffee from a styrofoam cup, was printing out everything in the computer directory. His face indicated a pleased competence. As the printer clacked away, an endless fan of computer paper unfurled through the office like a toy train, crossing desks and file cabinets, smothering an already sickly potted plant.

The FBI man looked familiar. With the dimples and pale blue eyes set slightly too close together, Ed Tarry didn't have the kind of face you see often. Tarry was sure that Malcolm looked familiar too. It took a couple of minutes of shuffling through Malcolm's social work and police photography, Ed Tarry's college days in Michigan and years on the Alaska pipeline, for them to realize that they were both local boys who had gone to St. Joe's Prep together, Tarry two years behind Malcolm.

"Weren't you on the football team?" Ed Tarry asked.

"Basketball."

"I worked on the yearbook," Ed told Malcolm. "Did you have Macklin for Greek?"

"God, yes. I wonder if they've straitjacketed him yet."

They beat up on Catholic schools for a while, then beat up on the city. Every time Philadelphia made the "Around the Nation" column in the *New York Times*, Malcolm remarked, it was for a trash strike or MOVE.

Ed agreed, then offered that crime in their city was a special breed too. "Speaking of which," he said, "you worked for Stone?"

"Yes."

"In what capacity?"

"Designer."

"This your bill?"

Ed handed him the first invoice, for the first couple of month's work, with DeWitt Associates across the top. Malcolm nodded yes.

Who owned the building to be renovated? What was the nature of the work to be done? After less than five minutes of such questions, Ed Tarry had thanked Malcolm for dropping by.

"Sorry I couldn't just ask you on the phone," Tarry said, "but it's procedure for the larger bills to get a signature." Ed located the form on a desk, and Malcolm bent over to sign.

"What's the charge?" Malcolm asked.

"I'm really not allowed to tell you."

"My suspicion is we're talking big," Malcolm said.

"Well, this one is definitely in your yellow pages under 'Crime—Federal.'"

"So I guess I shouldn't count on getting paid on my outstanding $6,800."

Ed Tarry threw his head back and laughed like Tarzan beating his chest.

Uptown, the snow had been trampled to death by the workers of the world, who moved fast as cockroaches headed for baseboards. Despite the Christmas decorations, everyone seemed emotionless, except for the people who had gotten splashed with mud by passing cars and buses: every few blocks the splash victims stood frozen in place at curbs, agape and indignant.

Nora would see Julie tonight, which meant Malcolm could play strange music at top volume during dinner, drink the vilest-smelling single-malt Scotch, and work on the plans for Stone's office, without having to account for his time. The office design was the most sophisticated, original work he had ever done, the first work he was proud of after too much nuts-and-bolts renovation, and he was less upset about losing the money than about not getting to see this work actualized. The truth was, he would do it for free.

Thinking about the plans made Malcolm feel so bad that instead of going straight home he decided to take in a movie at a theater he hadn't been to in years, since it was divided in half and began to show kung fu movies to hoodlums.

There were twenty-three other patrons in the huge theater—Malcolm knew, because he counted. Most of the patrons congregated in the middle seats of the middle section like castaways in a rowboat. The theater had a mildewed, brackish air. Luckily, Malcolm was some distance from where the school-skipping teens jabbered. He had chosen an aisle seat to stretch out his bad knee, but when he slumped his back hurt, and he realized how marginal he was when he noticed how unnaturally aware he was of his leg, as if he were one foot out of the grave, the foot placed on some kind of terra firma.

So he was frightened even before the movie began, and the movie didn't help. Countless people died against a backdrop of urban decay, in Sensurround. The teen-agers called *whoo-eee* for each bullet that hurtled off the screen. Malcolm tuned them out and concentrated on the path of the bullets until he was dizzy, stiff, and drained. The director had shot most of the action in a dusky half-light—the same kind of shadowless light the city had when Malcolm left the theater, making it even harder than it usually was after a matinee to adjust to real time. He experienced a surge of time-lapsed nerves about having spoken to an FBI agent, which quickly segued into anxiety about his foreclosure and the workless horizon.

Malcolm got into his car in a panic, and his friend Tobias Maxwell's office was where he found himself.

Tobias Maxwell was half-black, half-Jewish. His mother was the Jewish part. Despite the fact that his uncle was a famous retired basketball guard and one of his cousins had starred in a breakdance movie, Tobias was scrawny, stoop-shouldered, and in general about as black as Woody Allen. His glasses fell down his nose. For the couple of years that he'd worn a beard, he'd looked like a mangy, black, Jewish Abraham Lincoln scaled wrong.

Tobias and Malcolm had been social workers together in the late sixties. When Malcolm defected to filmmaking, Tobias moved to the city's Human Relations Commission. The commission did not solely represent blacks and women. In past years Tobias had defended a beer-bellied, balding forty-five-year-old man who wanted to be a waitress at a Polish restaurant and an orthodox Jew who wanted Friday afternoons off in winter to take public transportation to synagogue before it got dark.

Recently Tobias had been promoted to Housing Discrimination Supervisor, a position that dovetailed with his secret ambition: to make millions in real estate with no money down. He now had tips about the choicest inner-city dwellings, of the kind Malcolm called "milkers," as in "milk 'em for all they've got"—you slapped up new paint, jacked up the rent, got the tax benefit, and five years later, when the neighborhood improved, unloaded the building for a profit. There was little role for a designer in such projects, but Tobias had claimed to be getting more ambitious in the scope of work he wanted to undertake and had been threatening to rope Malcolm into a project soon.

As business partners, Nora often said, Tobias and Malcolm were unthinkable—except maybe as a comedy team with two straightmen. Still, they were always discussing deals, if a little less often since Tobias's milker kick. Now that he owned a couple of properties, Tobias seemed to believe he was both more realistic and more adventuresome than his friend, and that unvoiced but palpable claim to superiority had driven a wedge between them, though they could still keep up a comradely banter.

In his spartan office, Tobias was hidden behind stacks of folders on his desk, like a bureaucratic gnome. He brightened when he saw Malcolm, but stopped smiling at once to say, "What's wrong?"

Malcolm took off his wet shoes and proceeded to tell Tobias about Stone.

"You *knew* that guy was dire news," Tobias said. "It was just a matter of when you got the telegram. But here's timing. I finally talked with Rymer, and he actually sounded interested in the Ivy Street deal."

Months ago, Malcolm had drawn up plans to convert an immense old bank in the warehouse district into historically certified lofts, if only he could find an investor to cough up $800,000. Nathaniel Rymer was a wealthy citizen whose quiet power Tobias had been reverently following for years. Recently Tobias had stepped up his campaign to get friendly with the great man; he'd managed to have a long chat with Rymer during the annual Housing Discrimination Awards banquet and asked if he could present a potential real estate investment plan.

"If I wasn't such a mercenary guy these days," Tobias said, "I'd try to talk him into running for mayor. 'Time for Rymer.' He'd be great—I'd love to manage his campaign."

"Sure," Malcolm said.

"I'm telling you, the guy's magic," Tobias said. "He could get socialists to salute his Bentley. Silver hair. Strong, gentle face. Long, purposeful stride—distinguished enough to be president."

Malcolm rolled his eyes.

"I don't get this," Tobias objected. "You're suddenly unemployed, I hand you an extremely rich possible client, and you're not even excited. Your attitude—"

"You know how many extremely rich clients I've had? Enough to flatten out and use as pattern on wallpaper. Stone was an extremely rich *actual* client."

"That was a bad break. But you can't get discouraged."

"My 'attitude,'" Malcolm said, "no matter what the dress-for-success books say, is completely irrelevant."

"Don't get defensive."

"I'm just tired of being lectured on how to succeed in business by people who don't know anything *about* business. It's like Nora frothing at the mouth about how I should have made collecting money from Stone a top priority—as if architects billed daily. You want plans? I'll give you plans. I'll give you figures. I'll attend any meeting you can set up. But I'm not going to sit by the door panting."

"I'd hate to be reading your EKG right now," Tobias sighed. "How is Nora, anyway?"

"Nora and I haven't been getting along very well lately."

Tobias had time to put an *ah-hah* in his eyes before the phone rang. He answered and listened for long enough to pretend to kill whoever was on the line by strangulation and by poison darts (unbent paper clips) through the sound holes.

"I need a vacation," Tobias said when he got off, "or a hitman. That guy doesn't understand why you can't say you weren't promoted because you were black when your boss is black and the guy who was promoted was black, along with eighty percent of your co-workers. What's going on with Nora?"

"I'm out almost $7,000 from Stone. She didn't take that too well—I already owe her money."

Tobias nodded. Malcolm felt resentment rising: why tell Tobias about his financial problems, when Tobias was the kingpin of the get-aggressive-or-get-a-job mob? Why talk about his problems with Nora to a man whose experience with women amounted to noticing, in between bouts of eating take-out food in front of his home computer, that he didn't have any? But Malcolm forced himself to treat Tobias as a friend, and to continue.

"Plus she's getting on my nerves. She's always worked up about something."

"This is news?" Tobias asked.

Malcolm sighed. Everybody was always trying to get you to share your problems, so they could give advice. Say your back ached and right away someone shot back, *Did you take aspirin?* Always that very line, that identical syntax, as if the same brainwashing tape had played in everyone's sleep, the same conventional wisdom on throwing the perfect dinner party or achieving self-esteem. If, Malcolm thought, Tobias suggests that I take her out for a nice dinner and soothe her with affection, I'll kill.

Tobias suggested just that. "You've been at this for a while," he added, in the patient tone people use when it's obvious to them you're not thinking straight.

Malcolm grimaced, putting on the wet shoes.

"Call," Tobias said, "if you want to see a movie or something. And listen, if you need to borrow some money—"

"No thanks," Malcolm said. "But thanks anyway."

But what did it say about Malcolm that this was his oldest friend—these days (now that everyone was burrowed in with children) almost his only friend? And what if Tobias was right, Tobias and Nora and everyone else? What was he trying to prove? *Maybe I need therapy*, he thought, walking to his car. Or maybe he just needed a new career, something in film or photography, something regular and easy, like Nora's food styling. Maybe he could be a pornographic photographer. The idea made him smile, even intrigued him for a second, but then he realized it would be just as bad: instead of dealing with incompetent painters splattering the floors, he'd have to deal with incompetent makeup artists, pouting models, picketing fundamentalists. *Won't I ever learn? It's all the same.*

He felt, driving home, as if he were sleepwalking, in some kind of horrible hypnagogic dream, so he was hardly prepared to find, on his doorstep, the most beautiful woman he had ever seen.

He noticed her from the street, not only because she was at his door but because she wore a strange cape in a strange, shiny fabric. As he approached the house she turned, and he recognized her at once.

After a while the woman smiled and waved.

"Mr. DeWitt?" she said, when he finally arrived at the door.

She held out her hand, and he shook it.

"You're a hard man to get ahold of," she said. "Ann Marie Lewis. Internal Revenue Service."

Malcolm let go of her hand abruptly and grabbed his gut, because he was laughing so hard he thought that most of the internal organs located in that vicinity were going to sink.

ANN MARIE LEWIS was pale and high-cheekboned, with long green eyes like an Egyptian cat's, a Cleopatra hairdo, and the kind of oversized mouth currently fashionable for models. Her hands were big and her shoulders broad, but despite her size, something about her carriage suggested lightness, speed, a dancer's grace. She wore one of the most bizarre coats Malcolm had ever seen: voluminous, complicated folds of violet neon flecked with red and pink in a fabric that was nubby like coarse wool but also had an almost patent-leather sheen and slickness.

Malcolm was still laughing.

"The IRS rarely inspires mirth," she observed.

"No," Malcolm said, wiping his eyes. "Wait." He finally managed to speak. "I know you from Temple University."

He told her when she graduated and her major (English). She looked puzzled, unable to place him.

"You were in an antiwar protest third week of freshman year that got heckled," Malcolm said. "Remember that girl who squirted lighter fluid on everyone and recommended that you all burn yourself in protest?"

She nodded.

"Remember a menacing guy started to pace in front of the group, and another guy passing by watched for a while, then grabbed the crewcut by the collar and glared at him until he backed off? I had a beard then, reddish."

Laughing, Ann Marie's face was all mouth. The sound was as exotic as her face: a god-summoning harp for tribal ceremony. "That was you?" she asked. "I don't think I ever saw you again."

He had seen her. He had always been alert to the possibility of her head of then-waist-length black hair, straight and shiny as Pocahontas's, towering above the other women's heads. He had never learned her name. By sophomore year she was usually with a boyfriend whose name Malcolm didn't know either, until years after college when he met the man at an art opening through the friend of an acquaintance from the film department—the man, in fact, with whom Nora had shot the turkey commercial last week.

"I knew Andy Roth," Malcolm said.

"Andy!" she said, with the face that Malcolm had noticed other women adopt for old boyfriends: a nostalgic smile such as you might use for reminiscing about a goldfish that got flushed down the toilet.

"That was almost twenty years ago," Malcolm noted.

Both of them shook their heads, in the somewhat self-mocking disbelief that people use to admit they're aging.

From peace rallies to the IRS. Logical, finally: the political types wound up in social-service jobs, thus in government, both local and federal; each government agency was a slippery slope that led to the next, so finally HEW and IRS were alike—acronyms with benefit packages.

Malcolm was not, despite Nora's accusations, a nostalgic person, a memory-dweller. But seeing Ann Marie Lewis reminded him of how it felt to be strong, sure, and fast, the kind of man whose fist instinctively shot out to protect a woman. A man who would run to the rescue of a car stuck in snow, who single-handedly lifted up the rear end of a VW beetle and threw his back out for life. Ann Marie was even more beautiful than she'd been at eighteen, her features better defined.

"Well," she said. "I'm here on business."

"Come on up."

What percentage of the third floor was he deducting for a home office? Malcolm tried to calculate, then remembered—with much the same jolt he'd felt when he'd first seen Ann Marie—that fudged home office square footages were not the biggest lie on his tax returns. To harp on that would be to behave like the husband who, caught in a lunchtime infidelity in the marital bed, berates his wife for coming home from the mall early.

Upstairs, Ann Marie spun like a game-show model before the grand prize, as people often did on first seeing Malcolm's light-flooded, two-story living room. More panic: this wasn't the setting to tell the ex-socialist about his poverty. Ann Marie Lewis stood in the middle of the room holding her briefcase.

"Sorry," Malcolm said. "I should have offered to take your coat. Do you mind if I ask what it's made of?"

"It's a thick but loosely knit wool, you see"—she picked up a glob of fabric from somewhere on the coat's expanse and offered it to Malcolm—"tacked to raincoat vinyl."

"Whoa," Malcolm said, thumbing the material. "Strange. How does it close?"

"It doesn't. A time-honored principle—the principle of the toga or the muumuu, except looser."

"Or a mummy," Malcolm said, enjoying the Egyptian striptease that left her, some moments and turns later, in a black skirt, wintergreen sweater, and the green boots. She handed him the coat. He stared at it.

"Just throw it on a chair somewhere," she suggested.

"Can I get you a drink?" he asked.

"No, thank you," she said, flatly and automatically.

Of course she wouldn't be allowed to drink on the job. "How about coffee, tea?" Malcolm asked.

"No, thank you."

She walked to the table, put down her briefcase, opened it, and sat down. Malcolm sat too, his hands folded on the table. He was already smiling, because the mood reminded him of being called to the principal's office; so when she said "Mr. DeWitt, you haven't filed a tax return since 1977," he didn't have to grind any facial gears on the transition to laughter.

"Sorry," he said, when he recovered. "Please. Call me Malcolm." But the formality of this invitation made him laugh again.

"That's a lot of back taxes," she said sternly.

She had attended the same college as Malcolm at the same time and had watched the same late-night comedy shows; she would have to share his amusement at this scenario. Malcolm found himself looking around the living room for evidence of Nora. Her rug, her vase, her November *Vogue*.

"Sorry," he said. "I'm just so surprised."

For quite a while now, before he was killing himself for Stone, he had been in the process of falsifying the figures presented to him by his accountant. He was trying to match losses and earnings so they made some kind of human sense; otherwise, by the time he filed, he would have to pay about three hundred percent of his income a year in taxes, factoring in penalties—for years in which he earned just pennies above the poverty level. Impossible but true. He had tried to explain the problem to Nora many times: it concerned clients who paid very late, then paid in huge sums not offset by losses; and some property shuffling he'd engaged in with Beth. At the time, claiming some of her buildings as his seemed sensible for them both, since it reduced her tax liability and made it easier for Malcolm to get construction loans, should he arrive at a point where he wanted to do his own developing. It hadn't felt like much of a crime; they considered themselves business partners anyway, and the properties were, at the time, ghetto shells for which they'd paid $4,000 each. Only one bank in the city would offer them construction financing, and grudgingly at that. Didn't they deserve some credit for being visionary? But then Malcolm and Beth's working relationship had soured, she'd sold the properties, she'd made the profit, and *he'd* had to pay the sales taxes. She had promised to pay him under the table but never had.

Ludicrously, one of the only legal contracts Malcolm had made with Beth concerned their tax arrangement. So all he had in writing was a document about their silent partnership; he could turn her in—and get them both indicted for tax fraud.

The accountant, handing Malcolm the returns, had said, "These are great. Best shelter setup I've seen in years. I'm very impressed. By the way," he asked, as an afterthought, "how do you live?"

And this wasn't even counting state returns, or the city.

He told Ann Marie that he had finished 1978 and 1979 and was almost done with the rest.

"May I have the forms, please?"

"Well, I'm not *quite* done. I have to check some things. I could mail them—"

"Why haven't you already done that? You've received five letters."

"I know," Malcolm said. He again felt like a third-grader, being scolded for late homework. "Of increasing urgency. I'm sorry. I just haven't had time."

"For *nine years*?"

"I'm sorry," he smiled.

"Well, you have to get the rest of the forms to me real, real soon. Two weeks. Tops."

"Oh, God."

"Otherwise your friendly neighborhood IRS branch is going to get a subpoena and confiscate your records and have the auditing division help you file your returns, at a hefty fee, and believe me, you won't enjoy that much."

Malcolm removed his glasses to rub his eyes. The eyes were deep-set, the eyebrows craggy; without the wire-rims he was less woolly, more threatening and manly, but Ann Marie missed the transformation. She was skimming the paperwork in her lap, in the posture of Vermeer's woman reading by lamplight. She had an auburn glow. Malcolm needed to put his glasses on again to see that her face was bemused. True, Malcolm's tax story was faintly comic, at least how he would eventually tell it—the true story was more like Monty Python. He hadn't noticed how crooked her mouth was. Maybe it was only crooked for this half-smile. His groin and brain rallied: how he loved crooked mouths! Especially mouths that were straight in repose and then twisted, turned, or fluttered into imperfection, sexy and weird as the spasm of Venus fly-traps or the ordinary, gorgeous snaking of plants toward light.

She looked up, the smile vanishing in surprise at being watched.

"Freshman year," Malcolm said, "I thought you were the most beautiful woman I'd ever seen. I still—"

She might have thought the pause was for effect, but that was simply as far as he could get. He hadn't even brushed Nora's hand until their third date.

"I know I'm not supposed to say that," he said.

"No," she agreed, looking down.

"It's true, though. It's so odd to see you again."

"Not really," she said. "You're from here, right?"

He nodded.

"I just read a statistic somewhere, that Pennsylvania has the highest percentage of people in the country who grew up in the state, never moved, and whose parents always lived here too."

"Really?" Malcolm said. "Low turnover? That would explain a lot."

"Well," she said, "you've still got to file your taxes."

"I know that. I'm not trying to snow you. Why bother? I've never gotten out of anything in my life."

He couldn't believe he'd said that, but Ann Marie Lewis leaned back in the chair, crossed her arms.

He blurted out his whole story then, or rather what of the whole story was fit to tell an IRS agent: about how he had done all of Beth's work at slave wages for years without even getting credit in one newspaper article, how Beth had cut him out of the action in the first project on which he'd stood a chance of actually earning money; about the community development project that had gone bankrupt, leaving him with $13,000 in construction debts; about Stone. So here he was out the salary and the winter's work, months behind on his mortgage, years behind on his taxes. What could he do? He just had to slog through day by day.

"What rotten luck for you," Ann Marie said. "I've seen it over and over, though. Most of the people our age who get work they love wind up getting shafted. Or maybe getting shafted is the nature of any work involving money; maybe we just didn't know that."

"*I* certainly didn't," he said. "If I'd known architecture was going to be like this, I would have stayed in film."

"I know what you mean."

This was more sympathy than he'd gotten from anyone in what felt like decades. He was overwhelmed. Maybe he could just tell her what had happened with Beth and she'd help him invent the returns so they didn't look fishy—what was he thinking? He must have looked particularly stricken, because she said, "Listen, I can't do anything about the filing date. You've got to file in two weeks. But off the record, if you need help figuring anything out, I could answer any questions you have."

She was packing up her things, replacing the file that said "DeWitt, Malcolm." "Here's my card," she said.

He pocketed it, then helped her into her preposterous coat. They smiled at each other, and he walked her downstairs, Ann Marie first. The hallway was narrow; he had to get past her in order to turn the key in the deadbolt.

They were standing close enough to compete in an apple-bobbing competition. Her briefcase brushed his legs. He loved her height. If he had been a different kind of man he would have leaned the necessary inches and kissed her crooked smile right then, at the door to the building. But he wasn't that kind of man. Just as well. He did not need attempted seduction of a public official added to his list of woes. So he stood as she said, "Bye, now," and held out her hand to be shaken.

When the handshake was over he said, "Someday I'd love to know how this happened to you. I mean the IRS."

"It's one of those long stories," she said.

"How do you get a security clearance as an ex-socialist?"

She smiled. "Okay. After you file."

He hadn't had this great a foreboding of change since his father died. Or not even then, not like this. The last time was probably at age five, on his first day of school, and as she left he felt five: small, powerless, but full of promise. He would file his back taxes, be done with that part of his life, move on.

Malcolm watched Ann Marie Lewis walk around the corner, depressed that he wasn't going to see what kind of car she drove and feeling the most intense pressure he'd ever felt to get the damn taxes out of the way, so he could ask her out to dinner.

DAVID MARTELLA'S TOTAL screen time, in the romantic comedy presently being produced in Rome, was a little over two minutes. He had eight lines. But it was a big movie with a major director; he and his agent were thrilled. His biggest regret was that he couldn't stay longer, but it was the end of the semester at his university, and he was on deadline for a couple of freelance pieces.

14

"What's nicest," David was saying, "is that the part is sympathetic."

"I've always wondered about the people who play nasty cameos their whole lives," Nora said. "Pot-bellied thugs, peon Nazis. Do you think their children squeal 'There's Daddy!' when they see them in reruns?"

"Yes," David said, staring at her. "Nice to see you."

"You too."

The tuxedoed, earringed waiter appeared. David was ready to order because he always had pasta, and a diet Coke with lemon. He didn't drink at all, or watch television. Nora ordered soup, sweetbreads, and a glass of the recommended Beaujolais.

"I hope," David said, when the waiter left, "that after the bomb goes off the only uncarcinogenic thing left to drink is wine, and the oenophiles have to drink it and drink it."

"You know, David, just because you're not interested in something doesn't mean it's boring."

"There's nothing interesting about wine."

"I love wine. You see? We'd never get along."

"On the contrary, unlike you, I love people who disagree with me, as long as they can defend their opinions. That's why you're with Malcolm—you need a yesman."

"Then why have I never been able to get him to do one single thing I wanted him to do?"

The waiter returned with the drinks.

"He cooks for you and cleans for you," David said.

"We both just happen to be clean. That's hardly the problem with our relationship."

"I agree. Those are details you work out when you love someone."

"With you, *I'd* work them out, because you're not going to change, so who's going to pick up your dirty socks?"

"Actually, I've always imagined a butler doing that."

"I see," Nora said.

"We'll get a nice big house in town. You can even hire Malcolm to do the design."

"Low blow."

"Why? You can quit work if you want, just work on your screenplays." This was David's idea of her next career move: he thought she should be writing sharp-tongued, tender-hearted films about the pleasures and dissatisfactions of middle-class life. "We can have an apartment here and an apartment in New York. Maybe we'll win Oscars the same year."

Nora shook her head, fondly irritated: ten minutes together and they'd already slipped back to their codified disagreement about ambition and romance, with Nora cast as the timid bourgeoise.

"Aren't you embarrassed?" she asked. "You're an academic with some freelance pieces on your résumé and an acid indigestion commercial."

"Laugh. I'm still getting the residuals."

"Then why don't you own a car? Why are you living in a studio apartment with an unventilated, moldy bathroom?"

"Because interior design hasn't been a priority. But now I'm ready to settle down, and you're the person I want to settle down with."

"What about Rita?"

"You should know," David said, as Nora ate her soup, "that Rita has delivered something of an ultimatum. In a lot of ways, at least on paper, she's right for me."

"'On paper?'" Nora said, rolling her eyes. "So marry her."

"The only thing that has held me back is you."

"You'll marry in nine, ten years, when you're bald and paunchy and it's harder to get girls."

"I told Rita this—it caused a big fight. You're the only woman I ever knew I could be completely faithful to."

"Sure," Nora said.

"It's true. I'm a very romantic person."

"I'm a realist."

"No you're not," David said. "You're so deeply romantic that you have to hide it. You're a sweet little nut with a hard shell. I even love your hardness, which is odd, because—"

"We've had this conversation a hundred times," Nora noted.

"Doesn't that tell you something?"

"We like the sound of our own voices?"

"This isn't a crush, Nora. I mean, look at us."

They had been talking with enough concentration to miss the waiter removing the soup bowl. Nora ordered another glass of wine, despite David's censorious expression.

"We've never gotten over each other," David said, "because there's something there. If you'd ever just take a risk, you'd know what's there, how much."

"Now I say I have evidence from your past behavior—the infidelities, the endless negotiations just to agree on a time for dinner, much less build a life together—that we wouldn't get along, and you tell me that I don't know how you'd be if we were in a relationship."

"You haven't."

"If I make an argument based on your past behavior, you tell me to have imagination. If I make an argument based on my gut feelings, you tell me I didn't spend enough time with you to know how you'd be. It's impossible to win an argument with you."

"That's not true."

They paused to smile at that exchange.

"I assume things aren't going too well with Malcolm," David said.

"We're breaking up."

"Why didn't you tell me before? What wonderful news."

Their entrées came. For the rest of the meal Nora told David about her present situation with Malcolm. When she mentioned the amount of money she'd loaned Malcolm over the years, above her rent, David professed shock.

"You pay him *rent*?"

"Well, we split the cost of the mortgage."

"And it isn't half your house? That's *sick*."

Nora tried to present Malcolm's side of the story, but David shook his head. "You're his *girlfriend*. A girlfriend doesn't pay rent. And to have him still doing the petulant bachelor crap—I've always thought Malcolm wasn't good enough for you."

"Don't badmouth him," Nora warned.

When the check arrived he said, "Now that I know you run a charity outfit, I think I'll let you pay for this one."

"Forget it."

David skimmed the check, took a wrinkled fifty-dollar bill from his pants pocket, slapped it down, and said, "My place or mine?"

"I can't," Nora said.

David leaned across the table. "Tell me you don't want me and I'll back off."

"I've always wanted you. That's never been the problem. I just don't think it's right for us to plunge into anything before I settle things with Malcolm."

"Jesus, you're beautiful," David said. "Your long neck—you're like some fast, wild, vegetarian animal."

Nora smiled.

"Let's go," David said.

The air outside felt good. Nora's new shoes were the same grape as the snow-reflecting sky. The veal stock and wine on the back of her teeth tasted purplish too—a subtle, urban purple that just about caught her mood, which was something like glad to be alive, and when it registered after a silence that David was beside her, she felt so energized that she didn't even think to object when he began to kiss her. She just kissed back (this was a fairly deserted part of town), recalling at once the sharpness and hardness of his mouth, so different from Malcolm's. The feeling of the kiss was the exact opposite of those anxiety dreams in which you sleep through the final exam or take the test but don't know the answer to one single question. The kiss was more like you know the subject inside out intuitively: not tongue-tied, forgetting the lines, but just passing through and being begged to play the lead, so to oblige, you ad lib, do beautifully.

David leaned against a car, pulled Nora toward him, and kissed her more. His pelvis was as familiar as his mouth, and as gratifying.

"Where are you parked?" David asked.

"By your place. I took a cab. My car fritzed on Friday, and I haven't dealt with it yet."

They kissed more in the cab, which smelled of pine air freshener—better than Nora could say for David's apartment.

"See how I made the bed for you?" David said.

They sat on it. It was really the only place to sit. The bed, a desk, and a desk chair were the only furniture. The bed was at an odd angle in the tiny room, and not against the wall; this made room for a movie projector propped on an unsteady shelf at the head of the bed (Nora already knew his purist views on VCRs) so that David could lie down and watch movies, using the vinyl shade pulled over his window as a screen. The floor space was devoted to books, papers, reels of film, bills, boxed shirts from the cleaner's, and pyramids of dirty laundry, with a footpath so you could walk from bed to kitchenette to bath.

"Well, at least it's a nice neighborhood," she said. "Are you applying for a job at Harvard, or is that just alumni mail?"

"Don't look at my desk," David said. "I forgot to hide everything personal. But you'd find it anyway, wouldn't you?"

"Probably. David?"

"Yes?"

"You're naked."

He had undressed while she was surveying the scene. They both looked at David's body.

"This will go, I promise," he said, patting his little paunch in a Santa Claus posture. "I'll run a mile a day for a week or two and this'll look just like my legs."

His legs were more like a swimmer's, the muscles smooth and dense. Malcolm had the tendony runner's legs. If you gave scientists in lab coats a body checklist—height, weight, hair color and texture, amount of hair and hair placement; cock of course but also toe, nostril, and molar shape—David and Malcolm would differ on every characteristic. Nora was attracted to them both.

David began to undress her. "Look at this," he said with happy recognition at the revelation of each body part. "Look at these."

She had to help him with the boots and stockings.

Nora had astrally projected herself into this scene so many times recently that the pleasure was particularly intense—the pleasure of, as a child, coloring exactly inside the black lines of a coloring book. This was David, after all, and not a sailor. She knew the parameters. Because it was David, Nora found it difficult to feel guilty, at least until he was reaching into her underpants.

"Goopy," he said.

"We shouldn't," Nora said.

In response David sucked her entire nose into his mouth—a terrible sensation.

The flip side of knowing David: knowing David. He was a nose sucker. Foreplay was not a specialty. During Round One, Nora had rarely come, whereas with Malcolm she often came once before, once during, once after. Nora had told David this at one point, in anger, by way of explaining her impulse to stay with Malcolm. "Not only does he cook and clean," David had said, "but he'd a damn sex slave." Anyway, in David's view orgasm was overrated. People should relax about sex, stop being so goal-oriented. "By 'people,'" Nora had retorted, "I assume you mean 'women,' because in the orgasm department you're the white rabbit in a bowler hat who's always late for a very important date"—which had sucked them right into the conversation about how different he would be if they didn't have to keep meeting like this—"and anyway," he had added, "you should be flattered you get me this excited."

"No birth control," Nora said.

A lie. Her period was ending, at its lightest point; there was no danger.

"Have my baby," he said.

"Might be his."

"You mean we'd have to wait until it took the Stanford-Binet to know whose genes it got?"

"Very funny," Nora said.

She pushed him away, but he climbed right back on, holding up for her inspection a foil condom packet he apparently kept handy by bed-side.

They made love. It was engaging, while it lasted. Mid-act, Nora was distressed to get a flash of herself at a girl-lunch saying wryly, over white wine, *It was engaging, while it lasted*. So she tried to throw herself into the scene at hand, imagining, like a method actress, that this was her last evening with David before the authorities shipped them off to separate labor camps.

Unlike Malcolm, David made a great deal of noise. His chest was hair-ier, wider. Nora's guilt was a tingle, like the tenderness on her chin and cheeks from David's stubble.

"Come to Rome with me," he told her ear. "Let's elope."

"Are you proposing?"

"I'd marry you in a second. You know that."

"What about Rita?"

"Well, let's agree on forty-eight hours' notice so I can break the news to her."

"I've got it. This is ideal. How about we get married but I live with Malcolm so he can cook and clean for me?"

"Fine, as long as you sleep with me."

"It's terrible to joke like this," Nora said.

"If we marry," David said—he was stroking her back and she had be-gun, without quite noticing, to grind against him—"I'd be tolerant about your seeing him. You can even sleep with him. But you can't leave me. I'd be very angry. Do you plan to tell him about us? I think you should."

"Oh? Do you plan to tell Rita?"

"I'll tell Rita if you tell Malcolm."

As they sat up to talk naked on the bed, they kept cutting each other off with a "Wait!" or a raised hand. At one point, unable to agree on whose turn it was, they simply both talked, until the decibel level got so high they both had to stop and smile.

"If we ever get married," David said, "we're going to have to hire a tape scrambler, like Nixon and Haldeman."

"You're so cute. Sometimes you make me feel like I'm twelve years old, staying up all night at a slumber party."

"There's one thing you should know," David said. He had begun to dress. "I don't like being toyed with. I'm assuming you mean what you say about your feelings. Because we've been through this before, and you never seemed to acknowledge that my feelings were on the line."

"Likewise," Nora said, "I'm assuming you aren't just being an imp who's breaking up my quasi-happy home for sport."

"Maybe you can wait a minute while I pull my stuff together, and drop me at the station."

"I don't have a car, remember? Where are you going?"

"I was going to catch the 10:32 and try to work at the magazine office. If I stay up tonight I ought to be able to finish this piece, then tomorrow I'll have time to sleep a little before the flight."

"You'll never make it."

"Sure I will. Relax."

If Nora were going to Europe for a week, she would have spent the month before departure mentally packing. Which jacket to bring, which shoes. Each toiletry item in a plastic container: a toothbrush, a bar of soap. The travel alarm and the folding dual-voltage travel iron. She had always been the kind of packer who could fit enough clothes for a month in an overnight bag. Commuting for food shoots had made her even more efficient. While most stylists traveled in station wagons crammed with brushes, springform pans, waffle irons, and condiments, she had reduced the tools of her trade to take up the smallest possible space, so that for most shoots, if she planned carefully enough, she could take the train rather than drive, travel light. But David had gotten his passport only that morning and now, with complete concentration, was throwing items into an ancient, cheap suitcase of pebbled blue plastic. For a type-A personality his movements were strangely economical, almost Japanese, as though even in a room that small he didn't want to waste any motion. Still, he reminded Nora of someone who had just won the prize where anything you can stuff into your shopping cart in five minutes is yours. She watched him with the usual mix of affection and indignation: no doubt he thought the amount of time he'd spent in discussion after their quickie was a bequeathal of magnanimous proportions. They ran from the apartment at 10:22 and ran to a cab stand; a cab screeched to a halt, they jumped in, and David told the driver, "I hope the 10:32's late as usual. Do what you can without getting arrested." The driver left before David finished the sentence.

"Forget the whole thing," Nora said, as David reached into his wallet to ready bills for the driver. "Cardiac Arrestville. I'd be dead in a year."

"I'm staying at the Grand Hotel," David said. "I'll call. Keep the cab. Here," he said, thrusting money at the driver and kissing Nora loudly on the lips, as if the kiss noise compensated for kiss length. "I love you," he called over the slamming cab door. From where the cab was positioned at the station she could watch him vanish into a gate. Moments later, the train squealed off.

"Well," the cab driver said, "where next?"

Nora took the cab not home, but in the opposite direction, back into town, to her car.

Time and distance clacked away on the meter like sand through an hourglass. Whatever happened with David, her relationship with Malcolm was as dead as the car. She couldn't stall much longer.

The windows of her car were still encrusted with snow. The battery was dead. Nora sat at the wheel for a while, using the car as a kind of decompression chamber. She got out, removed the parking ticket from the windshield, and scraped a circle of visibility, like a porthole. Back inside, the car felt both claustrophobic and cozy. She sat there until she was too cold to sit there anymore, then extracted her turkey (still frozen) from the cooking equipment in the trunk and got a cab home, to face Malcolm.

BUT MALCOLM WAS already asleep, unusually early for him, having left his tax papers to decorate the living room.

He and Nora would succeed in avoiding each other for days—that had, after all, been the plan—so she wouldn't know how frustrated and fearful he was about the taxes. If fed the same column of numbers, each of his two calculators displayed a different total. One calculator couldn't even agree with itself. By the time Nora ordered her second Beaujolais, Malcolm's brain was twirling with tax vertigo—and he was only in 1981.

Malcolm dreamed that Ann Marie Lewis was the star of a movie he was directing in Paris. He was also the cameraman. Squatting by the Seine, his back and knee supple, he felt driven and committed. Except that Ann Marie wasn't altogether herself, he realized later, as the dream kept wafting back: she was also partly Laurel Mariani, an ex-girlfriend. A curious meld, given that Laurel was barely five feet tall—though at least she was also dark, and had "marie" in her name.

Soon after splitting with Beth, Malcolm had become involved with a woman who was in Philadelphia for the last year of her medical internship, and their time together was blissful enough that it was possible he'd made a mistake not moving to Boston with her for her residency, even though they'd only known each other half a year. Nora had always been jealous of Laurel. She knew how sweet Laurel was, how good a skier, how fast an achiever of orgasm. Laurel could prescribe medication for his bad back. In slide shows, Malcolm always looked happiest with Laurel. Nora had often claimed that Malcolm only got involved with women who were unavailable or leaving town, because after Beth he was too defensive to think about commitment. But other times Nora claimed that Laurel was just right for him, and he simply hadn't been brave enough to make the leap. Malcolm believed that either judgment could be true. Time was the acid test. He'd been happy with Beth too, and look how that turned out.

Still, it was disconcerting to think of Laurel Mariani now, to graft her with an attractive stranger, and to graft both women—the promise of romance new and improved—with the old, buried promise of his film career. And it haunted him that, just as he could never know whether he would have been happier with Laurel than he was with Nora, he had no method for determining whether the link of Ann Marie and Laurel with his film career was a pipe dream or a premonition. The hair color was wrong, but maybe the strawberry blonde in his and Nora's back-to-back dreams was some kind of psychic emmissary, auguring brave change.

After two days of internal auditing both financial and emotional, nothing quite added up. On Wednesday, Nora was once again already gone when he awoke. Malcolm put food in his stomach and soap in his armpits; he used his work on the Ivy Street plans for Tobias as a relief from the taxes, and the taxes as relief from Ivy Street—because Tobias, he believed, would never really pull off a meeting. At least Malcolm could show the set of working drawings to prospective employers, if he had to hunt for a job.

On Wednesday night, the late news was showing a candlelight picket outside one of his favorite buildings in the city. The Beaux-Arts Bulletin Building was designed in 1906 by the same architect who had produced the townhouse that Stone had bought for offices. Unless a federal judge signed a restraining order, demolition of the Bulletin Building would begin the next morning, despite the sweeping preservation bill that had just been ratified by City Council. The lovely historical landmark would be replaced by a $117 million Justice Center, with seventy-two court-rooms and a four-hundred-forty-bed detention center.

Only in Philadelphia, Malcolm thought, would the primest real es-tate in town be bestowed on prisoners, giving them a penthouse view of City Hall and the new convention center. He didn't believe it was possi-ble, but the wrecking equipment had already been moved in, the police barriers erected.

Malcolm thought he might cry. He should go to the library, find out what bureaucrat was responsible for destroying Frank Furness's mag-nificent, eccentric National Bank of the Republic Building, and shoot him. The moron would be retired now, no doubt, living off his fat city pension, while Louis Kahn died alone in a public restroom, no one even to identify the body. Malcolm needed to do something, however futile or misguided, so he went downtown and stayed up all night in the snow, on the picket line, with a handful of other die-hard preservationists and a bored television cameraman.

Most of the picketers were his age and looked as if they, like him, hadn't been in a picket line since the early seventies. All the other protesting architects had left. Not surprising: architects with jobs would not stay up all night picketing; they would have a more effective and less time-consuming strategy for making their outrage known.

When he got home at 6 A.M. on Thursday, Nora still wasn't there, or had already left. He was concerned, but he was also exhausted, so he went to sleep with the bedroom door open so he could listen for the phone. It woke him a couple of hours later.

"Run to a TV, quick," Tobias Maxwell commanded, and Malcolm complied, though half-asleep.

On television, Malcolm was being interviewed about the demolition.

His hands were in his pockets, his breath billowing crisply in the cold. Except for squinting into the cameraman's bright lights, he seemed handsome and articulate as he explained how important it was for the city to protect its architectural heritage.

Malcolm felt a burst of pride, then guilt as he imagined the reaction not of Nora, but of Ann Marie Lewis. He imagined her in her bathrobe, drinking her coffee. She somehow seemed the type to watch the morning news.

Tobias called back during the commercial break. "Did they get the restraining order?" Malcolm asked.

"Yes. Guess how. Rymer. There he is!"

The television crew was now interviewing, in daylight, a middle-aged man who was saying how happy he was to be able to do his part to keep the building alive. In his rod-straight topcoat, the man looked competent, elegant, well rested.

"The next mayor," Tobias said. "The builder of our Ivy Street condos—except now maybe we can get in on this place too. What a break!"

"You're not honestly telling me," Malcolm said wearily, "That you think we're going to be involved with the Bulletin Building."

"Why not?"

"I'm a one-man office specializing in custom residential."

"If you're not willing to grow—"

"What I'm not willing to do," Malcolm said, "is have this conversation with you at six in the morning."

"—Then you better just buckle down and look for a job, because—"

Malcolm slammed down the phone.

Tobias didn't call back. Malcolm sat numbly in front of the television for a minute, then brewed coffee and read the newspaper. Only when he found himself browsing aimlessly through the classifieds, hooking onto an ad near Architect for an Aquarium Maintenance Person ("to maintain the health and beauty of large aquariums in homes & businesses, saltwater fish experience helpful") did he remember that all-nighters were not something that he managed anymore. Awake ten minutes, he already had one of those brain-pickling, no-sleep headaches. He poured the coffee down the drain and headed back to bed.

When was the last time he had been awake this early in the morning? In 1977, when he'd stayed up all night to argue with Beth. The fight ended with her leaving for Haiti with another man.

That afternoon Malcolm had sat stunned in the mucky grass of the backyard for three or four hours. From the neighboring yards had come dog yelps, child squeals, and the perfume of barbecued steaks. True to character, Beth had left her dog for Malcolm to babysit while she sunbathed with Jack, and the smelly, shedding mutt panted beside him during his backyard vigil. The fact that Beth went to Haiti and Malcolm went to stand in line at the Magik-Mart for dog food seemed perfect.

Relationships, he thought, no matter how good the intentions, could turn out to be monstrous mistakes, like housing projects.

Beth and Jack had subsequently married, and divorced. Though Malcolm didn't even like Beth by the time she left, it had taken him all winter and most of the following spring to settle into a new house and recover, longer to meet and start seeing Laurel. It was going to take him much longer to recover from Nora.

Malcolm left a note taped to the bedroom door before he went to sleep: *Wake me*.

Where the hell was she?

16

ONCE THE HUSBAND of a friend of Nora's mother had gone mad.

Every day the man had donned his suit, kissed his wife good-bye, loaded his briefcase, and left for work—except he wasn't going to work. He was going to the zoo, the movies. For months his wife didn't know he had been fired. Only when all the checks bounced did she realize that he was wearing the same suit to the office every day, that the suit was becoming more and more wrinkled and stained. By the end, he was putting the suit on over his pajamas.

Nora remembered this story on the train to New York, the morning after her David encounter. Amazingly, Nora's mother's friend had stayed with her husband. They'd medicated him, found him another job; the marriage had survived hell and high water.

The $27,900 question: When, for modern folks, was enough enough?

Nora knew the conflicting answers she'd get if she polled her friends and relations. The real dividing line was more basic than whether the advisor believed in marriage. The line was how much possibility the advisor in question felt that a life—any life—holds forth. Is life a limited thing from which you wrench whatever comfort you can? Or is life an open book, the only limits the limits of imagination?

Both views were seductive. She could imagine herself and Malcolm adorably eccentric at ninety, all the small stuff having already been sweated. But as David said, *You live like an old lady, shut up in the house with him.* True, but did freedom mean washing David's clothes while he globe-trotted? The third hand: maybe she should be alone until she met the man who was *between* Malcolm and David, neither catatonic nor hyperactive. The perfect man, in short. If he existed. If he wasn't already married, or in a different city—not that Nora couldn't move herself.

She would, in fact, have an offer from the photographer she worked with on Tuesday: he needed someone posthaste for a shoot in Richmond, Virginia. In the kind of low-grade deception that was starting to seem rampant, Richmond would pass for snowy Boston in the beer ad— cheaper to blow snow in Richmond than to rent a house for an imaginary hockey team in Boston. Nora thought that it might be nice to get away.

On the train to New York she studied the people around her, to play a game she often played to pass commuting time. If she shared a disaster with these people, a hotel fire or hostage situation, how would they act? Who would be resourceful, who the whiner? One man motored through a huge stack of job applications. Another, who read a pile of air-mail letters from places like Zambia signed "Yours in Christ," appeared to be a religious medical charity organizer.

There are odder things to do with a life than food styling, Nora told herself. Proctologists. Slum landlords. Still, as she flipped the pages of her *Advertising Age*, she began to feel odder and odder.

A feature on the economic repercussions of AIDS reported that business was booming in Alabama, the rubber glove capital of America: rubber glove sales were up eight percent, to 2 billion pairs a year. But AYDS, the diet candy, refused to be swayed. "The product," the company president said, "has been around for forty-five years. Let the disease change its name." McDonald's spent $35 million a year on advertising targeted at children aged five to twelve, who spent $2 billion a year on fast food. $2 billion a year, and Nora was risking jail for $30,000! A confused, bitter woman on a commuter train with a huge immigrant's suitcase and a toolchest big as a carpenter's, ashamed of herself for noticing, at this late date—she'd read *Das Kapital* in college, for God's sake—that money, not love, makes the world go round.

New York was not the place to send a nervous person, especially before Christmas, and a commercial shoot was not the place to send a person who was questioning the value of life on earth. Nora went through the four crates of apples she'd called ahead to have delivered, looking for the apple that would be the first close-up shot in an ad for frozen apple pie: a lone apple nestled in velvet. The apple had to be perfect but not artificially so; the red should be deep and dappled, the shape tapered, like a pulled molar. An easy shoot, as food shoots go. She did not have to blow-torch a steak to make it look grilled or deal with butter, a food stylist's nightmare. All she had to do was discard about fifty cooked frozen apple pies before she found the eight or nine that didn't look dry, dull colored, or lopsided. Then she got to apply the calcium chips that made the hero pie steam as though it had just come out of the oven. The company insisted on an on-camera cut, which meant they had to go through twenty-five takes before the pie could be sliced in a pristine wedge.

Five minutes on rush-hour Fifth Avenue, and Nora thought she would self-combust. After the rarefied air of the studio, the heaving street made her feel like one of those bubble kids, allergic to life. Her gloved hands were already stinging from the weight of her suitcase and tool chest. All of the elevators, subway cars, and stores were full. The happy hour drink patrons thronged four deep around the bars. When she turned to look downtown, at the people moving so densely that no motion was visible, she got vertigo.

What did she have in cash, $60? That would get her to the airport. She could charge a ticket. In Rome she could charge a change of clothes. As she walked furiously uptown, she imagined David's pleasure as he opened the door. It was only as she lowered herself over the pee-splattered toilet at Bonwit's ladies' room that she considered the snags. How would she get a cab to the airport in rush-hour traffic? What if the flights to Rome had already left, or were all booked?

She fought past the women at the mirrors to reach a sink and splash off her hands. One woman was drawing an outline around her mouth that did not exactly match the true contours of her lips. Nora's own lips were bare and chapped. Her hair was wild, and so were her eyes. She watched the other women watching themselves in the mirror and felt proud and sure, disdainful of their conventionality and fastidiousness.

At the phone outside the beauty parlor Nora got the international operator, got the phone number of the Grand Hotel, and dialed the number on her phone credit card.

"Pronto," an Italian man said.

Nora asked for David. Centuries later, the man connected her to David's room. The phone rang fifteen times, twenty. The operator wouldn't intercept to take a message. She jiggled the bar and cut herself off. When she redialed, reading the number from her palm where she'd written it, the line was busy; then a testy woman showed up with dime in hand. Nora let her go first and listened: *I'll leave at seven and get booze*, the woman said, *but could you stop by the bakery? Get the chocolate thing*. Nora thought, *I never want to marry*. By the time Nora got the Grand Hotel again, she made the message simple, so as not to challenge the operator's English or David's credulity.

"Tell him it's Nora," she said. "On my way."

Spontaneity, however, had never been her long suit. She called Alitalia and TWA before she left for the airport on Tuesday, to learn that flights to Rome were minutes from takeoff. Besides, it was not a good week for continent hopping, so she had dinner with her old buddy Ralph in New York and let him distract her with his baroque postmarital woes.

When Ralph and Nora were lovers in college, she'd been charmed by his seriousness about art and how that seriousness played against his slightly parodic Texas macho. He had a heart-melting way of slinging the word "darlin'" into a sentence. It was long enough ago now that Nora rarely even thought about their romance. Boxy and good-old-boyish, Ralph wasn't really Nora's type. He was the most successful artist from her old group. For a while, when he'd invite her to shows and parties, she'd always sensed a patronizing *I told you so*. But she'd later put that down to her own paranoia. Ralph certainly inspired it: now, every time a show of his opened, his ex-wife left a death threat on his answering machine.

"What's most bizarre," Ralph said, "is that when I call friends to say I'm truly afraid, they say, 'Poor Cynthia. She must be so jealous. How's *her* work doing?' This town is really sick. You're lucky not to have to deal with it."

"You don't really mean that. You love it here."

"Not anymore. I feel like I'm in ancient Rome seconds before the fall."

"So how about a couple of acres in Connecticutt?"

"If I weren't single."

"You don't think you could talk a woman into spending the night with you there?"

"People don't spend the night anymore. They kiss good-bye on the cheek and go home and dream about each other."

"Did you ever meet my friend Julie? She can have sex without touching. A sort of undress real slowly, stand next to someone, touch them wetly with an intense expression kind of thing. She can actually come that way."

"Yeah? The psychologist with the short arms?"

"*That's* what you remember about her?"

"For some reason. Haven't you noticed that?"

"No," Nora said, rather roughly.

"Well, tell her she ought to write a book. She'd make a fucking fortune."

On the way to the train station some time later, she gave a dollar to each blind and crippled beggar in her path.

On the train she was still shaking her head over the short arm business. She had kept in touch with Ralph at some pains, against his busy schedule and her own embarrassment at her lack of comparative riches, and it bothered her that she didn't like him more wholeheartedly, that she found him niggardly and overjudgmental. But dismissing someone for that reason is a niggardly, overjudgmental thing to do. One of those double binds: once you're resentful that a friend is stiffing you on a lunch check, you're just as cheap.

At home, Malcolm's tax papers mummifed. This was a man who had taken two years to select paint colors for the living room. By the time he noticed she was gone, she'd probably have grandchildren by someone else.

Too bad they couldn't enter a cryogenic sleep and wake up later, solvent, married: a curtain drawn across their porter bed after much travail, as in the last shot of *North by Northwest*. Or her moved out, with David, who still wasn't in his hotel room.

A phone call on Wednesday morning confirmed that the check, praise the Lord, had cleared the money market.

She left for a local shoot before Malcolm awoke, then wandered around like the city's homeless. She bought shoes she didn't need (shoes, Malcolm claimed, were the closest thing she had to a hobby) and dealt with her car. The battery, the triple-A man told her, was defunct. She couldn't bear to have the car towed so a spanking new battery could be installed; she would do it later. The snow had left salt and soot stains that made the car look like something dredged up from the sea bottom from prehistoric times, which was about how long it seemed since she'd talked to David.

She finally got him from the gladiola phone booth near her car. It had just begun to snow again. She was starting to be sentimentally attached to this snowy booth; she and David might have to hold their wedding ceremony there.

"We've got to stop not meeting like this," David said. "How are you? Where are you?"

"At home, falling apart."

"Poor baby."

"I miss you," Nora said.

"I miss you too, but there's a hitch. Rita's here."

There was a moment of silence while that registered.

David said, "I invited her months ago. I would have been more worried about the two of you crossing paths if I thought you'd actually show up."

"Forget it," Nora said.

"There's a silver lining. I told her we might be seeing each other again. She knows how I feel about you, and needless to say she wasn't happy. We slept together, but we didn't make love."

"Horrors."

"Hey. You only told me you might be available a week ago. What did you expect, a monk? I swear to God I'll do whatever you want. Just tell me what that is and try to stick to it for a couple of days. You want to come to Rome? Fine. Tell me when, and I'll be at the airport."

"When I leave Malcolm for you, is it going to be me getting sent home from Rome while you meet with Rita?"

"Where's your sense of humor?" David asked.

"Or I'll be home, Rita will sulk in whatever love nest you've set her up in, and you'll be off screwing some little actress on the set."

"Nora."

"Or some undergraduate, or whatever editorial assistant they have at the magazine. Why, I don't know—you're lousy in bed."

"Aren't you lucky I find your foul mouth cute? *You're living with someone.* This presents certain logistical difficulties. I can't even call you at home. You want foreplay? Let's make more than an hour for sex—"

"I can't believe we're having this talk on my bill."

"Do you want me to call you back?"

"No." She was crying now. "Forget the whole thing."

"When do you want me to call?"

"Don't."

"Listen," David said. "I love you. Now concentrate: *everything will work out*—"

Nora hung up.

Never had she been so tempted to ditch her diaphragm and devote her life to something useful. Join Mother Teresa in Calcutta or become an abortion rights activist, or at least volunteer herself as a nanny for her brothers' children and work quietly, cheerfully on her art again. Follow Freud's advice and sublimate, sublimate.

She took a cab home. Malcolm was upstairs, listening to music far too loud for him to hear the key in the lock or her movement downstairs. She packed quickly and took the bus to the train station.

She panicked for a moment at the car rental stand—the police might already have tagged her credit card—but the agent gave her the keys, exhorting her to drive carefully, a traveler's advisory was in effect.

Once she was in the car, concentrating on staying on the road, alive, she felt much better. Anyway, she loved rental cars. They always made her feel free and breezy—maybe whatever they sprayed the interiors with to make the cars smell fresh was better than airplane glue.

JULIE PESZKO AND the insane computer programmer had not yet made love. They hadn't held hands, or even discussed their attraction.

"Are you kidding?" Julie said. "I could lose my license. I could go to jail."

Approached in the snow, up the long elm-arched driveway, the mental institution looked like a postcard of Monticello. Julie's office could have been any business executive's, with a pencil cup, in box, and plant on the windowsill; but during past visits Nora had seen patients with "poor impulse control" throw food at each other or have "assaultive episodes." She had seen the padded Quiet Room and a mass hysteria when the art therapist tried to conduct a scissor count.

"Why are you doing it, then?" Nora asked.

"I'm not doing anything yet. But he's a voluntary admission. He was here as a teen, after his parents died, and a lot of people with a history of emotional problems, especially without families, come back when they feel they're losing control."

"What's he losing control of?"

"He has ambivalence."

"Don't we all?"

"The worst cases just look at the doorway and deliberate about whether they want to walk through. They can stand there for a half-hour with one foot in the air. Sometimes Chris can't decide what TV show to watch. He's a tad morbid. Also, he tends to retreat into details. He goes off on these tangents without really coming back to the point."

"Sounds like Malcolm."

"Just try to gently steer him back to the topic. But go easy with him. Don't push him too hard."

What Julie hadn't mentioned to Nora was that Chris was stunning—but then, all of Julie's boyfriends were strong-chested and strong-chinned, with an edge of danger. Julie had such a talent for ravishing these fellows that Nora had often suggested she bottle her hormones and sell them as scent—Peszko no. 78, or whatever her current lover-count was.

They found Chris in the art therapy room, to which he had a special pass. The room was furnished with rubber-backed Italian chairs that Nora recognized from *Abitare*, except that in *Abitare* the chairs weren't screwed to the floor. Dark-haired, dark-eyed Chris was working on a sketch that was bright, aggressive, and rather good, in the Chicago style.

"How are you?" Nora asked Chris, who stood to shake her hand when Julie introduced them.

"Better," he said. "I heard about your $30,000. What bank is it?"

She told him.

"Sums that large are pretty easy to trace," he said. "They'll track you down eventually."

"What then?"

"They'll ask for the money."

"What if I just say I don't have it?"

"They'll prosecute. If it were less, they might not bother. I knew a guy who got $10,000—they caught him in one day, but he'd already withdrawn the money and he said, 'Want it? Sue me.' The legal hassle wasn't worth it for them, especially since it isn't good PR for banks to lose money. Of course, that was New York. You know who else earns $10,000 a day? More now, probably. Frank Wallace. School chum. He used to do video games. Now he's with the Department of Defense, designing their missile detection systems. Know about them?"

"No," Nora answered.

"From Flight Simulator to the real thing—what difference does it make if the target's real?"

Julie wore a concerned expression that meant, Steer him back. So Nora did. "Do you think my money could be some kind of scam?"

He shrugged.

"What kinds of scams are there?" Nora asked, and Chris counted off on his fingers: data diddling, Trojan horses, logic bombs, superzapping, scavenging, piggybacking, salamis, round-down frauds, and some other terms—Nora couldn't tell if he was wandering because she didn't know what he was talking about.

"Tell me about salamis," Nora said. "In layman's terms, now."

"You randomly reduce a few hundred accounts by ten or fifteen cents disguised as a service charge—it's too small for anyone to bother asking about—and transfer the money to a created account where it can be withdrawn by normal methods. But that wouldn't apply to you. $30,000 is too much for a salami. It's too much for a round-down fraud. Probably just a computer error. Happens all the time. I'm afraid of when they start happening with missiles. The Soviets have this system—"

"Chris," Julie said gently. "What should Nora do?"

"Call the bank," Chris said, "and give the money back."

"No chance they'll just not notice?" Nora asked.

"They have every deposit slip, every withdrawal on microfilm. Every transaction is coded with a teller's name and the time; they've got cameras going all day and all night at all the branches, all the ATMs."

"If it *is* some kind of scam—say some mousy, balding bureaucrat trying to steal the money and getting the wrong account number— wouldn't he entrap himself by catching me?"

"May I ask you something personal?"

"Sure," Nora said.

"Why do you want the money?"

Chris and Julie folded their hands on the paint-splattered table and studied Nora like therapists.

"You mean other than the obvious?"

They nodded.

"I didn't exactly plan this, but I must say I really hate banks. Think if you were Russian, watching a documentary of Americans lined up on payday—how's it different, finally, from migrant workers buying milk at $20 a gallon from the company store?"

"Right, " Julie said. " 'A long and elegant culture,' no?"

Julie was alluding to a previous discussion, in which Nora had argued that the Soviet Union was probably full of fine folk, descended from "a long and elegant culture" that included many great novelists, composers, and thinkers. Julie, who studied Russian in college and had actually been to the Soviet Union (where she'd endured a strip search by somber policemen after she paid the cab driver who took her to the airport in American dollars), had added long-and-elegant jokes to their friendship's routines.

"If you're thinking revolutionary gesture," Christ said, "the trouble is, most banks aren't doing too well, though I understand the impulse—like us screwing Ma Bell in college."

Chris inclined himself toward Nora, his lips pursed. A tight mouth any girl would want to run her tongue across. Maybe Nora and Chris could elope in the rental car, ditch it in an Avis lot, take a bus to somewhere obscure, and live curled in each other's arms. Such things happen, at least on television, and in Julie Peszko's life.

"All that money," Chris was saying, "traveling by electronic transfer, not clean green bills in a safe, not even numbers in a ledger, but just sounds in the air, impulses over wire. Somewhere they print the money, invent how much should be in circulation, invent the size of the deficit."

"Right," Nora said. "The guy I live with had a client, Stone, who had something like $200 million in forged securities. On this Monopoly money he rented limos, courted the maitre d's of all the best restaurants, bought cocaine which is how much an ounce? A lot."

Chris nodded. Julie watched him proudly. Despite the setting he could be any boyfriend trotted out for inspection.

"The trouble is," Chris said, "once you get into that frame of mind, where does it stop? Because back in what passes for the world, a 'slippery slope' isn't merely a logical term. Mafia enemies do wind up dead. The CIA exists. Bombs. So the trick is to make up some rules, because otherwise your brain is like electronic funds transfer—it's happening somewhere else, to someone else. Know what I mean?"

"Yes," Nora said.

"Christopher," Julie said.

"Torture still happens on most of the surface of the planet not covered by water, which luckily is not much. Less than you'd think."

"Audience over," Julie told Nora, then put her hand lightly on her patient's forearm. "Christopher."

"Sorry." He turned to Nora. "I'll make a deal with you. You're an artist, right?"

"Ex."

"You still know artist-types?"

"Unfortunately."

"I can feel the thing out for you," Chris said. "I know people at your bank. What I was wondering is, do you know any dealers? Because I'd kind of like to show this stuff."

He held up the crayon sketch he had been doing when they came in: a blue pig with spooky teeth.

"Neo-expressionism doesn't go over too big here," Nora said. "But I could tell you places to try. I don't have much in the way of connections, though—if I did, I wouldn't be filming soft drink commercials today."

"Is that what this is?" he asked. "Neo-expressionist?"

"But about the money: maybe I ought to lie low for a while."

All Nora needed was this guy calling the bank to deliver the short form of *Being and Nothingness* in the context of her name.

Outside, real snow fell. Julie forbade Nora to drive home, so they brewed tea and ate yogurt and Cup-a-Soup for dinner in the nurse's lounge, which, despite the homey touches of any employee lounge—the monogrammed mugs lined up on a paper towel by the Mr. Coffee, the cute cat poster—still had a sour institutional smell, that smell of elementary schools which Nora had never been able to place: the cafeteria food, the solution they use to mop the floors.

They talked about Christopher's chances of recovery—Julie had confidence in him, especially if they could stabilize his medication—and about Julie's attraction to him. Then they talked about Malcolm and David.

"I don't know what to do," Nora said. "It wouldn't be very nice to leave Malcolm now, though he might go on with bad business as usual, unless he killed himself—drove his car into a tree late at night on a twisting road in rain. How could I settle his estate, sell his records? I'd feel so guilty."

Julie smiled.

"Except with my luck," Nora continued, "he wouldn't die. He'd be a drooling quadriplegic, his piddling assets wiped out by the accident—he has no health insurance—and I'd have to care for him the rest of his life."

"At least all this is useful if you ever decide to be a stand-up comic," Julie said.

"As for David, he better move fast. I can hear him now: 'Why does Malcolm get five years, and I only get five days? It isn't fair.' Tough. If it's supposed to be love at first sight, let us bite the bullet, wed, produce the bambinos."

"Why not just live with him?" Julie suggested. "If it doesn't work out, Malcolm's slowness would be an asset—he doesn't seem likely to marry in the next couple of months."

"He'd never forgive me two David episodes. Anyway, on the rebound, Malcolm might be a sucker for a divorcée with similar reservations about commitment, or even a marriage-and-family type who could outwait him, if that were possible."

"You don't sound like you want either of them," Julie observed. "It's hardly like you have to settle or be a maiden aunt. If things are so awful with Malcolm, why would you want to preserve the relationship?"

"Have you seen the statistics lately on the man-woman ratio?" Nora asked. "At least he's a good cook."

"Cute and sad, if that's as hard as you've thought about what you want in a relationship."

"I want Malcolm to say 'I love you,' period. Tie the knot, get it over with."

"The way you get life over with, Nora, is to be dead."

"But then sometimes I look at him and there's absolutely nothing there."

"Maybe there isn't. Or maybe it's in a place you can't get to."

"So?"

"So you move on."

"To what?"

"Now *that*," Julie said, "is the question. Because I don't think you're unhappy with Malcolm. Or rather, you might be, but that's not the problem. You're unhappy with yourself."

"Here goes," Nora sighed. "I'm not 'hard on myself.' I'm just realistic about my talents and about what I'm likely to get in a mate."

"I disagree," Julie said. "I think you're conflicted. There's a difference between realism and masochism—"

"Or as my mother would say, with a more Marxist, less Freudian metaphor, I'm 'selling myself short.' We can't all be you, Jule. I mean, sometimes you remind me of—what was that woman's name? The one who dated Freud and Nietzsche and Mahler?"

"Lou Andreas-Salomé," Julie said, looking pleased despite herself. "Not Mahler, I don't think."

"Well, some of us have to go out with the CPAs and dentists."

"Sure," Julie said. "Self-effacement is a winning stance, but it doesn't exonerate you from making peace with yourself—either finding a way to be content with your lot or struggling to better it, rather than just nattering away about how rotten everything is."

"True, I'm sorry."

"Why are you apologizing?"

"Malcolm always complains about my complaining too."

"I'm not complaining. You're a wonderful friend. You've always been there for me. You're funny and you're nice. But I don't think you like yourself much."

"What's to like?" Nora said. "I'm a food stylist. I live with this guy whose chief interest is moldings. He doesn't like me, I don't like him, and I'm having an affair with a guy I like even less, from whom I'll probably get AIDS."

"Plus you're a bank robber," Julie said. "Hear yourself? You've got to think of a way to say, 'I deserve to be happy. My happiness matters.'"

Nora began to cry.

Julie moved closer to the couch to put her arm around her friend, but Nora felt strangely removed from the contact, as she had with Alan at Richard's wedding.

Soon Nora got her gear from the car trunk and went to sleep in an empty guest room, tearfully. If she kept up at this rate, she could use the $27,900 to camp out here for a couple of months and produce some nice potholders.

In Richmond, Virginia, for the shoot on Thursday, Nora got beer to the right temperature to look cold, but not too cold, and to froth, but not too much. The photographer and prop stylist invited her to dinner; she refused, feeling monkish. Every week on the job she met attractive, witty, artistic men—many rich, some even heterosexual—and she had to choose David Martella, twice? In a room much like her mental institution room, but much cheaper (the very hotel, recently renovated, that had the grand staircase Scarlett O'Hara had been carried up in *Gone with the Wind*), Nora picked up the phone to call Malcolm, or David, and controlled herself. Different as they were, Malcolm and David counted as eggs in one basket, the basket called "Man." Any woman's group would tell her to find other sources of satisfaction: work, family, friends. She'd certainly been trying, but maybe not hard enough. Even in the midst of her own feminist lecture, she got a glint of wanting either Malcolm or David to track her down, appear at her door with flowers.

She embarked on a walk, empty-handed except for her room key, a ten-dollar bill in her pocket. Richmond was not New York, or even Philadelphia; almost no one was about. Deserted, the streets took on a stage-setty, day-for-night cast under the glare of the crime-deterring street-lamps.

She stopped at a Chinese restaurant and ordered some takeout. She liked the idea of eating cross-legged on the floor of her hotel room with chopsticks. When the woman brought the bag of food from the kitchen she said, "Thank you very much," smiled, and walked away without asking Nora to pay. "Thank *you*," Nora said. She actually left and had walked a brisk half-block before she thought: *What are you doing? What the fuck are you doing?*

Had it come to this, stealing won ton soup?

Back at the restaurant, the woman who had given her the food was chatting on the phone, had not noticed the error. She made a questioning expression. "I didn't pay," Nora said. The woman said "Ah" and rang up the sale while talking in Chinese to the receiver. She didn't seem at all grateful for Nora's honesty.

And why should she be? Nora asked herself as she left. She vowed that redepositing the stolen money to her checking account would be the first thing she'd do when she got home. She would give the check a day or two to clear, then call her bank. And the comedy was that Malcolm wouldn't know a thing about any of it. In her absence he would have fed himself, slept, worked out. She would ask him if he'd had any thoughts about their relationship, and he'd say no, he hadn't had time. *I don't know what to tell you*, he'd say, sinking deeper and deeper into his armchair, until, like the akinetic patients Julie described, he couldn't move at all.

But Nora was wrong.

WHEN SHE GOT home on Friday, Malcolm was waiting for her in the hallway near the glorious, chipped dressing table, glaring, arms crossed. "Where have you been?"

"Richmond," she said.

"Why?"

"A shoot."

"Why didn't you call?"

"I did, 857 times. Busy, busy, out."

"You couldn't have tried very hard. I've been here."

"I thought I was supposed to leave you alone."

"If I didn't check in for five days you'd have me declared legally dead. Do you have something to tell me?"

"What do you mean?"

"Come here," Malcolm said.

She followed, still in her coat, to his office. One small step for mankind, one giant step for Malcolm DeWitt: he had actually picked up the answering machine at the repair shop. David Martella could not possibly be so dumb and dastardly as to leave a fishy message. Malcolm rewound the tape for her. "Nora?" the message began. "This is Chris."

She exhaled, relieved.

"Your bank," Chris said, "is in the middle of a major audit. That either lends credence to your fraud theory or simply means they're freaked, just making mistakes. I'm still inclined to think the latter, but the audit certainly means there might be something fishy. Meanwhile, on another front, I'm in a therapy group here with a lawyer who was talking about his last boss. The forged securities rang a bell. The guy's in bad shape—drawing treasure maps, organizational charts with the president on top and himself at the bottom—so everything he says has to be taken with a grain of salt. But it seems the CEO of the brokerage house his boss dealt with is a guy who did a lot of business with my bank once.

I know the guy, and I wouldn't put anything past him. No wonder the FBI's involved. Anyhow, good luck, I hope this helps."

"Sit down," Malcolm told Nora, "and talk."

She did.

"Oh my God," Malcolm said. "You actually moved the money out of your account?"

Nora nodded in the sheepish way he had about the Empire dressing table.

"Why didn't you tell me before?"

"I've been under some stress," Nora said, "because of our relationship falling apart."

"You're going to try to pin this on me? Is that what you'll tell the bank? 'Sorry, guys, I had a fight with my boyfriend'? I can't believe it. Did you make announcements to everyone in your address book?"

"Just Alan, Julie, and Chris."

"And we went through that whole mortgage argument without your even mentioning the money?"

"I tried. But why? It's not like we can spend it. Chris seems to think I'll get caught."

"You will."

"What have you heard about Stone?" Nora asked.

"Nothing." Malcolm told her about the IRS deadline (minus his attraction to Ann Marie) and his TV appearance in the picket line.

"Looks like it might work," he said, "at least for a while. They got a wrecking ball through the hotel adjacent to the Bulletin this morning before the restraining order came through, partly because of the intervention of this mover-and-shaker, Nathaniel Rymer—the guy Tobias kept claiming was going to do a real estate investment with us. So guess what? Tobias has an appointment with him next week, for us to talk about Ivy Street."

"That's wonderful!"

"Tobe let me know it, too. I hung up on him when he tried to give me his Carnegie crash course on how to make friends and influence people."

"He's been doing that to you for years," Nora said. Malcolm refrained from adding, *So have you.*

"Philadelphia has to be the only city in the world that's still tearing down historic structures," he said. "I'm so fed up I'm starting to have Rambo fantasies."

Nora smiled as she always did when she thought of Sylvester Stallone, a Philadelphian exactly Malcolm's age—actually they'd attended grade school together at Notre Dame Academy, until Stallone got kicked out. Malcolm smiled back, but his lower lip jutted out the way it did when he was genuinely troubled. Nora patted his bad knee.

"I feel," he said, "like the Bulletin Building. Like I'm in one of those movies where the unjustly accused makes his final plea to the governor and hopes against all hope for the appeal. By sunrise, it's either freedom or the noose—except in my case I wait and wait and wait, with no idea how long the movie is going to run."

"I know," Nora said.

"I can really understand why death row folks ask for the chair, just to kill the suspense."

"For weeks," Nora agreed, "I've been prodding myself to take some decisive, immediate action. But I haven't been able to figure out what. And meanwhile I keep getting these goofy moral messages, like one of Julie's patients." She told him about the Chinese takeout incident. "Then I was at a phone booth, the line was busy, and when I hung up a handful of coins tumbled out. One was an Indian nickel, very worn and smooth. I kept thinking it meant something."

Malcolm smiled. "About the taxes—do you know what'll happen to me if I get caught? About what's happening to Stone. He broke the law to get rich, and I'm breaking the law to get by, but we're equally criminal."

"So what about Stone?"

"I talked to Lucy. Despite the FBI's involvement, she thinks he was just crazy, coked up, and suffering from delusions of grandeur. Once, she said, they were at lunch with a business associate who kept staring at an Oriental woman he found attractive. Stone picked the woman up for his friend and invited her to dinner that night; then he called over the maitre d' and said, 'I have a very special visitor tonight. Chiang Kai-shek's granddaughter.' If he liked the driver he got at the limousine company, he'd set the guy up in business. Once he fell for a clerk in a clothing store in Florida—he was always collecting these boys—and when he found out he was an illegal alien, he tried to arrange a marriage with the sister of a friend. Once he was trying to buy a big company. He kept asking Lucy to photocopy things, but he'd say, 'Don't read it. Don't even *look* at it.' He'd hand her documents and say, 'Put this right in the safe.' There was evidently a lot of back-and-forth about cocaine too. Plain brown bags delivered by specific boys, but then each restaurant had a special table and a special waiter."

"That might explain the lawyer's treasure map."

"Lucy said one of his dealings was in Florida with some Moroccan Jews who were having trouble getting their money over here. Presumably their money would be illegal, so they couldn't show their assets, but they could get a bank loan for a huge construction job and use the bucks to pay back the loan. Obviously Stone's lawyer would know about things like that, which would explain his paranoia."

"Speaking of lawyers, you really should—"

"I did," Malcolm said.

"What?"

"I went to one. Yesterday."

"Really? So fast? I can't believe it. How did you get his name?"

"Called some architect friends. The guy I saw wasn't too positive about my odds of getting any money back, but that wasn't the worst part of our meeting. I'd brought all the paperwork on Stone. He looked at the contract—kind of held it up like rotten food, with two fingers—and asked me if I was insured, if I'd been sued. When I said no to both, he said, 'You're lucky.' Turns out I can't get architectural insurance anyway because I'm not a registered architect, but if I could it's twenty percent of gross billables with a deductible is $5,000—basically a lawyer's fee."

"What's the point, then?"

"If a beam falls on someone's head, it covers the zillion-dollar award But if a homeowner sues for spite, because the dishwasher makes a funny noise, you still have to pay for the lawyer. No matter how idiotic the case is, it's five or six grand. He said suing architects is the latest rage and that I should start covering my ass, writing down everything I ever say or do or even think on a job. 'Documentation.' For what I charge, there's just no way."

"Maybe you'd better not think about all this now," Nora suggested. "Why not try to feel good that this Rymer guy has shown up at just the right moment? That's so lucky."

"It's hardly in the bag."

"Listen," Nora said. "About my bank money—maybe I should just call them up."

"Now that you've moved it around, I'm not so sure."

They sat in silence for a minute, staring at each other.

Then Nora said, "This is all probably red herrings. They catch me for a simple bank error, I give the money back. No big deal. Stone gets his wrist slapped for a forged signature, and what's it to us? Just the house foreclosed upon."

"There was an ad in the paper today," Malcolm said, "for a fire-damaged place on Pine. Great block. I know the houses—neat details, south-facing bays."

"And you're telling me *I'm* acting weird, when you're househunting amidst all this?"

"More as an investment for someone."

"Have you had any further thoughts," Nora asked, "about our relationship?"

Malcolm said, "Have you?"

"I asked first."

"You always ask first, and you always ask just that way. Why not share *your* thoughts for a change?"

"I thought I shared my thoughts too much."

"Yes, your thoughts on what I'm doing wrong."

Nora said, "I can't believe how much you've gotten done. Working on the taxes, and seeing the lawyer, and trying to work on Ivy Street—"

"See what happens when you don't interrogate me every other second?"

"Aren't you proud of *me*?" Nora asked. "I haven't even asked you how things went with the FBI."

"Good girl," Malcolm said, patting the top of her head dog fashion.

"How *did* things go?"

"Routine."

"That's good. Listen, could you drive me to the train station? If I don't get there in twenty minutes I'm going to have to pay a whole other day on the rental car."

"Give me a kiss first," he said.

"Right here?" she asked, straddling him, still in her coat.

"Change of venue."

"Does this mean you love me?"

"Yes," Malcolm said, "for what it's worth."

"What's it worth, on the open market?"

"I'm not sure."

"You're sure unsure about a lot."

"Life in the big city," Malcolm responded, looking at her in a way that wasn't entirely fond but wasn't entirely hostile either—the way you look at a lover you haven't seen for a while, whose face is still sifting back into familiarity.

NATHANIEL RYMER'S ESTATE nestled in Haverford, a suburb that made Mortimer Street look like Harlem. "If you fuck this up," Tobias warned Malcolm the next Tuesday, as they took the private drive—past a man proprietarily polishing the midnight-blue Bentley, past tapered firs erect as sentries—"you die by midnight."

19 Tobias had scheduled the meeting about Ivy Street so fast that Malcolm had to rush on presentation drawings, putting his taxes and everything else in his life on hold for a week, including Nora, who daily was becoming more panic-stricken. She wasn't sleeping well. Each night around 3 A.M. she woke up expecting to see FBI men at her bedside, like punk Grim Reapers.

Rymer greeted Malcolm and Tobias at the immense door: gray hair, perfect posture, slim tie, eyes blue as a husky's. Not Rymer, it turned out, but the butler. The entrance court was completely free of snow; Malcolm wouldn't have known where to wipe his shoes. The rug in the granite foyer was antique Persian, each silken knot hand tied.

"This way, gentleman," the butler said.

They walked past a football field–sized living room with heroic wainscoting and a fireplace similar to the one before which Citizen Kane's wife had sighed over jigsaw puzzles. Malcolm glimpsed a Mackintosh chair, a Ruhlmann sideboard. A painting of a pale woman in a plunging gown, maybe a Sargent. The house must have been fifteen thousand square feet. While everything in Malcolm's life was a last-minute stay against disaster—fumbling to knot his tie while Tobias honked in the car outside—everything in Rymer's suggested leisurely layers of accumulation.

Nathaniel Rymer was relaxing in the library at a desk that could have seated eight for dinner. He wore a sweatshirt and jeans. Like Malcolm, he worked at home, though "home" in this context took on a different meaning. Even his jeans looked regal, with a faded crease where they'd been pressed. Tobias was right: the man had a senatorial stage presence, the handshake and clear-eyed gaze of an honest man.

"Coffee?" Rymer asked. Malcolm and Tobias nodded dumbly and sat as the butler whispered off.

"I saw you on the news about the Bulletin Building," Rymer told Malcolm. "You know it well?"

"Yes," Malcolm said. "Great building. One of the best in the city."

"Better than Lit's?" Rymer asked, referring to a huge department store slated for demolition.

"I like it more," Malcolm said. "It's more idiosyncratic."

Rymer pressed his hands together and raised them to his lips—a gesture which Malcolm associated with priests—as Malcolm tried to do the kind of self-marketing he was so bad at: dropping names and facts, with eye contact, and all within the guise of ease and informality. He could be relaxed, and he could be emphatic, but not emphatically relaxed; in client meetings he always resented feeling like a trained seal. He managed to mention that he knew the developers who were packaging the Lit's Building.

"I know," Rymer said. "They speak highly of you. They recommended you to me, then Tobias did, then I saw you on the news. So your name stuck. I must tell you, though, that I haven't been involved in any real estate, and I'm afraid now may not be the best time to start."

"Maybe not," Malcolm agreed, as Tobias gave him a veiled glare. Well, it was true, given the proposed tax laws. Malcolm's other business problem: he could not tell a lie. For years he'd quoted real bottom lines, and what for? So he could be a nice guy and finish last.

"What do you have?" Rymer asked.

Malcolm unwrapped the Ivy Street plans and made a presentation in a wan voice, shaking—though his hands were, too much to pick up his coffee mug. Rymer asked the standard questions about historical certification and tax credits, and made the standard sounds of approval as he flipped the pages of Malcolm's portfolio. They discussed other developers Malcolm had worked for—Rymer registered the names in a way that meant he was remembering them, would check Malcolm out. "Have you ever done a project this big?" Rymer asked, and Malcolm said no.

"But he could," Tobias said.

What a jerk! What was Tobias, Malcolm's press rep? What did he think they were selling, Girl Scout cookies? But Rymer smiled benignly.

"I'll run this by my people," he said. "By the way, maybe while you're here you could look at the basement. I'd like to have work done on the wine cellar—a storage system, temperature and humidity control— then finish off an adjacent space for tastings. Service bar, a powder room, maybe some kind of opening onto the west garden. My daughter's getting married in June, so I'd like to finish the work by then."

"I'd be happy to look," Malcolm said, repressing excitement: maybe he could recycle all the wine cellar product research he'd done for Stone. But the excitement turned edgy as Rymer walked him through the space. Basements are architectural ballbreakers—damp, viewless, with a tangle of wiring and heating pipes on the ceilings. In front of the biggest heater he'd ever seen (it looked like a submarine), Malcolm listed potential problems as if trying to discourage Rymer.

"It can be done, right?" Rymer asked, puzzled.

Peripherally, Malcolm caught Tobias's scolding expression.

"Sure," Malcolm said. "But it'll cost—"

Rymer made the subtlest of price-is-no-object shrugs.

Fine. Rymer would spend. But what would he want? No doubt clichéd "caves," with dark, aged wood, antique lights—something "in keeping with the house."

"I don't want an amusement park effect," Rymer warned. "I want it cozy and warm, relaxed yet elegant, open and airy at the garden . . . I can't quite envision it. Can you—"

Sure, Malcolm thought. *You want everything, all at once, yesterday*. But he managed to murmur some conceptual- and technical-sounding things as Rymer, nodding vigorously, unlocked the wine cellar.

"Malcolm knows a lot about wine," Tobias offered, as they entered the makeshift room (Malcolm suppressed an urge to strangle his friend).

Once Malcolm saw the hundreds of cases stacked in the wine cellar, he wanted to get a job as Nate Rymer's janitor, so he could sneak down here for his lunch breaks. He could barely get his mouth to close at the hills of Haut-Brion, the mounds of Montrachet, but he somehow managed to talk shop with Rymer for a couple of minutes. Why was he telling a man with a Ruhlmann sideboard that cost more than a house when it was new in 1920, no less now, what a good buy Portuguese cabernets were? But Rymer looked impressed, as Stone had. It turned out that Malcolm and Rymer frequented the same bargain wine stores in New York. They talked about vintages and importers for long enough to bore Tobias, until Mrs. Rymer came down to introduce herself.

"Claire Rymer," she said, offering her hand with a respectful dip of her head. She looked like an astronaut's wife. Though her hair was pulled back into a crisp knot, like Kim Novak's in *Vertigo*, she managed to seem unstarched. So easy to imagine Claire and Nate in their jeans, still in love after all these years, eating Cornish game hens in front of the fire; their children off somewhere enjoying full, rich lives; their money in the bank, unpretentiously growing. Mrs. Rymer was clearly not all that interested in the basement or the wine cellar, and for that Malcolm was grateful. With any luck he'd only have one client to please, not two pulling in different directions.

Nora didn't have a shoot for a week. While Malcolm returned to Haverford to measure the basement and then worked on preliminary sketches for Rymer, Nora attempted to deal with dirty clothes; unreturned phone calls; unwatered plants; coats with crucial missing buttons; a message from Alan, who was concerned about her; a message from David Martella, delayed in Rome (on the answering machine he posed as an ad job from a fictitious agency, for discretion's sake); and Malcolm, who, a week after their mutual revelations and hint of reconciliation, now hunkered over plans at his desk, unavailable to her.

In her studio, she set to work on a mobile for her imminent nephew: bobbing fish, pigs, elephants, and giraffes in the cheeriest of colors. Among the papier mâché animals was one human, a little guy with a scowl, a bowler hat, and a briefcase so overflowing with dirty money that one bill the size of a pinkie nail was caught in the clasp.

A decade ago she would have been fueled by the fantasy of displaying this piece in a museum. But the art world had lost interest in the kind of

whimsical vision to which Nora had aspired and still did, anachronisti-
cally. For years she had waited for the sensibility to circle back, as it had
to long hair and miniskirts. It hadn't. To ride with the times, Nora decided, she would do better to manufacture these mobiles for her friends'
better babies.

So this was what Julie Peszko meant by "conflicted." Nora couldn't
even afford to quit her job and devote herself to raising a child. Her only
hope was to hold tight to what, in graduate school, is called "the work
itself": the pleasure of slopping newspaper in goop or creating the perfect orange for the pig's snout. If she couldn't enjoy herself, what was the
point? What was the point of there being no point?

If it weren't winter, she thought, and if their backyard even in summer didn't look like Appalachia, maybe she should take up gardening.

While Malcolm met with his potential client, Nora screwed up the
courage to throw good money after bad and paid for a new battery to re-
suscitate her car. She brought the filthy old girl to a car wash and
watched sadly through the glass, knowing that the vehicle would
emerge looking exactly as it had on the other end. The paint was worn
unevenly thin and didn't shine at all; the sight of the car gave her the
same overblown sadness that chipped fingernail polish had, back when
she tended to such things. But somehow the car also inspired her to return the stolen money. She did this in much the same spirit she'd taken
the money with in the first place, without much advanced planning—
the way, some people claim, you should jump into marriage, because if
you think about it too much for too long, you're guaranteed doubts.

The money machine closest to their house was seven blocks uptown, at
the invisible boundary where the interracial neighborhood turned all
black. With the neon sign for the Church of Christ, and the State Store
displaying strange-but-true cognac blends—including, Nora noted
with dreadful glee, cognac and papaya juice—this was still a neighborhood. Drivers double-parked to greet men emerging from the corner
bar. Nora was the only white, except for a policeman passing by on a list-
less horse. The couple of times that her parents had visited her here, from
North Hills in Pittsburgh, they'd locked their car wistfully, prepared
never to see it again. But Nora had lived in West Philadelphia long

enough to instinctively both acknowledge and downplay her white-ness—a friendly yet protective attitude that said, *I live here too*. She knew how to look first at threatening people who passed, a full, bold, aware look that would disarm in any city, but especially in Philadelphia with its low eye contact.

Why this money machine? She couldn't say. She couldn't use prox-imity as an excuse: she could now drive to any money machine in the city or, if the automatic teller networking advertisements were true, in the country. Nor did she know whether it was safer or more dangerous to use the unfamiliar branch—whether this branch would be more used to large cash transactions from workers cashing their paychecks or would assume (since they didn't know her) that the size of her transac-tion was typical. *Either or neither or both* was what she said to herself as she parked near the ghettoish money machine and deposited a money market check for $27,900 to herself and her bank. The line sounded ee-rily familiar; she must have said it recently, to Ralph or David or her brothers, on another subject. In her head *either or neither or both* had a cartoonish gallop, like *lions or tigers or bears*.

After she'd redeposited the money into her checking account, the machine clacked out an emotionless receipt to verify the transaction. *That's that, then*, she told herself primly—though it obviously wasn't.

20 FILLING OUT TAX forms made Malcolm philosophical. How could you tamp your life into bureaucratic language and not think, pugnaciously, about how little the government understood you? The government or anyone else: preposterous that journalists would use the word "yuppie" to describe him, despite his non-income, simply because he didn't live in a tract house, eat TV dinners with the kids at sunset, and buy toilet paper by the twenty-roll pack. "Yuppie" now meant anyone with aspirations to taste.

He would say this later, to Ann Marie Lewis. He would point out as well that you could know someone and not know them at all. Nora could name the things he didn't like: mint, lemon, light blue. Big breasts, sitcoms, rock and roll. And he could provide the same service for her, listing noise and crowds, hot and cold, or any meat that, served, looked too much like a butchered animal. But what did any of that say, finally?

"I guess," Ann Marie would observe, "that 'your wife doesn't understand you'—and you're not even married."

Lunch with Ann Marie Lewis would stretch into dinner, and dinner would be followed by what often follows between people who brush hands when they reach for the butter concurrently. When Malcolm said, "Good bread," and Ann Marie said, "Very fresh," and Malcolm added, "Hot too," they would lower their eyes, as if they were speaking in code about their future together.

Malcolm met her at the IRS office. She wore a sweater dress in turquoise that curled about her brightly as she approached him across the huge desk-filled room. The turquoise, the black hair, and the pale, pale skin—Irish, he thought, but there was a touch of something else, Italian maybe. (He turned out to be exactly right.) He handed her the fictitious forms. "Congratulations," she said; she went to put the forms on her desk and fetch her coat.

At lunch she told him about how she'd become an IRS case worker. As Malcolm had guessed, she'd started out in Welfare, had moved to the IRS for the usual reasons: better money, sick of the grittiness of urban poverty. Not that you needed a security clearance for the kind of work she did, but her socialism had never been hardcore enough to ruin it. "My politics at the time were pretty much decorative," she admitted.

"And now?"

"Well, I make less noise, but I'm more careful to vote. I know the records of all the local judges."

She had been at the IRS for five years, and though she had always assumed she'd get out momentarily, she found that she enjoyed the work. Some of the messy cases were challenging.

In her spare time she had begun work on an MBA at Wharton. Malcolm drew back some. As if catching his wince, she offered justification—just because you had an MBA didn't mean you had to become an automaton: you could do organizing or fundraising for charities or the arts, or even make policy for monsters like the IRS.

"And you?" she asked.

Malcolm told her about his own career history, which made her laugh. Behind the laughter he could feel her asking herself, How big a flop *is* this guy, anyhow? But beneath that layer was the other, truer one. The one that meant she was ready for what would follow.

After lunch she asked if he'd return to her office, to make sure his forms were in order. He agreed readily, hoping that this was a ploy to spend more time with him and not a sign that she suspected him of the federal crime that he had, in fact, committed. He watched anxiously as she speed-read the forms, but then she just smiled her crooked smile, put them down.

Malcolm asked, "Would you have dinner with me? After work, I mean?"

She smiled, said, "Why not?"

He would tell her about the forms. If not at dinner, then eventually. So easy to imagine them in bed, his postcoital confession; she'd interrupt, just say, *I know.*

It was three by the time he left. There was no point in going home before dinner. He wandered around awhile, doing errands. For a half-hour or so he was in almost a trance of happiness: Ann Marie, getting Ivy Street and taxes out of his life. But downtown was thick with Muzak, Christmas aggression, blind and legless beggars; he had to concentrate to stay confident and lighthearted in the thin December light.

On his way back to Ann Marie he bought a bunch of tiger lilies wrapped in soggy green paper. Flowers were a source of some uneasiness: after Nora's standard burst of delight in being given flowers, she usually gave him postpurchase tips on how to choose the freshest ones. He didn't exactly think about this, certainly not for long enough to feel angry at her, but he was brushed by a waft of the heaviness that she and their relationship brought. As if in planned contrast, Ann Marie was waiting for him outside the Federal Building, swinging her briefcase and looking down at one of her shoes; she appeared to be lining the point of her pump up with the corners of the entrance walkway's marble.

"Thanks," he said, holding out the flowers at a right angle that he suddenly found stupid, but how exactly were you supposed to thrust them forth—at hip level, like a pickpocket?

"Oh! You're welcome. Thanks. What are we supposed to do with them while we eat?"

"It's too early to eat. Let's get a drink."

"Can I put these in water here?" she asked.

"Sure."

"Do you want to come up?"

"Do you want me to?"

She smiled, with a shrug to suggest that this was only the first of many tough decisions he might face that evening.

He made a gesture to indicate that he would follow.

They were the only people on the elevator up, going against traffic. It was both disturbing and strangely pleasant that she made him feel self-conscious about assuming elevator posture—heading for the corner, watching the floor lights. He quickly corrected himself, and stood with his back to the door, facing her. It was not a long enough trip for her to become uncomfortable, or for him to pin her features, which shifted, becoming Eskimo at the three-quarters angle of broadest cheekbone. Full-face she was somewhat plain, but it was a good sort of plain, the kind that would look expressive, rather than unfinished, in the morning.

On her floor he waited by the elevator holding the packages he'd acquired on his errands. From there he could watch her motor to her desk among the many desks, unlock her drawer to get a vase, head to the water fountain, shove in the flowers, and spend that satisfied, private second as she surveyed how the flowers enhanced her turf.

"Makes it better here in the morning," she said when she returned. "Thanks."

He let her choose the restaurant, which gave them something to talk about as they walked other than deciding whose car to take—his, since hers was in the shop (he regretted that he'd neglected to remove the tire iron, empty soda bottles, and papers from the floor). His heart jumped when she confessed that she drove a Pacer.

"I always wished I'd bought one of those," he said.

"Well, I think *Consumers Reports* rates it the worst car of the century."

"What color is it?"

"Green. Want to buy it, if I can ever afford another?"

"Maybe. Seriously. I think it's a modern masterpiece. Totally ahead of its time. Wait and see, it'll be in a museum someday, along with the Olivetti typewriter and the fur teacup."

She just looked at him.

At the restaurant they determined that both of them had been born in the city, had grown up there, and longed to move, but where could you move that was better, where you could afford to live in the style to which you'd grown accustomed? They stayed because it was easy. Well, maybe not easy—the city had more than its share of urban difficulties—but at least familiar.

They noted that they both kept losing friends. The city couldn't hold on to good people. Part of the blame, of course, had to go to old age—everyone had become less energetic. *I never even get out to the movies anymore*, all their friends complained, in the same plaintive tone.

Not that the movies were so great these days. Which movies they'd liked, which they hadn't. The changes VCRs had made in their viewing habits. Malcolm was aware of how easy it was to talk to her. He had never heard her IRS stories, so of course she would seem charming relating them; but what surprised him was how effortlessly they segued to more personal recollections. By the end of the meal she knew, by some automatic transition, about his long-standing fascination with Italian women, which went back to the third grade and Julia, the consulate's daughter who, at however old you are then, was already sexy.

Malcolm didn't feel the least bit guilty. He didn't think about Nora at all as he drove Ann Marie home and she invited him in for cognac. He didn't feel bad, in fact, until she'd handed him the snifter and they were side by side on her couch. Soon they would kiss. The question was whether they should have the inevitable relationship discussion before or after. Malcolm didn't want to instigate it, but he also didn't want to withhold information she thought she should have. Only then did he actively remember Nora. What he remembered was their first kiss—the last first kiss he'd had. For some reason they had been fooling with his calculator, trying to figure out how to make it do percentages. "What if you press that button?" Nora had said, and Malcolm said, "No, that's not it." "How 'bout that?" No, Malcolm had said, it was some formula, but he didn't remember what. "I thought if you didn't kiss me," Nora later told him, "I'd die."

Malcolm opted for kiss now, talk later.

First kisses should be sure and new at once, like stepping into bright sunlight in a foreign city. When Malcolm and Nora went to Paris and got off the Metro at the Left Bank, Malcolm looked at the sun, the river, the spire of Notre Dame across the river, and knew immediately where he was, where their hotel would be, without consulting the map. "This way," he'd said, and Nora, who had been to Paris before, said, "No, this way." They'd had a tug-of-war in the middle of the square. Nora's sense of direction was worthless. Some kind of right brain/left brain difficulty—she couldn't reap a map, or, rather, always read a map exactly flipped. The trouble with the present kiss with Ann Marie was that Malcolm was distracted. A mental shift like sunlight through clouds or clouds over sunlight, through which Paris peeked. Malcolm pulled away, eyes closed; when their mouths re-engaged they seemed better matched. Not that he didn't love Paris. But Paris was Nora. So this was—

well, Barcelona: steamy, golden, ornate, and, if truth be told, a little surreal, like Gaudí towers.

This went on for some time, with Malcolm's hands in her wonderful
thick black hair. He was kissing, not theorizing, but had a thought seen
the light it would have concerned how close sex can be to a certain artistic purity of thought: the strands of hair seemed magnified, particular,
truths with which the lines of their hands and lips seemed to rhyme.

They stopped and held hands for a while, looking at each other.

"Excuse me for asking this," Ann Marie said, "but who is the infa-
mous 'Worth' who answered your doorbell?"

"Oh," Malcolm said.

"The woman you live with?"

He nodded.

"You're not married?"

He shook his head no.

"Things not going so well?"

He looked at their intertwined hands and shrugged.

"I see," she said.

She didn't seem particularly upset.

After a while she reclaimed her hand to straighten her hair and began
to talk.

Ann Marie Lewis had lived with someone for three years. He'd been
transferred a year ago, and they had been attempting a commuter relationship, with the usual difficulties wrought by distance. Of course
when he was in town they'd had the usual difficulties wrought by close-
ness. The seesaw could probably continue indefinitely. It was so hard for
her to disentangle herself from the history of a long-term relationship.
Of course, new things were nice too. Ann Marie had enjoyed their evening, even though she'd assumed he had someone else, which damp-
ened her spirits some—not that she was anyone to talk—but it was hard
to know how to proceed.

"I agree," Malcolm said, enjoying the sound of her voice.

"I don't feel myself getting younger by the minute," Ann Marie said,
"and I've always kind of assumed I'd have a family. Not like it's all over.
I've got six, seven years left. Maybe more with the miracle of modern sci-

ence. I don't even know if I *want* kids. I mean, they're noisy, messy, time-consuming. I'd want to keep working, have full-time child care, and you know what that's supposed to do to them. They'd probably hate you. But I figure, hey, they're going to hate you until they're thirty anyway, the way we hated our parents, so what's the difference? But . . . I don't know. I feel like I'm missing something."

"I know what you mean," Malcolm said. "Half the buildings I pass in this city I tried to get someone to buy at some point." He shook his head sadly, but when he looked at Ann Marie he realized that this was not what she had in mind in the way of commiseration. He kissed her again.

What he'd meant to say was how impossible it was to tell if the timing was right on anything. That balance of bravery and caution—the proving, in the movies, of soldiers—now applied to everyone and everything: when to buy buildings in an iffy neighborhood, when to leave or stay in a relationship.

She pulled away and excused herself to use the bathroom. When she left, Malcolm pounced on the phone, about to leave a message for Nora using Tobias as his alibi, hoping she had stayed in New York for dinner as she often did and would not be so tacky as to call him back at Tobias's when she got in. But he didn't dial. He just sat, awash in guilt and panic.

When Ann Marie returned, she suggested that maybe they should cool it for a while, until they got more of a feel of their mutual situations. Malcolm agreed.

In the minute between her departure and her return, he had managed to compose a long list of her flaws: she was beautiful, but she worked for the IRS. An MBA-type who didn't seem to have much sense of humor. For all he knew she was a believer, wanted her children—the children she wanted—raised in the faith. Over her dining room table (why did so many women collect such dark, heavy furniture? The table gave off an air of spinsterhood), a Degas poster. *Degas*, for God's sake! Again, he didn't think of her critically so much as see her form, when she walked back in, as less tinged with golden light—a perception that he realized was either realistic or overly negative.

They said affectionate, encouraging good-byes.

Only as he drove home did the longing for Ann Marie settle back over him like fairy dust. Why hadn't he been more optimistic, more romantic? So she had mentioned children—all women do that. It was just something you had to deal with. Maybe he should go back, point out how when he saw her at his door he had a sense of destiny—it wouldn't be a lie.

Malcolm had slowed for a traffic light several blocks from his house when he noticed a man sitting cross-legged, guru-style, in the slush in the middle of the intersection. As he came to a stop he saw that the man was young, naked, and covered in blood. He appeared to have a head wound; under the glare of the street lamps, Malcolm could see that blood dripped down the man's face and clotted in his chest hair.

A cab had just turned the corner. The cabbie stopped, rolled down the window, and said something to the man, who stood up and walked laconically in the cold toward the taxi. He was barefoot. His penis bobbed. He said a couple of words to the driver, then got in the cab as the light changed.

That was it.

It was after 2 A.M. There was not a soul out to confirm that this had actually happened.

He was delighted to discover from the answering machine that Nora had stayed in New York. He had been dreading their hello kiss: she would smell Ann Marie on his breath. What Nora lacked in sense of direction she made up for in sense of smell—she had, alas, the nose of a birddog.

21 THE DAY OF David Martella's scheduled return flight, a terrorist bomb exploded at the Rome airport. David was not there, having found himself at an intimate lunch with the film's star, who was even more stunning in real life. He had cinched a deal for a feature on the reclusive actress in the *Times Sunday Magazine*. While the interview was being taped, bloody civilians were loaded onto ambulances.

"Your chances of being caught in terrorist fire," an expert on the late-night news would offer, "are about the same as your chances of winning the lottery. But remember, people *do* win the lottery."

David called to assure Nora that he was safe at the moment she finished reading his letter, which had arrived (amid bills and advertising circulars, but no letter from the bank) the afternoon of the explosion and of Malcolm's meeting with Ann Marie:

> I'm thinking of your warm white skin in my hotel room. Am I allowed to say that? Will you have to burn this? I hope not. I still have the note you shoved through the holes in my mailbox on day two of Round One. Remember how *sure* everything was? You in that bizarre green dress, like Robin Hood—the whole night had a sort of Arden Forest feel.
>
> So why do you have to wear me down with doubts? I wish you understood—it's not magic, it's the same old shit. You have the destination and the ticket, but it's like you sit there wishing you knew exactly what the weather was going to be like so you knew what to pack, then cancel the trip for fear of rain. Why not sing in it?
>
> The rain, I mean.

Nora scrutinized the cursive of her heartthrob. She tried to conjure up the old ardor for David's mouth but was disconcerted by a close-up of his earlobes—rather too long and loose, like an old woman's.

When the phone rang she picked it up with shaking voice, expecting the bank as she did every time it rang now.

"Don't worry," David Martella said, "I'm not dead."

"That's nice," Nora responded.

"You haven't heard?"

"What?"

"What planet do you live on? Don't you watch the news?"

David told Nora about his brush with disaster and the lunch that had delayed him. Nora had to clutch her chest just thinking about terrorists on planes.

"Oh David, you must be terrified about flying home."

"Actually, I was more worried that when I got there you and Malcolm would have made up."

Nora didn't have time to respond. "I should have known," David accused. "You're so predictable."

"This is sexy," Nora said. "Especially long distance."

"Sorry. Did you get my letter?"

"It appears to have been written before Rita's visit."

He emitted a stagy sigh. "You know how I feel about you. What will any of that matter if my face gets blown off?"

True. Nothing would matter if she found herself in jail tomorrow, or if her brother's baby, due any second, was less than perfect. As he tried to convince her to meet his flight at J. F. K., as a test of her affection, bone cancer could be brewing in her right arm, which would have to be amputated, so she'd never be able to draw again. She wouldn't even be able to dial a phone, except with her toes. If Nora were a Stanislavski actress, she could weep torrents by conjuring limblessness. Would Malcolm still love her? Maybe. David? Probably not. But then, life is full of surprises.

The next afternoon, in New York, Nora made a sales pitch to produce a fire-breathing dragon costume for a mouthwash commercial. Five advertising executives were concerned full-time with this campaign, one of whom deep-sea fished with a food photographer Nora knew. They examined her presentation boards and looked at her book. Art dealers couldn't be more earnest, or drug dealers. Her bid for the E.T.-like critter was carefully positioned to be neither the highest nor the lowest, and her boards were terrific if she did say so herself: part Rauschenberg, part Rube Goldberg, green and exuberant. If she got the job, she could begin to overspecialize in a new direction. She was not alone in this, she reassured herself, remembering Malcolm's prison-accessory catalogs as she fought for sidewalk space with thousands of other pedestrians, each of whom juggled Christmas packages in addition to their ordinary burdens: briefcases, grocery bags, babies in strollers.

Assuming that few of these people were Einstein, Picasso, or President, she knew that they, too, had to convince themselves that their absence would cause at least a pockmark in life's surface. So they had affairs, or babies.

Walking during rush hour, Nora counted options—a more staggering exercise than figuring out the number of ways you can seat twelve at dinner. David could leave her, Malcolm could leave her; both of them could marry someone else; any pair could marry and divorce, and this was only the options in the narrowest spectrum. She wasn't even considering homosexuality, bestiality, transexuality.

She was calm at the airport, having ingested half a Valium to help her make her decision while David Martella flew over the cold ocean. Disconcertingly, she crossed the arch that said TICKETED PASSENGERS ONLY with no trouble (all articles on terrorism said to stay out of public areas) and waited. Her heart leaped, stupid and predictable as a leashed dog, when she saw David's feet, then body, then head, emerge from the gate.

He smiled, put his arm around her, and kissed her ear as they walked to baggage claim. "I'm so glad you're here. I didn't think you'd come."

"You look tired," Nora observed.

But not so tired that he couldn't entertain her while they waited for his luggage, with a string of stories about the making of the film and his trip. When his suitcase arrived, though, he said, "End of the line," put his head on her shoulder, and made a snoring sound.

"Poor baby," Nora said, patting his wiry hair.

"Would you mind watching me sleep for a couple of minutes?"

"All my work stuff is in a locker in Penn Station. I checked it earlier so I wouldn't have to—"

David sighed in a way that meant, *Don't clutter up your life with details.*
"Okay," Nora said.

So they took a cab to the airport hotel and checked in. They were silent in the cab, silent as David flopped on the bed without undressing. Nora snuggled against him, breathing in his smell—a kind of clean-but-dirty smell that reminded her of children in a playground and called forth, from her, a gruff tenderness.

"Christ," David said. "Down, boy, *down*. Please let me sleep," but he unzipped his pants to unleash an erection.

Nora had actually remembered to put her diaphragm in her purse before leaving for work. She felt determined to be erotic, open. But when they began to make love, the Valium was not enough to quell her discomfort—an empty skittishness, like arriving at the grocery store without your list. She pushed David away.

"Here we go," David said.

"Not now," Nora said. "The timing isn't right."

"Faster?" David asked. "Slower? Harder? Softer? What do you *want* from me?"

"I'm sorry."

"I've been awake for thirty-nine hours," David accused.

Nora stroked his chest.

"You," David said, "are a bore. Bore bore bore."

He glared at her. Then he fell asleep. Nora did too; the Valium was good for at least that much.

In her dream, it was love at first sight for her and someone blond with an accent—German, Swedish, maybe Israeli. He was an actor or a rock star or a tennis player. He wore white shorts; the muscles on his legs were incredibly well articulated, burnished with golden hair. There were obstacles, the man was world-renowned, everyone wanted a minute of his time, but Nora was atop him, so overwhelmed by lust that she didn't even care they were in a public place—the United Nations, it appeared, or Congress, for there were curved rows of seats, like an amphitheater, each seat with a microphone, except each man held a large menu, and waiters in tuxedos transcribed dinner orders.

Just as Nora was about to come (she rarely got to come in dreams, though she often got to die), the sound of a plane awoke her to the bland hotel room. She preferred to dwell in the misty glow of the dream, in which she had had both the thrill of the chase and the comfort of a man's unequivocal love. It was after ten, too late to return to Philadelphia. That pleased David. "Now we stay up for an hour or two. This is perfect for jet lag," he said.

"I really should go. My brother's baby is due any second."

"You have a patent to speed that up?" David asked.

"I just want to be available when they call."

"Don't you have remote?" he asked. "Relax."

While he was in the bathroom showering, Nora called Malcolm, blessedly got the answering machine, and talked fast so Malcolm didn't have time to pick up. "Got tied up at the shoot. Crazy. I'm crashing at Ralph's" (Ralph's number was unlisted). "Hope you're okay. See you tomorrow."

David emerged from the bathroom rubbing his hair with a towel. She'd seen him do this before, and it always puzzled her how vigorously he swatted at his hair, as if any remaining drop of water was an offense to God.

"And now," David said, "your presents."

He rifled through his suitcase. He had brought her a writing book, with handmade paper and a pretty marbleized cover. Also, a pair of emerald earrings, tiny enough to seem consciously positioned against the current fashion of gladiator-sized accessories rather than just outmoded. "The whole time I thought of you in Rome," he said, "I kept seeing green."

"They're beautiful," Nora said, then added, "Did you get the same things for Rita?"

David glared again.

"Sorry," she said, meaning it. "Thank you, David."

They did make love then. What was she supposed to do, having checked into the hotel with him? The dream lover hovered about; Nora concentrated on transferring the lust to David. It wasn't easy, because the dream demon seemed to understand that women respond to some space and light and air between strokes—the kind of fluttery touching that, in porno flicks, is always attributed to lesbians—whereas David thrummed right on the button. When she liked David, his Horatio Alger crassness seemed lusty, endearing. In the low swings of her affection for him, he seemed like a boor. *Sex isn't everything*, she was surprised to remind herself as she performed, tricky as a poltergeist. (David found her talented sexually: flattering, since Malcolm found her average, but then Malcolm was indifferent to fellatio, one of her college minors; further- more, they'd been together long enough so sex was often mostly effi- cient—not that efficency doesn't have its rewards. Sometimes Malcolm, tired, would catnap while she "got herself ready" for orgasm or, if she was tired, would "borrow her leg" for his own pleasure. No doubt David would find this disgusting. It was hard to imagine David being amused, if he rubbed on her thigh too roughly for too long, by Nora plagiarizing a line from Hitchcock to suggest, in hick drawl, "Mind mah leg, Mar- nie.") *Just because I slept with David,* she continued to herself, *doesn't mean* . . . mean what? Probably not nearly as much as the fact that, her hands on his hips, she was busy constructing self-defenses for a jury, which might not understand how she felt she was getting closer, thrust by thrust, to some kind of closure, how this encounter would perversely al- low her to put a lid on things.

Afterward, David propped himself up on one elbow and smiled. She smiled back. After sex, his teeth always looked different to her, maybe because his mouth, wordless and trusting, took on a different shape.

"What are you doing for Christmas?" he asked.

"Pittsburgh, I assume, at least for part of it. You?"

"Family too. But I was thinking. How would you like to spend New Year's somewhere warm? Have you ever snorkeled?"

"No."

"You'd love watching the little fishes pass. And I wouldn't mind watching your legs, especially with some color on them. Why *are* you so pale?"

"Winter?"

"I love your legs." He kneaded one, for emphasis. "The flesh is hard and soft at once."

"That is called," Nora observed, "poor muscle tone."

"I know you're not very adventurous, but you've taken the first step. Why not alone for some period of time, somewhere romantic? My treat."

"David, what does it mean that every single time we finish making love, you propose a vacation?"

"You tell me."

"You could have a T-shirt printed 'Run Away with Me.' What do you do after sex when you're actually *on* vacation with someone?"

"Why not find out?"

Impossible to believe that David meant this, yet he looked earnest enough, smiling with his postcoital teeth, as he proposed ways that Nora could finesse a week's absence from Malcolm. Nora felt a pang of conscience, not for Malcolm, but for David, especially as he ran tender fingers through the hair at the base of her skull (a technique that Malcolm adamantly refused to master: he massaged her scalp as you'd rub the belly of a spayed old dog that rolled over, panting, every time you passed). What if David was right, and she was merely diddling him? Because she felt no urgency. The sad part was that if David noticed, he'd attribute her languor to satiation. He seemed to believe that she had a ferocious and simple sexual appetite, like a man's, and she had never seen the point in correcting the impression.

This was the part of the night that Nora liked best, and would remember in retrospect. David, naked and unhurried late at night, tickling her back as he offered theories about their future together, along with gossip, movie judgments (not a single one of which she agreed with), and compliments. "You can't have everything scripted for you, you know," he warned her. "Some parts of your life you have to live." She felt warm and woodsy, tuned into the mysteries, like a teen-ager in a movie about an upper-crust boarding school where she read by flashlight way past curfew and, speaking in whispers, formed deep friendships which she'd maintain for her whole life.

That Ken and Annie Worth's second child was a boy surprised no one. Amniocentesis had also already revealed that, barring ugly surprises, health was in the cards. But nobody could have predicted the ease of the delivery. Joshua Worth slipped out the next morning at eleven o'clock.

Nora got this information from Ken and Annie's answering machine. "I've never done this before," the frantic message began (Ken referred not to fatherhood, but to the fact that he was recording the message via remote control, from the hospital pay phone). "His name is Joshua. He's six pounds, ten ounces. Why do people always say the weight?"

From this point on Ken spoke so quickly, racing against the message time, that he'd revealed all the major details with time left on the message loop. Then he just broke down. Nora couldn't tell if he was crying or simply speechless.

Nora liked other people's babies much better than their weddings. The traffic on the way to the hospital echoed her excitement. She was the first to arrive. Annie's parents were en route, as were the elder Worths. Various other siblings (Annie had two of her own) were due as well.

Ken was watching the babies through the glass. Despite the other spectators (Nora knew from the last go-round that New York maternity wards were rather like the subways), his posture was unguarded. Nora felt hugely tender toward his bony back as she put her hand on it. He hadn't expected her and laughed, hugging her hard enough to knock her visitor's card from her hand. "I just left a message for you in Philadelphia," he said. "How did you get here so fast?" Then, before she could answer: "Guess which." He pointed to the twenty-odd cocoons on view behind the glass, one of which had just begun to cry. Ken and Nora watched the space creatures fall into an odd rondo of mewling. "Really," Ken said. "Guess."

Nora pointed to the most serene baby, the only one who wasn't crying now other than the rear-row preemies. "That one?"

"C'mon," Ken said. "That one's black."

"Really? They all look sort of red."

"Yeah, but the black ones have much better hair. Remember how dark Emily was for the first couple of months? Look for the one who looks like Winston Churchill."

"They *all* look like Winston Churchill."

"Not true," Ken said. "Some of them look like Eraserhead."

Ken pointed to the second row, third baby from the left, who, it was true, suffered from no deformities of head and had the further distinction of eyebrows.

"Eyebrows!" Nora said.

Not only eyebrows, but Ken's identical eyebrows, as exaggerated as proofreader's marks. Nora was deeply touched, as she'd been the last time. Goosebumps crept up her forearms,—and once the goosebumps started, her eyes always filled with tears. Seeing her cry, Ken crooked her head into his shoulder and ruffled her hair in the way only Ken did. A baby couldn't wish for a better father.

"How do you think he got your eyebrows?" she asked, pulling away to wipe her eyes with the back of her hand. "Are genes a computer-generated list, or some kind of automatic zip-code sort like the post office, or what?"

"I always imagine a committee at an oval table saying, 'Now boys. About that nose.'"

She and Ken stared reverently.

After a while Annie joined them in her bathrobe. Compared to the other shuffling, disheveled mothers, Annie looked as if she'd just won a tennis match. She greeted Nora effusively, but then she looked at Ken, Ken looked back, and both of them looked at the baby in a way that seemed to Nora like extraterrestrial sex: they could touch without touching, the glass no barrier to perfect union.

Soon Nora surrended her visitor's pass to Annie's parents. With Alan and Jane, who were now in the lobby waiting their turn—Alan had heard the message too—she allowed herself a touch of the mopiness appropriate to a single sibling confronting the miracle of birth. But as Alan and Jane joined her in the routine, Jane wore a guarded expression that Nora recognized. She had been through this before with sister-in-laws: both Annie and Laurie had adored Nora until their weddings, but then they'd grown distant—just distant enough to not be offensive, not make waves—and there was nothing that Nora could say, either to the women or to her brothers. Alan and Jane would marry soon. Then the baby. And Nora?

Nora could think only far enough ahead to imagine her parents' arrival. The thought of her mother's expression—the subtlest of recriminations, part pity—made Nora wonder whether she could fulfill her walk-on role here. It's hard to look forward to seeing your mother after a night of illicit sex at an airport hotel. Besides, with her cheer and energy, Sylvia Worth often made Nora feel somewhat barren and brittle, a failed Little Mother. And Ted Worth would cup his dry hand around her cheek to kiss her hello, smelling of cigars and fabric softener, distant and adult—but why was she thinking of her parents now with this uncharacteristic bitterness?

She didn't know, but it made her feel a pressing need to be home, with Malcolm.

MALCOLM DIDN'T GET around to Christmas shopping until Christmas Eve. He had been working fiercely on plans for Rymer. Everything else in his life—Nora, Ann Marie, Stone, poverty—blurred by the wayside, and he didn't mind. He didn't share Nora's faith that thinking had the slightest power to change anything. Not only did the mental peregrinations not get you to the bottom of things, but they stirred up the water, scared the fish. So while Nora darted all over the place in between panic attacks about her bank money (she still hadn't heard from the bank, picked up phones like Mary Queen of Scots), Malcolm tried to be still and focus.

He had no choice. To his surprise, even before he presented the basement plans, Rymer called to ask if Malcolm would be interested in working on a potential package for adaptive re-use of some buildings owned by the College of Physicians, more historic structures slated for demolition. Malcolm agreed, of course, though he had no CAD system, no army of drafting drones, so the work would be time-consuming. And nerve-wracking: self-taught, his approach to buildings was intuitive, with many on-site revisions. He could enter a building and quickly grasp how to make efficient use of the existing partitions, but he couldn't free-hand the square letters that every architect learns in school. He had to trace the letters from a template, and even then he often needed to call architect friends for advice on the best kind of paper and lead.

He had work, and the promise of more work. But he was still reeling from the last threat of collapse. Every time he remembered what he'd earn if he did get the basement job, he felt as if he were plugging the deep hole of his debts with shrinking spackle.

"Babies," Nora had said one evening when she checked into his progress and he shared these doubts. "Babies put an end to all questions about the meaning of life. They have this real clarity of purpose. They're happy, sad, hungry, tired—"

"For that," Malcolm suggested, "you could get a dog. And may I ask if you think I really need to consider parenthood at this particular moment?"

"You're right," Nora said. "Need anything? Coffee? Your heating pad?"

"Just leave me alone," he suggested, and she stroked his shoulder in melodramatic commiseration, as if he had some joke disorder like postmenstrual syndrome, though she knew very well—or should have known, by this time—that, after weddings, Christmas was the one time most likely to inspire in him an existential crankiness.

The $30,000 deposit was credited the very week a month ago that Stone was busted. There the figure was, bland as unbuttered bread, in the credit column of Nora's November statement. In the debit, the $27,900 withdrawal. Then, the amount credited again.

Usually Nora loved to balance her checkbook, maybe because her math was bad but, curiously, often against her favor, so with her monthly statements she got bonuses. She even liked paying bills. She had no serious debts and always paid on time, feeling righteously adult. She penned the checks with a rolling writer that she kept in her bill basket; the pen made her cursive glisten for a second under the desk lamp. Then she recorded the checks on a budget form. There was an orderly pleasure whenever a month's line of expenses was filled in. But the $30,000 threw her. She and Malcolm had agreed that it made the most sense for her to sit tight, rather than draw attention to herself so soon after the psychotic spasm of her withdrawal and redeposit. But it wasn't easy to ignore the extra cash.

On Christmas Day they would go to Malcolm's sister's house, eat overcooked vegetables, receive unwanted gifts, and feel guilty around his mother (whom he should visit more). Then there was Nora's family: more overcooked vegetables (what did vegetables ever do to these people?), children, and dogs. Though Nora had fond familial memories of the holidays, she also generally had anxieties to share with Malcolm about buying gifts for an ever-expanding number of relatives. Because of its size, her family managed Christmas gifts by the lottery system: at Thanksgiving the siblings drew straws to give one big, nice gift to one other sibling or sibling family unit. This year Nora had drawn Ken, which meant she had to factor in two kids as well as a sister-in-law.

Another question: should she buy Christmas gifts for David? She had returned from New York ready to renounce her sin and snuggle back into domestic life, but Malcolm was so busy that if she stayed out all night with David now and again, he might not even notice. He could work right through the holidays, thin and shivering, like Bob Cratchit. Lovely as it was to see him employed, his absorption meant he had less time for Nora. David and the promise of David hung in the air, like the bank money; and like the bank money, the resolution seemed rote. Their affair would end. But why did she feel so sure of that, even as she enjoyed pondering what she could give him (a new earth-tone suitcase) and had so little problem imagining the Caribbean jaunt he'd proposed, however cavalierly?

Nate Rymer called Malcolm the day before Christmas to enthusiastically approve the basement design and budget. The deposit on the design would be enough to pay the overdue mortgage, if not any other bills. The pleasure of getting the job—a normal job with what seemed likely to be a normal client, gotten through normal, respectable channels—even leaked through the discomfort of Christmas. It would make a fine gift for Nora, though it wouldn't do as the *only* gift.

No one was at the antique mart Malcolm went to first. By dusk on Christmas Eve the department stores were almost empty as well. The only patrons were other men. Some looked glad, as Malcolm was, to move last-minute against traffic, but many were grim or panicked.

Malcolm knew exactly what to get for Nora; he kept a running list all year of objects she stopped to admire. But Ann Marie Lewis was more difficult. The thought of buying for Ann Marie made him feel more guilty than kissing her had—how could he do this to Nora, who at this very moment was perhaps out selecting trinkets for his mother and sister and nephews, to save him the trouble? Who had been so supportive while he pushed out the drawings, bringing him milk and cookies and aspirin, cashing checks for him, and generally cheering him on?

At his last stop Malcolm approached the perfume counter and found himself beside a dark man who looked familiar. At first he registered *dark* and thought *Stone*, but this man, though the right height, was far too hefty. It bothered Malcolm that he couldn't place the face. The man seemed to be looking at Malcolm too. Eventually Malcolm got curious enough to ask, "Do I know you?"

"I don't think so," the man said, almost crossly. "Why?"

"Thought I did," Malcolm said amiably.

He spent a long time deliberating on a perfume for Ann Marie Lewis and at the last minute simply couldn't do it.

It was only after he'd left the store that Malcolm remembered the man at the counter. The face was hazy—they'd only met once—but the voice was familiar from the phone. David Martella, whom Nora had almost left Malcolm for years ago. The guy had really put on weight! Malcolm remembered him as leaner, more intense—now he barely had a chin. He was not, Malcolm observed with some satisfaction, aging very well.

Malcolm and Nora ate dinner out on Christmas Eve. Every year they put a tin-foil star on the Swedish ivy, went to their favorite restaurant, then came home to open presents and make love. At the restaurant, which was always deserted—everyone else already with families—the candles shimmered in golden light. Oysters and mussels, venison and sweetbreads appeared exquisitely arranged on gleaming plates. Nora was always happy at these meals. She was a sucker for dressing up and getting fed. A sucker, too, for men in ties and jackets—she always exclaimed how handsome Malcolm was when she saw him like this. She was even happier than usual that night, once Malcolm told her about Rymer.

"Our troubles are over!" she said, looking milkily skyward, like an El Greco.

"Not entirely," Malcolm said. "I'm not going to feel secure until I get something more substantial, and until this Stone business is settled. How am I supposed to feel great about Rymer with Stone as a precedent?

And of course I'm going to be in my usual double bind: while I'm working I won't have time to pursue more work."

"Don't remind me," Nora said. "Say something else that points to hope and prosperity."

"I just have to plug away and hope something goes right someday. Keep up the faith—hard, because there's such a backlog of bad luck and bad blood."

Like our relationship, Nora thought. She had long suspected that their fate as a couple was tied to Malcolm's confidence in his financial future.

"I forgot to tell you," Malcolm said. "I made an appointment for us to see the house on Pine Street."

"How can we plan on a new house with so much up in the air?"

"We can't," Malcolm agreed. "But for an investor—"

"If we break up, neither of us can afford the mortgage alone. Or will you get one floor, me another?"

"I agree it wouldn't make any sense to buy a house until we know what we're doing."

"What *are* we doing?"

"Seeing how things go."

"You know, Mal, I've been thinking—I even told Julie—that relationships may simply be something you can't think too much about, because if you do you'll discover you're dissatisfied. Like sitting around trying to figure out if your life is worth living—the answer is going to be no. You can't get an answer, so why ask?"

"I disagree. That's what I hate about marriage. People stop thinking. Things just freeze."

"They don't have to."

"But they always do," Malcolm said. "Freeze or get worse."

"That's not what I hear. Mal, please don't tell me we're *never* going to get married."

"I didn't say that. In fact, I thought we decided we would."

"We did?"

"That's what I thought."

Nora was speechless. It wasn't easy to render her speechless. She squinted at Malcolm, who was speechless himself, having had no idea he was about to say what he'd just said. Once he said it, though, he thought he did remember that was what they'd agreed, the last time they discussed the topic—months ago, before the Stone job. He was sure they'd decided that if all went as planned, they'd marry. He distinctly remembered having agreed to this because, indifferent as he was to marriage, it would probably make Nora feel better, more secure.

"We did?" Nora repeated after a while.

"I thought so," Malcolm said, puzzled.

"Oh. You mean our recent near-split counted for naught?"

Malcolm sat silently, looking confused.

"Malcolm," Nora said. "Let's concentrate here."

"I thought—" Malcolm said.

The waiter came. They ordered coffee, dessert. When the waiter left, Nora said, "Okay."

"Okay what?"

"When?" she asked.

"Someday," Malcolm said.

"Oh," Nora said. "*Some*day."

"When our situation stabilizes."

"Meaning when hell freezes over. So in other words, we're back where we were to begin with."

"No. Soon."

"Oh," Nora said. "Soon. *I* see."

Malcolm's face was earnest and uneasy. This was as close as he was going to get, it seemed, to one of the bashful proposals in romantic novels. Nora could be irritated or enchanted, depending on her mood. What she mainly found herself feeling was amused. She covered her mouth with her hand and started to laugh.

She laughed for a long time. Malcolm laughed too. When she drew her hand away from her mouth she was smiling enough to show all her teeth, which were stained from the wine. Malcolm smiled back.

"Well," she said, "I'm certainly glad we got *that* settled."

Three

THENCEFORTH, NORA WORTH was wildly in love. It was as if she'd discovered, after a lifetime of wheezing, that she was allergic to her goosedown pillow. Now the air and her brain were clear. For decades her beloved would be across the table in his bathrobe, in excellent health (if bran, vitamins, and weight lifting did their jobs), surprising her with goofy news.

Malcolm DeWitt had become an aficionado of the city pages; bankruptcies and sheriff's sales, notices of intent not to pay, busts as inconsequential as hiccups. It was Malcolm who discovered that the FBI had raided Stone's brokerage house, "armed with a search warrant authorizing them to seize evidence of the crimes of conspiracy, aiding and abetting in the commission of a felony, and failing to report domestic cash transactions in excess of $10,000." And it was Malcolm who circled the ad the next week in the real estate section, for a house so expensive the broker could afford vowels:

> CITY CASTLE! Unique 1852 townhouse on best block in city exquisitely restored w/ finest European amenities. Marble foyer, huge living rm w/ 6 ft mirror, formal dining rm, gourmet kitchen, breakfst rm, 8 bedrm, 4½ bth, Jacuzzi, 4th flr library w/ bookcases & skylite, basement gym w/ sauna, wine cellar, parquet & mahogany flrs thruout, chandeliers, 8 fireplaces, all orig trim & mouldngs, sundeck, garden, parking. Gracious living for the truly discriminating. $800,000. EASILY $3 MIL IN NYC!

So Stone was going to have to sell his manse. The proceeds would go to his wife, who, Lucy heard, had filed for divorce. It was only fair, since Malcolm and Nora couldn't afford their dream house on Pine Street downtown.

They made an appointment anyway, and poked around a long time. Malcolm's eyes got hot and focused. Old houses were his element; he was at home as a big, bright fish darting through sunken galleons. Nora smiled at him, and he responded with his benevolent, subtle, knowing dolphin's smile, which barely altered the curves of his face.

The house would need new everything in the way of systems, so it was relatively inexpensive for Center City. They still couldn't afford it. They'd have to stay in their present house in University City, a neighborhood that at least had the distinction of being quirky. From their dinner table, to the tune of passing traffic and the beat of melting roof snow hitting the bucket under their leaking skylight, they could oversee an urban parade: an old, bald hippie with a chest-length beard; a priest lurching as if drunk—maybe mild Parkinson's disease. An albino. An interracial couple with a child. Nora had seen the family before—the man was black and seven feet tall, the woman had a thalidomide arm (maybe two, but she always passed the window in profile), and the baby was Vietnamese.

Malcolm argued that their peanut gallery–eye's view was entertaining—as entertaining, at least (even if they *could* afford it), as paying triple their present monthly mortgage for an equivalent house in the Art Museum area, where they could be thrust into an active turf war between Puerto Ricans and gentrifiers, or near the Naval Home, where they could deal with Irish bar brawls.

"This is what I do," Malcolm pointed out. "Of course I'd like a new space. But I don't want to be a mortgage slave."

Nora concurred, though she couldn't quite shake her mental connection between love and real estate. A new, joint house would be starting afresh, rather than dealing makeshift with scraps of their pasts.

Soon thereafter, Julie Peszko called to report that she had been summoned to the FBI.

She was livid. The patients had confidentiality—not that she knew anything. She wasn't even Stone's lawyer's therapist. Ed Tarry had asked her how long she'd known Chris. Then he invited her to join him for dinner. Over the course of two hours and a bottle of wine, Julie used her Mata Hari talents for extracting the lowdown.

An envelope had been received by the FBI. (How an envelope mailed anonymously to "FBI Philadelphia" got traced to Ed Tarry and this case must have been a story in itself, one that Tarry didn't relate.) Inside the envelope was a key to a locker in the 30th Street train station, in a row of lockers reserved mostly for the belongings of sleeping vagrants. Inside the locker, five white cardboard cartons, the kind used for take-out Chinese food, which contained five keys of cocaine, worth about $32,000 a key.

The cocaine, Ed told Julie, was no big deal. It was clearly Benjamin Stone's—he'd probably asked the lawyer to play errand boy, as he'd done in the past, and the lawyer got scared—but they wouldn't bring charges. What they planned to crack, he bragged, was the infrastructure of the city's banking elite.

The bank under attack was Stone's bank—and Nora's.

"$32,000 is a familiar figure, no?" Julie asked Nora.

"You're not suggesting—"

"You have mystery money in your account, and your bank is shady."

"Come on. You think of all the accounts at the bank, they chose mine to hide coke cash?"

"They're talking to Chris. If a connection is paranoid, Chris will make it. Chris knows about Malcom and Stone, and he knows about you and your bank."

"That's true."

"Fun's fun. Confess."

"I put the money back in the account. I don't think it's a good idea to highlight its comings and goings."

"Have you spoken to a lawyer?"

"Why should I? I haven't done anything wrong."

"That guy Tarry—"

"Uh-oh," Nora said.

"Tricky fellow. I liked his eyes—such a clear blue. He was hard to read. I half thought he was just an ordinary accountant-type, hiding behind the mystery of his job, and half of me thought his job was what stabilized him and in fact he is very marginal, very dangerous."

"Sounds right up your alley. How's Chris?"

"Out. Looking for work. Pretty much stabilized. Sort of back with his wife."

"Really? Are you disappointed?"

"Yes and no," Julie said, and discoursed for a while on Chris's recovery ("amazing when we can actually help") and her feelings for him, before returning to Tarry.

"He asked if he could call me. I said yes. A weird night—me trying to draw him out, him trying to draw me out. I must say, I didn't at all appreciate protecting you. What I can't understand is why you're taking this so lightly. *You've committed fraud*, Nora, and all for a lousy $30,000. Why? This is a federal investigation."

"You might be right. I'll think about it. Meanwhile, I have some other news. I didn't tell you before because we agreed to let it sink in first, but we're getting married."

Nora wasn't sure why it had happened, she told her friend, but it was like how you look up one day in April and suddenly all the trees have leaves. It was clear now that her fights with Malcolm had been caused by stress over finances, stress aggravated by the fact that they dealt with stress differently. Malcolm's slower, more patient way had its advantages. Now Malcolm had work and she'd been energetically pursuing her new career direction. She had actually gotten the mouthwash-dragon bid, and that might open doors. Even her food shoots had been more amusing. She was sorry she'd been so hasty to announce their troubles to everyone. All her talk, Nora confessed, only served to tangle her in theories and countertheories.

"How do you know," Julie asked, "that what you're saying now isn't just another theory added to the pile?"

"Right. It's hard to tell. Maybe, as my mother would say, you have to take it on faith, take the leap."

"And David?"

Nora told Julie about the Rome debacle and their encounter in the airport hotel. A man who screws for five minutes in the blush of first love was not going to get more attentive after a couple of decades of marriage. "Anyway," Nora said, "I could never live with him. We were deadlocked. At two different points when I was ready to leave Malcolm, David didn't do a thing to propel me. He pursued me the same way he applies for jobs and grants—just to see if he can get them. For all his 'range,' his real specialty is David. What the actress in Rome thought of him, what the *Times* thought of his article. What I think of him and what Malcolm and Rita are going to think when we run off together."

"What did you expect him to do when you called him from Bonwit's?" Julie asked. "If you'd really wanted to go, you would have gone. He would have dealt with Rita."

"'Dealt' with her. Very attractive. What if he really loves her? It's quite possible. David always let it be known he loves me madly and is merely waiting for me to act. How convenient. I'm just not convinced that's worth much."

(Nora didn't tell Julie about the Christmas Day phone call. As arranged, Nora's and David's answering machines had communicated by remote the whereabouts of their owners, and Nora had been sitting by her phone at ten in the morning, before she went to Malcolm's sister's house, ready to receive David's call from a phone booth near Rita's family's house. They had wished each other a Merry Christmas and agreed, as Julie surely would now, that the secrecy was absurd.)

"I've heard all this before," Julie said. "Then half a year later you tell me how adorable he is."

"I'll always have a soft spot for him. But I like the imagined David best. The real one wears on me, whereas Malcolm keeps growing—"

"Well," Julie said, "that's great, Nora. It's been a long time, and I'm glad it worked out. But I'd suggest that you tear yourself away from the bridal registry for long enough to think of a way to keep yourself out of jail, because my educated guess is you'll find the inmate experience unrewarding."

"I don't know. Malcolm might enjoy a prison ceremony. That way we won't have to invite our families."

Malcolm and Nora agreed to postpone the date until the fall. Spring was too soon, summer too hot. And if the date was in the fall, what was the point of telling people now? Nora could tell her parents if she insisted, but he certainly wasn't going to tell his.

As she filled Julie in on the wedding plans, Nora was surprised to find herself bubbly. These details would hardly qualify her for a spotlight in *Modern Bride*, though from what she had begun to hear, engagements were rarely trouble-free. Parents—especially fathers—were often only guardedly thrilled, and grooms were often reluctant.

When you decide to marry, you become the automatic recipient of wedding lore. Similar as the horror stories were—guest lists as wild as golems, overbearing in-laws, hideous gifts, cold feet, gastrointestinally troubled honeymoons—everyone seemed to recall their own events fondly. Nora found this touching. Malcolm found it smug—but then, Malcolm's views on weddings were no cause to interrupt the programming for a flash bulletin.

Ann Marie Lewis was not the first thing in Malcolm's head when he woke up, or the last thing in his head when he went to sleep, but she came to him in glints: a fragment of voice or laugh, the blunt edge of black hair against the line of her chin. He didn't seem to have the right lens to see her whole. Sometimes, making love with Nora, a phantom Ann Marie would drift over the scene, making Nora seem lightweight, insubstantial in comparison.

Malcolm and Ann Marie had a strange phone conversation shortly after Christmas, in which they didn't discuss relationships at all—they discussed real estate, a compare-contrast look at Philadelphia and Boston, where she'd spent Christmas with her boyfriend. Malcolm's neighborhood had just experienced a surge of growth, which meant that if, a decade ago, he'd simply acquired some properties and run them into the ground rather than improving them, he'd be a millionaire today.

"Hindsight's easier than foresight, though," he said.

"True, but even if you'd known, would you have acted differently? I didn't get the impression that you wanted to be a developer."

"Making money was never a top priority," he agreed, feeling somewhat stunned that she realized that about him. Still, he couldn't help but wonder whether she'd be so quick to dismiss him if he were closer to a millionaire. As they chatted about their respective work—it was a busy time for the IRS—there was nothing in Ann Marie's voice to indicate that she wanted further romantic contact.

He didn't call her again. What would he say? The promise of Ann Marie, he told himself, had helped him through a rough period with Nora and in his life in general, and the image of her as the Good Witch was a large component of the attraction.

But if it was only a trick of mind that made Ann Marie seem so appealing, wasn't it possible that his mental image—for whatever reasons he held it—would make the relationship work more easily, just as a patient's mood can determine the rate of recovery? Certainly the Uncertainty Principle applied to love as well as medicine. Nora's new cheer about the relationship, since he'd waved the magic wand of imminent marriage, attested to the importance of the proverbial positive attitude.

How simple women were about marriage, like dogs getting fed. If, as Malcolm often claimed, he'd already made a commitment to her when she moved in—for therein lay the crucial loss of freedom—then marriage hardly mattered. If it made her feel more trusting, no skin off his back.

That was the logic, anyway.

They had agreed to have the actual ceremony offstage privately and let Nora's parents throw an informal party. Famous last words. A basic rule of life on earth: you pay, you get your way. The guest list would be dominated by dull strangers; there would be a dance band and a "rehearsal dinner"; Malcolm's poor friends would be obligated to travel to Pittsburgh, pay for a hotel, and he wouldn't even get to talk with them. He'd be pumping hands all night as usual, only this time it would be worse because he wouldn't be able to skulk in a corner. And he had to speak to Nora about the plans *now*, in the middle of a crunch.

He concentrated on his work and stifled his dismay. Since the wedding was to please Nora to begin with, it hardly mattered what he thought. But he was finding it more and more difficult to deal with her impression that *she* was humoring *him*. He could guess how he was being portrayed in the endless phone calls with Julie, Jessica, Ralph, her brothers: the boyish, aging bachelor who has overcome his "fear of commitment" but cherishes illusions of himself as the Lone Ranger. As if not choosing to restage the wedding from *The Godfather* was wildly eccentric.

With the down payment on the basement design, Malcolm had enough to take care of the back mortgage, but not his three-months-delinquent credit card or utility bills. He had to borrow money from Nora. Now that they were "engaged," she was sympathetic, cheerful as a loanshark—not at all the way she'd acted when making him loans in the past, which was more as if her newborn had been wrested from her

breast and dumped into an open manhole. It was also easier to be gen-
erous with $30,000 in the bank. When Malcolm reminded her that fi-
nancial disaster was still very much a threat for him, she'd pat him on
head or chest and offer a pep talk. Was there no stance in his future wife
between hysteria and complacency?

Rymer was taking too long to size up Ivy Street. His accountant had
been away, and by the time the accountant returned, his lawyer was out
of town. By mid-February Rymer had definitive support for the project
from both of his advisors; but by the time that he, Tobias, Malcolm, lawyer, and accountant ironed out the details, there was another bid on the
building.

"Why didn't you make it clearer to him," Tobias Maxwell demanded,
"that he had to move fast?" Malcolm said he did, both of them had—as
much as they could. The building had been on the market for over a year;
they could hardly portray it as a hot potato. The College of Physicians
deal was still a possibility, but that would be a complicated package—
complicated enough that Malcolm couldn't pursue anything else, like
finding an investor for Pine Street. He could be homeless by the time it
came through.

At the beginning of March (the IRS was experiencing notorious pro-
cessing problems), Malcolm received his tax refund—with, absurdly,
five years' worth of interest—which was enough to get him through another month.

"So why don't you get a job for a while?" Tobias suggested, when
Malcolm tried to pour out his sorrows.

"'For a while'? How am I supposed to work on the College of Physicians if I'm employed full-time? I don't even have time for it now, with
Rymer's basement."

"Couldn't you get something part-time?"

"What? Counter work at a Burger King?"

"An architecture firm, obviously."

"I don't have an architecture degree."

"Maybe this would be a good time to get a loan, go back to school."

"Tobe, that'd be years, and anyway, most beginning architects earn
slave wages."

"I've got it!" Tobias said. "How about a job with the City Rehabilitation Commission? Maybe Rymer could pull some strings for you."

Never had Malcolm felt so distant from his friend. A desk job would be a prison sentence for Malcolm. He had been trying to be in business for himself without losing his soul, to earn money without stepping on people. He didn't want a lot of money. But even his modest goals might be impossible, and if so, he had nothing. Why should he expect Tobias to understand? Working nine to five, Malcolm thought, was a line you crossed. Once you adjusted to being indentured for fifty weeks a year, you had to dismiss people who weren't as weak, lazy, or juvenile.

In March, several weeks before the court date with Stone, Malcolm's lawyer called. Stone's lawyer had offered to settle out of court for $2,000, less than a third of the contested amount.

"I'd take it," the lawyer advised. "Even if we win the whole judgment, he'd appeal, and by the time you get a date for the appeal and go through the continuances, there's a good chance he'll be indicted, or bankrupt. I'd cut your losses and get out."

That made sense—for the lawyer at least. But did it make sense for Malcolm? People always said you could only command respect if you charged enough. For years he'd undersold his services to get himself out of financial catastrophes. Sooner or later the pattern would have to stop.

He refused the settlement, without discussing the decision with Nora. Nor did he tell her when the lawyer called to report (a tad triumphantly, Malcolm thought) that the court date had been continued. Malcolm had enough work that he could table thoughts of Stone, and when he did think of him, he was surprised by his lack of bitterness— about Stone, at least.

He was bitter toward Beth. His dreams were full of gruesome revenges against his ex-girlfriend and ex-boss. He hadn't seen or spoken to her since she'd moved to Buenos Aires, hardly ever thought about her, but his resentment of her, for taking advantage of his skill and energy under the guise of doing him a favor, seemed bottomless. In the dreams he plunged a knife into her stomach or held her babbling head underwater until she drowned—and woke from them with a deep fatigue, worse than a hangover. Certainly he was no more accountable for dream murder than Jimmy Carter was for dream adultery, but he didn't tell Nora, fearing her interpretation—that the dreams were sexual, or spelled veiled aggression toward her, or meant that he deeply wished to blame others for his fate. In the mornings, shaving, the contrast between his hopelessly plain, mild-mannered face— Christ was he sick of looking at himself—and his private anger terrified him. He thought about getting glasses with darker rims. He considered growing a beard again. In July he would be thirty-nine.

At the beginning of April, on a day when Nora was in New York on a shoot, Chris Mann, Julie's ex-patient, called. Since Nora wasn't home, Malcolm talked to him. He knew the story from Nora. Unlike Stone's lawyer, Chris' stay at the mental institution had been short. Now he was out, back to computer consulting, making art on the side.

Chris also socialized with Julie Peszko and her new boyfriend—Ed Tarry of the FBI. This was a subject over which Nora engaged in much breast-beating: the Peszko-Tarry liaison was over three months old, but Nora had only recently been told, and she still hadn't been introduced to Ed. She didn't understand why her oldest friend had cut her out.

"I wanted to let Nora know," Chris told Malcolm, "that there's going to be a bank showdown sometime this week. I'm not sure what day, but there'll be some rolling heads."

"What's happening?"

"From what I can gather, the buck is going to stop."

"Oh," Malcolm said. "Well, keep us apprised."

"Want to get together sometime soon for a drink?" Chris asked. "I wanted to show Nora some stuff I've been working on."

Malcolm said sure, said he'd call back later to make more definite plans. He wrote "Chris-bust" on his message pad, then "Drink?" He thanked Chris, hung up, and looked around his office. His eye snagged on the huge pile of product materials on the floor, papers he had no place to file and, with the deadline on Rymer's renovation looming, no time.

If Benjamin Stone was indicted before Malcolm's court date against him—and that looked likely now—Malcolm wouldn't get a cent.

That meant that after April the gig was up. Again.

The next time the phone rang and he picked it up, the caller asked immediately, "What's wrong?"

It was Ann Marie Lewis.

"Ann Marie?" he asked, and his surprise made her laugh.

"I've been meaning to call you," he said. "How are—actually, no. Are you busy?"

Time was running out. Of course, time had been running out forever. But it was as if the hourglass had gotten wet, the sand stuck, and any second it would fall in a clump, without warning. For months, ten or fifteen times a day in his office, Malcolm had been paralyzed by pure panic. But for some reason, that day the panic lifted him up like a tornado and whorled him to Ann Marie Lewis's apartment, months after he'd even talked to her.

STUPIDLY, HE WAS always surprised when he visited people he hadn't seen for a while and their apartments were exactly as they'd been the last time. Same posters on the wall, pillows on the couch, magazines in the magazine rack.

Ann Marie Lewis had been reading. Her face was gently distant; a paperback novel with bright graphics on the cover rested face down on her coffee table. She wore jeans and a man's shirt with a frayed, unpressed collar. Her bare feet were, like her hands, strong and shapely.

24

What force field had prevented Malcolm from pursuing her further? Nora could not say much; he had been understanding about her affair with David Martella years ago. He imagined Nora's self-righteous tears: *But at that point we weren't getting married!* She was a master of moral weights and balances that always put her on top—not an eye for an eye, but an eye, ear, nose, and throat for an eyelash.

"How have you been?" Ann Marie asked.

"I'm sorry I haven't—" Malcolm started to say, but Ann Marie just smiled and shrugged.

"Sit down," she said. "Can I get you anything?"

He shook his head no and sat. She sat beside him. Malcolm and Nora often sat this way on a couch, hands in their laps, with Nora staring, expectant, head cocked (she always reminded him of the RCA Victor dog); but Ann Marie's expression was softer, a *What's wrong?* in her eyes.

He didn't know where to begin. *I may be losing it*, he could tell Ann Marie. On the radio, a patient confessional: *A few months ago, my life began to fall apart. Most days, I couldn't drag myself out of bed and into work. When I did get in, I just couldn't concentrate. At home, I'd yell at my poor kids for every little thing. . . . In the old days they called it a 'nervous breakdown.'*

"Malcolm?" Ann Marie prompted.

"I've been busy," he said. "Dumb-busy. My whole life kind of fell through the cracks. I've been wound up about that Stone business I told you about. This morning I got a call—" How would he do this, without mentioning Nora, or her money? The fact that he had falsified his tax returns, that he was accessory to a fraud? Carefully, he told her about the call from Chris.

"Of course, if Stone gets busted I'm out the money, but it's not just that. I mean, I'm not involved, but—it's like when I opened the letter from the IRS. I wasn't exactly expecting a refund check. I saw the return address, and—"

Ann Marie nodded. "The FBI and IRS are such big wheels," she said, "people are afraid of getting run over. But in truth The Wheels of Justice are kind of creaky."

"But then," he said, "you read about the Great Falls grandma whose $925 tax return gets audited five times."

"Sure. But think of the tax returns that go right through, all the letters delivered each day to the right address."

"Modern miracle," Malcolm said.

"Even when you get that letter from the IRS saying any minute you'll be tied to the train tracks, your wife and kids sold into slavery, it can be *years* before anything happens."

"You mean I didn't really have to file my returns?"

"You were creeping up our list. But even then the process is hardly airtight."

"That's encouraging in a way," Malcolm noted, "but in another way that's just what's spooky."

"True."

"And then everything's so webbed up. I mean, knowing you from college, and the FBI guy handling Stone's case from high school, and now Julie dating Tarry—and not even telling Nora."

"Who's Julie?" Ann Marie asked. "Who's Tarry?"

"Julie is Nora's old college roommate. Tarry's the FBI agent. They're both hanging out with Chris Mann, an ex-patient of Julie's who—" Well, he *couldn't* do this part without mentioning Nora's bank windfall. "Complicated, as you can see. And my friend Lucy, who worked for Stone too—"

"You got her the job?"

"She got me mine."

"Small town."

"Stone's house on Mortimer? I visited my mother the other day, she'd seen the ad too—"

"She lives around here?"

"Near Rittenhouse Square. And she reminded me that . . . wait, I'll backtrack. When I was a kid, we had boarders on the third floor. One of the boarders was a deaf-mute who retrieved balls at the stadium. Each morning he put on a suit, a bow tie, and a hat and set off to retrieve balls for ten cents a week. Regular as a bank executive. His room and board were paid for him by a rich old dowager—my French grandmother did all of her tailoring—who lived all alone in a big old house on Mortimer."

"Stone's house."

"Right. She was its second owner. Stone was third. Then Stone hiring me when I'm not really qualified—I mean I *am* qualified, but I don't have the diploma, so it's hard to get people to believe it. Then it happening again, right away, with Rymer."

"It sounds," Ann Marie observed, "like your self-confidence could use some fattening up."

"Probably."

"Aren't you good at what you do?"

"Not as good as I could be. Not as good as lots of people."

She made an automatic gesture, a *That's life* shrug that rolled off her shoulders and puffed out her lips for a second. Almost a French gesture—a tiny affirmation of defeat.

"I miss you," Malcolm said. "I want—"

Ann Marie looked down, as she had at his house, in her tax collector role, when he'd first told her how beautiful she was.

Malcolm thought of the scenes in old movies where the hero, escaping a war or murder plot, seeks sanctuary with a woman he can trust, the brothel madam with the golden heart or the fond ex-wife. He thought of the scenes where the hero gets the woman just as the ring is slipped onto her finger or the train chugs off. He did not feel up to these plots. Ann Marie, beside him on the couch, put her hand on his knee consolingly and he took it—*savoring like a blind man*, the busy voice-over in his brain supplied, *the contours of her fingers.*

"I feel really dumb," he said after a while.

"The timing isn't great," Ann Marie said, slipping her hand away. "Things finally look like they're going to work out for me and Ted. I'll be marrying end of June, moving to Boston. Quitting my job. Commuting here to finish my degree."

Malcolm looked stricken. "Why didn't you tell me?"

She just stared at him.

"I'm sorry," he said. "I should have called you."

"Why didn't you?"

"Nora," he said.

And he told her about their wedding plans, even though he realized it would make him seem like even more of a heel than he already was.

"Do you want to get married?" Ann Marie asked.

"Not particularly."

"Why are you doing it, then?"

"She wants to. There are problems, but I'm not an idiot—I realize there would be problems with anyone. And I realize it's a hard time in my life, so I can't be too enthusiastic. She doesn't think I know all this, but I do. It just doesn't make it easier. And then there's you. I know what anyone would say, but that's not how it feels. I'm not saying it's not the case. Maybe it is. But how it feels is—I just want you."

"Why?" Ann Marie asked.

He was tempted to mock his own desire: *Something in the way you walk.* . . . Instead he answered in grave detail. She listened the way women do when complimented—with a certain mistrusting detachment tempered by a strong desire to be seduced. Not just how she looked, Malcolm told her, but how the way she looked seemed to mean something to him about the way she was. The straight, serious line of her hair offset by its soft texture, the way her serious nature seemed offset by gentility and humor. How her walk was at once mysterious and no-nonsense, as she was herself: he knew this without knowing her, and it was the very balance he wanted in his life, so how could he not be drawn to her, her directness and depth?

"Don't oversimplify me," she warned, "for your last fling."

"I don't. I'm not. I just—"

Sometime while he talked he took her hand again, and soon thereafter they found themselves in bed.

If Nora was a cat—a "domesticated" creature that dove into your lap but would also, with no warning, bite the hair on your chest—then Ann Marie Lewis was some exotic variation of wild and foreign deer. Such a strange combination of grace and strength. Her sexual style was completely different from Nora's, both shyer and more self-assured. Every time Malcolm opened his eyes, he had the feeling of being a documentary cameraman who startles the creature while it is idling in the field, chewing grass. The creature looks up, blinks, bolts.

Like film heroes who return, through time capsules, to their childhoods, Malcolm was conscious of savoring details he was bound to forget. Through the long stretch of kissing and disrobing he was aware of the noise of the pipes when the toilet in the next apartment flushed; of Ann Marie's cheerful, Matisse-like curves, her body fuller than Nora's and firmer; of her perfume, something vanilla-lemony that he wasn't crazy about but forgave, breathed past.

Ann Marie did not act skittish or standoffish. But he wasn't surprised when she pulled away from him, naked, and said, "I guess we shouldn't. At a certain point, you have to stop searching, go with what you have."

Ann Marie sat up and talked about Ted. She didn't pull the sheet around her. She didn't gesture, and held her head very still, as if the stillness would inch her closer to some kind of truth. No music played. Her bedroom walls were the cold white that landlords paint apartments, to camouflage the shoddy condition of the woodwork. Though the room was pleasant—a basket of dried flowers on the dresser, another ballet print (she must have danced once, which would explain her carriage), a downy spread with blue flowers—this could have been a hotel room, or a room in a model home. Malcolm knew from the room, if not from her words, that she hadn't fully inhabited her life, that she'd been stopping over in her job and city until a marriage provided her with a destiny. This disturbed him: the sense of how much starting from scratch, with Ann Marie or anyone else, would entail. All those objects to acquire! How Nora always got into bed, then got up again to fetch a Kleenex—lying down made her nose run. Her passionate, party-line liberal Democratic leanings on every single issue, from national health care to capital punishment. She was like a Democratic Stepford wife. The way he thought of Nora—with a sigh, a smile—would not be the way he thought of Ann Marie.

Maybe the way he thought about Ann Marie would be better. If Ann Marie were the better woman, as Boston was the better city—if a new life was within reach and it was just a lack of conviction and drive that kept him from laying claim to greater happiness—then he was failing miserably. If, on the other hand, Ann Marie was right—both of them had mates and careers, and now they needed patience and perseverance to make things work—then the fact that he hadn't called her earlier, before it was too late, was a triumph of his wiser side. He had not, after all, been swept away by her, though perhaps he wouldn't be swept away by anyone. It wasn't his nature to kidnap Ann Marie for a month in Europe. What would that tell them? Only whether they could tolerate each other on vacations. They wouldn't know if, three years down the line, they'd be tempted to cheat on each other, as both of them had been tempted to cheat on their present mates.

They talked until late. He didn't spend the night. They promised to stay in touch, as friends. Although Ann Marie insisted on playing the scene as a poignant last act, and he'd agreed that this was probably best, he didn't really believe it was over.

When Nora got back from New York even later that night, Malcolm was asleep in their bed, mouth open, sunk in a dream full of shadowy bureaucracies. She slipped naked into bed and pressed herself against the motor of his heaving chest. He put his arms around her. "Ann Marie," he said. But because he was asleep, not enunciating, it sounded more like *hurry*.

FOOD STYLING MAY be a stupid job, but it isn't always easy. Truth in advertising laws govern the ways you can make a product look appetizing. You can imply that a yogurt is studded with whole, fresh fruit (flash to the fruit, then back to the yogurt, being lustily stirred by a fit young woman), but when you present the yogurt itself, the strawber-**25** ries have to be the true strawberries found in the real product. To get a yogurt turned upside down with the fruit neatly packed to hold the shape of the container you need a seasoned professional. For the day's play with yogurt, Nora earned a flat $600. Then she walked three blocks (wearing a tiny Walkman, a Christmas gift from Malcolm, which gave a beat to her thoughts and the traffic) to pick up the part of the mouthwash fire-breathing-dragon costume that was hers to keep, post-filming.

Her first work in this silly genre had given her pleasure: the dragon at once realistic and whimsical. The body of the costume would stay with the ad director, who planned to fit it, headless, over his office hat rack. The head Nora would give to Ken and Annie for baby Joshua. She hadn't seen the commercial yet, but she had received the check—$5,000. (Almost the amount she'd given Malcolm to pay bills, but she tried not to think about that.) Not only had the agency been pleased with the costume, but she'd gotten along quite well with the art director, who had hinted at other work possibilities and taken her card to give to another art director.

It was exactly the hopeful self-image she needed in order to meet David Martella.

David had invited her to attend the screening of the rough cut of his film, then an informal cast party. The invitation had surprised her. For starters, he had a girlfriend. The press screenings and parties were supposed to be the advantage of dating him—the perks that Nora, by choosing Malcolm and a provincial life, would miss. Furthermore, David had not been at all pleased with the way Nora had ended their affair.

Mostly she'd stalled. After Christmas David was busy, then Nora was. When she'd finally told him, mid-January, that she and Malcolm planned to marry in the fall, David had pronounced, "That's so far away it's not even worth thinking about." The airport hotel incident had bought his goodwill and delayed his fury until the beginning of February, when after a lunch date she'd gone home rather than to his apartment and he'd called to accuse her of superficiality, egocentricity, and some other flaws. "If you think all that," Nora had tearfully demanded, "why would you want me anyway?" David said he didn't. In subsequent phone calls he provided the speech about why he was too focused to afford the luxury of nonsexual friendships. Then he offered her another chance to renew their affair, on whatever terms.

It was a sign of either Nora's perpetual fondness for him or her self-delusion that she didn't believe he was that monomaniacal about sex. She believed that he did still love her—or thought he did, which is close to the same thing—and was simply too male to admit it.

She didn't miss their sex at all. She barely missed sex with Malcolm, when they forgot about it for a week or so. Not one of the times that she'd waited for the phone during the last three months, her fate on the line, was it David she expected. It was the bank, or word on her dragon bid, or news for Malcolm. But she did miss David. She missed missing him. She missed the tingle of conviction that there was someone out there who, scanning Fifth Avenue, wanted to see her very person emerging from the bright ripple of rush-hour pedestrians.

The more things change, the more they stay the same: David was late. Very late, so they'd have to rush dinner. "I'm so glad you could make it," Nora greeted him, in an Ingrid Bergman voice of gentle gratitude, and he said, Come on, give him a break, then summarized the office politics that had detained him at the magazine.

He wore a suntan and a ratty jacket, once corduroy, which could have used being let out some. The jacket actually had elbow patches. Why did a jazzy girl like herself always wind up with men who kept their high school jackets? Or maybe all men keep all the clothes they ever owned? Malcolm's jackets, at this point, were over twenty years old, which at least was long enough to cycle them back into fashion. She skittered through these thoughts in the time it took David to get a waitress to their table and flirt her into rushing their order.

"You have a tan," Nora remarked.

"Remnants. Martinique. I went without you."

"With Rita?" When he nodded, Nora asked, "How is she?"

"Terrific."

"How are things going with you two?"

"None of your business," David said, and made Nora do their usual fishing-and-begging routine before he'd give her the scoop.

Probably at the moment their entrées arrived, Rita was wrapping up a job interview in California. Nora had long ago undergone Rita envy—David had been seeing her, on and off but usually on, for the close to four years that Nora had known him. Like David, Rita was a racy academic. Her field was American Studies, popular culture, with a specialty in images of women. Since meeting David she'd taken to writing, in addition to academic essays, freelance articles for women's magazines on issues like weight or day care. Rita now found herself with an unusually flexible marketability: she could teach not only in graduate departments of American studies or popular culture, but in communications and women's studies departments as well. And an entrepreneurial past boyfriend (who would "remain nameless" to Nora, though she was assured that he was quite notorious, an Iacocca or a Steve Jobs) had helped her hook up with marketing organizations, which paid her five hundred dollars a pop for lectures.

"I've been really proud of her," David said, "of the way she's turned things around for herself in the last year or so."

"What'll you do if she goes to California?"

"I might be able to talk the magazine into sending me there. Or I might just take a sabbatical, try to get some writing done, get some sun, meet some people, pursue the acting. Then again, she may stay here. She's ready to get married."

"Are you?"

"Maybe. She wants to have children."

"Do you?"

"Yes."

Nora found herself listening hungrily, with a wet click in her eyes that David must have taken for jealousy but wasn't—it was detached awareness, of a new sort. She saw David and Rita for a moment as a couple, as they must see themselves: thoroughly modern careerists who were spontaneous and soulful enough to take off for Rome, for Martinique, to allow each other to pursue affairs so they weren't just "settling" for each other. Nora would be what David had to get out of his system, by way of "avoiding commitment," before he recognized the richness of the possibilities with Rita. In this scenario, Nora was the flaky blonde, a failed artist, who lived with the dolt who had failed as an architect. Why not?

She didn't discuss this with David. Actually, she didn't discuss anything having to do with her life. Her recognition, small and dry, even a touch resentful: she wasn't going to know him anymore, and he certainly wouldn't know her. He would be, to her, the fast talker that he was at parties, with waitresses. Or not even that, because each stranger was a fresh opportunity. She wasn't going to get the boyish, open side of him again, the side that served as antidote to the self-centered workaholic, no matter how rampantly she courted him over chaste dinners.

Nora had never been to a private screening before. What a wonderful way to see movies! The screening room chairs swiveled, each with an ashtray attached to the seat (Nora wished she still smoked) and a handy table for your drink; if you waved, a waiter discreetly appeared, to whom you could whisper your order.

The film's original (derivative) title, *Roman Holiday*, had been nixed by the studio. The now untitled film had been pushed through production so it would precede another European-vacation film slated for the summer, starring the year's other hot actress, who was, in real life, a good buddy of this one—they jogged together in SoHo, had even, according to *People*, taken a joint vacation with their respective unfamous spouses. Both brought babies in slings on location; both were smaller in real life than you'd think. The actress from David's film (what David thought of as "David's film") was downright tiny, with a tiny woman's spunk and a winning smile that transformed her face. Even if she weren't famous, you'd notice her on the street.

The actress played a dizzy heiress on holiday who stumbles onto an international plot to smuggle contraband material onto space shuttles and use the moon as something of a Swiss bank—a comic, sci-fi version of *The Wrong Man*. In the way of the genre, everything works out in the end, order restored, man and woman united. David played a waiter who helps the heiress in her moment of need. The waiter's restaurant becomes a meeting place; David gets to deliver several messages from the actress to her man, and vice versa. Not much of a part: David had to look Italian and make comical Italian gestures.

While the leads looked better on the screen, David looked chubbier, older. How strange to sit beside him as he watched himself. Every time he was about to appear he would stiffen, reach for Nora's hand. Then when his face filled the screen he'd pull the hand away, as if to say, *Come and get me, ladies!* The screen David would utter his line. It was pathetic but also touching—Nora felt as if she were his mother, at his high school graduation, waiting for him to be summoned to the stage for his diploma.

The group was small, a hundred people or so—just the director, producer, actors, head cameraman, and film editor, and their spouses. If David had brought her to the screening to remind her how suave, worldly, and indispensable he was, the plan almost worked. As the lights came on, everyone clapped, and they adjourned to another room for drinks and food and chatter, Nora was impressed by how easily David spoke with these people. But she also felt somewhat embarrassed as she detected people drawing back from him, treating him like a journalist (he would, after all, be writing a clever piece on the making of the film for his magazine); as he asked questions, trying to be both familiar and respectful, she could feel them downshift into public relations gear.

When Nora and Malcolm attended parties together, they usually wound up by themselves holding hands in a corner. David circulated. In this case his abandonment was an advantage, as it left Nora free to pursue her own conversations.

The dragon head was naturally too big to fit in Nora's portfolio, so she'd had to carry it loose, and it turned out to be a good conversation piece at the screening party: a stylish, long-legged woman with a dragon head. "Mouthwash," she explained a couple of times after trying to extend her hand to be shaken, the head tucked awkwardly under her arm like a football helmet. Eventually she put it in a corner, near a pile of coats, so she could hold her drink.

Next thing she knew, she was, face to face with the latest TV heart-throb, discussing the ad business! "Nice dragon," he said, and intro-duced himself, as if she didn't know who he was. "Nora Worth," she said, extending her hand, and he asked her what the dragon was for. She told him what she did. They determined that they were both ex-artists. Did he know her friend Ralph? Yes he did, he owned a couple of his paint-ings! How had Nora forgotten this? Years ago, when Nora was between men and before this actor married, Ralph had volunteered an introduc-tion.

But why was *People*'s recent Bachelor of the Year "chatting her up" (David's term), anyhow? Was he one of the legion men who hit on al-most everyone? Was he stoking the envy of another woman here? And why was Nora wondering why she deserved to be spoken to? Wasn't it possible for her to appear in public without these layers of self-consciousness and self-doubt?

From across the room, David was watching them talk, half proud of Nora, half jealous. Within a minute he motored across the room to mus-cle into their conversation.

Seconds later the actor excused himself, and so did David—to greet another woman as if they were old buddies. When Nora tried to join their conversation, David thrust his back toward her, failing to intro-duce her to his companion. He would do this several times over the course of the evening, taking off midsentence without a "Pardon" or hand on her arm. Yet whenever Nora managed to get a conversation of her own going, David would immediately materialize.

The art director of the movie commented on her dragon too. He thought it was good, a funny green; he liked its eyes. Nora thanked him very much and complimented his work on the film; he asked if she did movie work—"Sure," she said—and he took her card. "Nice card," he said, and had asked her one or two questions about her work before

David came along and changed the subject. The art director excused himself.

In the ladies' room (one place David couldn't penetrate), the actress was changing her baby's diapers. "Cute baby," Nora said. "Isn't she?" the actress agreed. They discussed babies for a couple of minutes—when they smile, when they teethe, the pleasure they bring, how much attention they need.

"Just for the record," Nora blurted out, "I love you in comic roles. I loved you as Alice. You were great in *Tell It to the Judge*. It's so unfair how some critics have typecast you as too serious."

"You can't win," the actress agreed. "What do you do?"

"Artist," Nora said. "Ad work, part-time."

"Was that you out there with that green head?"

"Yes," Nora said. "Dragon. Actually, I usually do food styling."

"Really?" the actress said. "We've been kicking around food styling as an idea in a script. You done that long?"

"Six, seven years."

"What's it like?" the actress asked, and Nora began to tell her, feeling humiliated—how tacky, how positively Martella-like, to inflict herself on the poor woman this way! But she reminded herself that she had been asked for this information. The actress listened with interest, then said, "Would you be willing to sit down with me and the screenwriter sometime and discuss this?"

"Sure," Nora said.

On scraps of paper towels they exchanged addresses and phone numbers.

Wait until Malcolm heard!

Nora was ecstatic. One of those nights when you've had enough wine to take the edge off your shyness but not so much as to make you sloppy or loquacious; when your dress doesn't wrinkle, you spill no drinks, and have no crackers stuck in your teeth; when everyone seems ordinary in the most positive sense, with whole lives behind them, whole histories you'd love to hear about, given world enough and time.

David and Nora caught the last train back to Philadelphia together. On the train he suggested that, if she was pulling into town this late, she hardly had to pull into town at all. She could say she spent the night in New York.

"Don't you get it?" Nora interrupted. "I'm monogamous."

"I've noticed."

"You just told me, in great detail, how well things are going with Rita. Can't we just be friendly?"

"You know what I'm going to answer to that," David said, "so what's the point?"

"The point is, I *do* know how you're going to answer. Four years, David—it's worth something, isn't it?"

"How was your evening, anyway?" he asked, cutting her off, carefully intoning that he didn't care (if she didn't love him, she was an ass), that he was deeply wounded, and that she hadn't done her share—he'd offered her this opportunity to hobnob, had gotten nothing in return. When Nora reported that the art director had taken her card, he offered a comment in the vein of "You see? What did I tell you?" then warned her not to get her hopes up about anything. People were always discussing deals at these things, but very, very little ever came of it. You had to see people over and over, and after you'd been introduced to them twenty, thirty times at countless parties, they might remember your face.

"In other words," Nora said, "'Stick with me, baby.' That's mean. Can't I even think I had a nice time at a party if we're not fucking?"

"I don't know. I wonder. You're really torn. You want to be rich and famous, and I think you *could* be, but for some reason you affect some sick kind of disdain toward the whole process of becoming successful."

"Here we go."

"So rather than settle your ambivalence, you simply bring yourself down to Malcolm's level."

"Right. That's why I stopped dating Beethoven, too, and Henry Kissinger. You boys are just too much for me."

"The Nora I wanted was driven, gutsy. At that party you just—"

"I'm sorry I'm such a disappointment. Feel free not to invite me anymore."

"Why should I, anyway?"

Nora grabbed David's hand and pressed. Not seductively, but hard, as if to squeeze the venom out. She succeeded in shutting him up for a second or two—watched, tender and irritated, as his face drained of comment so he could concentrate on their joined hands. "I love you, David," she said. "I always will. Try to be nice."

She didn't at all feel that she was lying. But she had the distinct and not entirely satisfying feeling that she didn't need him anymore.

THE CALL FROM the bank came the next morning, while Nora, at the window with her coffee, watched the street with canine curiosity, except that she tried not to get nose prints on the glass. She'd been following the mime of a domestic argument below for a while now, a young black couple on their way to work. The man endured a surfeit of finger-wagging, occasionally gesturing toward himself incredulously, as if the woman might be accusing someone else. One of the virtues of living at this address: it provided human drama as well as the more essential amenities.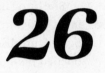

Malcolm had told her, before he rushed off to Rymer's that morning to meet workmen, about the call from Chris Mann. Chris was to set up a meeting with Ed and Julie and call back. Nora was anxious to work out the details, and when the phone rang she picked it up eagerly. But it wasn't Chris. She knew who it was the second the man on the other end of the line said, in a firm, friendly voice, "Is this Nora Worth?"

"Yes."

"Miss Worth, this is Joe Infante, Assistant Vice President at—" But of course she knew. "We're verifying a $30,000 deposit made to your checking account last November. We believe there was an error. Do you remember the deposit?"

Nora had rehearsed a variety of responses to this question over the months, from the stance of the harassed businessperson ("I make so many large deposits") to more creative options (she could belong to an obscure religious sect, think the money had been wired directly into her account by God). Now her response emerged effortlessly.

"Yes," she said. "My parents gave me that money."

"You claim to have made the deposit, then?"

"Yes. I was going to make a down payment on a house."

"I'll need to see a deposit slip or canceled check," Mr. Infante said.

"I believe my parents wired it straight through from their bank."

"I'll need a wire transfer receipt, then. Or if you give me the name of your parents' bank, I can call directly to verify. We have the date of a withdrawal, then a redeposit of $27,900—"

"Yes. I put the money back. Unfortunately, the house deal fell through."

"I see. Do you know the date of your parents' deposit?"

"No."

"Will you check on that information and get back to us as quickly as possible?"

"Of course," Nora said.

She hung up the receiver gingerly, then waited a second before picking it up again. She called her supermarket client, said she was ill, apologized profusely, and rescheduled her afternoon shoot. Then she opened her address book to "R." She had been instructed to call Malcolm at Rymer's only for emergencies; this surely qualified. She picked up the phone, but then thought better of it. Malcolm, she knew, would tell her to wait. She felt like getting it over with.

When she called back, Mr. Infante greeted her with conviviality.

"I talked to my father at his office," Nora said, "and—I'm quite surprised. It appears that he didn't wire the deposit."

"I see. Do you still have the money?"

"All of it but around . . . $4,000."

"We'll need that money back right away, then," Mr. Infante said sternly. "As far as the $4,000, how soon could you repay that?"

"I'm not sure."

"We don't know what you've done with the money"—a hint of restrained censure—"but we'll need to discuss repayment. Why don't you come in?"

"When?" Nora asked.

"Are you free this afternoon?"

"Yes."

"Why don't we meet at two o'clock, then?"

"Do I need to bring a lawyer?"

"I don't see why you should bring a lawyer, unless you think that we need a lawyer."

So, Nora thought, as she hung up. *I could have been belligerent, made them fight.* Taken a week or so to "trace" her parents' gift—lame, *lame!*— and another couple of weeks to meet with the bank. If Malcolm was right in his theory about the IRS and Water Department, you could foul operations terminally just by stalling. How much (with overhead) would it cost the bank to prosecute her? Maybe more than . . . no, the bank was going to be courteous, and she should respond.

She showered and groomed herself step by step, and dressed as defendants are urged to dress for trials—conservative, not too natty. Only then did she think to check the time. She didn't have much. Calmly, however, she went downstairs for the mail (gas bill, department store makeup promotion), then sat down to confront her finances.

Unlike the day of Nora's "robbery" last November, the bank was calm. No birthday girl, no snow, no long holiday weekend. The usual number of customers spoke with employees at desks and waited in line for the tellers. Midweek, midday, middling weather. An exasperated assistant manager type scuttled across the room with a file folder. At one desk, a customer waved a bank statement emphatically: "I have the evidence! It's right here! I'm showing it to you! You retarded or something?" The employee to whom these comments were addressed had long since hidden behind a sourly patient banker's smile, and was in truth concentrating on her cuticles.

As Nora approached the guard to ask for Joe Infante, the man with the bank statement stood and began to shout: "I demand to see the manager this instant!" Several people, including the guard, turned to watch.

"Twelfth floor," the guard said.

Nora emerged from the elevator to find herself on a huge, open floor surrounded by windows. The reception desk was a sexy twist of black glass floating on thick gray carpeting. In front of the reception desk a sign said, INTERNATIONAL CURRENCY—LOANS, with arrows pointing in opposite directions. But Nora wasn't looking at the sign.

She was looking at the art.

The first painting that confronted her was a Rauschenberg. An original. On the opposite wall, an architectural drawing—Carlo Scarpa. Next to the waiting area, with its Bertoia chairs and magazines arranged on a Nelson coffee table, was a mixed-media glass ball sculpture. Nora walked toward it. She knew the sculptor—Mary Bauermeister. Stockhausen's wife or significant other.

She stood like an Iowan on her first trip to New York City, transfixed. Where on earth did the bank get this stuff?

The receptionist asked if she could help. Nora asked for Joe Infante, was told to wait while he was dialed. "If you could come this way," the receptionist commanded, and led Nora down the hallway, which was bland and institutional, devoid of museum-quality art. But she was ushered into a small conference room with a table and six chairs—Saarinen chairs from Cranbrook, which Nora happened to know from Malcolm's product literature cost almost $2,000 each, and that's net. Out the window, a view of a slice of the neighboring building, an old high rise with blackened brick and ancient air conditioners in each window. When Infante arrived, Nora was pressed against the glass to look out and down: she had discovered that she could see into her dentist's office, where she thought she could make out the crane of the hygienist's tool.

Nora felt a pang of pity for her hygienist, a decade with the same dentist, trapped in that minuscule room with her rubber-gloved hands shoved in a mouth.

"Miss Worth," Infante said, offering his hand heartily.

She had expected someone older. Infante might have just hit thirty, and the man who accompanied him—"This is X," Infante said (she forgot the name as soon as she heard it), "who will be assisting me. Have a seat"—was even younger. Infante and his assistant put their writing pads and calculators on the table and smiled. Nora withdrew a writing pad from her briefcase and smiled back.

"I'm awfully sorry about this misunderstanding," Nora said. "I brought you what of the money I can at this point." She withdrew her checkbook, in which she'd already neatly penned the check for $26,000.

Infante took the check, studied it. "Now about the other $4,000—"

"I realize we'll need to arrange repayment," Nora said.

"Right," the assistant said. "You can't return any of that sum at this point?"

Her morning bookkeeping had confirmed that she'd spent all of the dragon money on Malcolm's bill crunch. She had only $3,000 of her own money left in her money market, plus another $1,600 in her checking account. She didn't feel it prudent to throw her money market savings into the pot—what if she didn't get work for months? What if Malcolm's financial life fell apart further, as was its wont?

Her brother Alan would probably see it as evidence of complete madness that, once cornered, she would still attempt to weasel something out of the bank's mistake. But she felt instinctively that she didn't have to be cleaned out.

"Well, I have $1,600 in my checking account," she said, "but I need it for bills."

"No savings?" Infante asked.

She shook her head no.

"We'll need to get an approximate idea of your monthly income and expenses," Infante said. "We'll need to see your tax returns for the last couple of years—"

"I brought them," Nora said, withdrawing the forms from her briefcase. This was how thoroughly she'd plotted the inevitable day: the best-case scenario had always been just this, that the bank would treat the money as a loan and ask for "verification of income." She had actually xeroxed her tax forms on her way to the bank. They certainly couldn't accuse her of being uncooperative.

Nora sat, hands folded on the table, while the men reviewed her papers. They asked if they could be excused. When they returned, they had filled out a loan worksheet, with a proposed monthly payment of $258.

"That's too high," Nora said, alarmed. "My income is erratic because I freelance."

They excused themselves again. When they returned, the monthly payment was down to $178. Nora said she could almost be comfortable with that, if she stretched. Again the men left the room, and again returned with a series of papers, which had clearly been drawn up before her arrival, because the monthly payment sum, the repayment schedule, the interest rate, and the date had been added separately, and the typist hadn't quite aligned the numbers with the rest of the text. All that art and they couldn't afford word processors? *Note*, the paper was titled, *Re: $4,000 Deposit in Error*. Nora read carefully:

Bank is hereby given a security interest in all property of the undersigned now or hereafter in Bank's possession in any capacity whatsoever, including but not limited to any balance or share of any deposit, trust, or agency account, as security for the payment of this note and any other liabilities of the undersigned to Bank, which security interest shall be enforceable and subject to all provisions of this note, as if such property were specifically pledged hereunder and such property shall on default immediately become subject to set-off and may be appropriated and applied against any of said obligations without demand upon or notice to or further consent from the undersigned.

Fair enough, Nora thought. Completely standard, too, that if default was made in payment, liabilities "shall become instantly due and payable, without demand or notice." Then the sticky part:

The undersigned hereby waives presentment, demand for payment, notice of dishonor, protest and notice of protest, and any or all other notices or demands in connection with this note. Any failure of Bank to exercise any right hereunder shall not be construed as a waiver of the right to exercise the same or any other right at any time and from time to time thereafter.

"In other words," Nora said, "I give up the right to suddenly claim the money is mine, but if you get so motivated you can at any time still bring me to court?"

"No, no," Infante said. "The next paragraph explains that"—he pointed. "Our terms are firm except in case of default."

So it did, although it added that should they have to sue her, she would pay attorney fees and fifteen percent collection. Then a last page, with a gentle closing:

As a condition of this repayment agreement, we require that you continue to do your banking with us. Kindly indicate your acceptance of the terms of this agreement by signing the attached copy of this agreement and returning same to myself. Very truly yours.

"So," Nora said. "I sign here?"

Infante nodded, pointing to the line under which her name had already been typed.

Shortly thereafter, X signed the line marked "Witness."

"That's it, then," Infante said, standing. "We thank you for making this process so fast and pleasant."

"I thank *you*," Nora said.

Hands were shaken. Nora was given her copy of the forms and her original tax returns. No one said, "It was nice to meet you" or "See you again." No one, in the hour or so the transaction took, mentioned the word "crime," or "jail." Very British, very low-key, except Nora's heart was beating fast enough to make the scene feel like a climax, and as Infante led her back to the elevators, past the incomprehensibly expensive furniture and art, a tiny outrage welled up in her: What was a couple thousand to them? She should have fought. She should have made them sweat as they'd made her sweat, thrown around words like "audit" and "fraud"—especially when she realized how sweet and understanding they'd been. They may have been in real danger to refrain from threatening her.

She would feel that even more strongly when she finally saw Malcolm. In transit, he'd already intercepted Chris Mann's call by remote and set up a meeting with Chris, Ed Tarry, and Julie Peszko for that evening to get the last installment in the tale of Stone's investigation. It would be hard not to take it as a meaningful coincidence that Nora and the bank were called to task on the same afternoon.

But when Nora left the bank and left a message at home, she didn't know this. She only knew that, overnight, she'd shed both David Martella and her bank business. She felt very light, almost giddy, partly from hunger—she hadn't eaten. So she ate a late lunch, then window-shopped for a postcrime present to celebrate the fact that after all that, she'd wound up with a $4,000 loan at a decent rate, without even having to apply for it.

"You brought your *tax returns*?" Malcolm would ask. "You mean you went to the bank the very day they called, with your tax returns for the last five years? You're not serious."

What more joyful purchase could she make than a hiply goofy spring hat? Lime green, with a spray of careful black roses at the brim. Malcolm had finally figured out how to record a message by remote indicating his whereabouts. In the hat, going to meet the FBI crew, Nora felt like Gidget. Or Miss Marple.

MALCOLM WAS THE first to arrive at the designated bar for the happy hour summit. Chris Mann was second. He wore a rock star get-up—baggy pants in silvery seersucker, a fuchsia tie, and petroleum in his hair to sculpt it, as Malcolm used to do with shampoo as a child during labor-intensive rubber duck baths. Though they'd never met, Malcolm recognized Chris at once from Nora's description. Even in the silly clothes, Chris Mann emitted some kind of testosterone buzz keyed for female sonar.

Julie Peszko arrived next, frazzled from a hard day at the office (a suicide attempt). She kissed Chris on the cheek, then Malcolm. "Congratulations," she said. "I haven't seen you since—"

"Oh," Malcolm said, remembering his engagement (and his recent episode with Ann Marie) in his stomach, as if an elevator had just thudded still.

Next Nora, in the hat. They discussed the hat while awaiting Ed Tarry. Nora did not bring up the bank. When Tarry arrived, names were exchanged along with brief vitae for the recently introduced. Then the FBI story began. Nora and Malcolm would both feel like they were in one of those TV crime shows where the lawyers or policemen loaf around the office, summing up for the last minute before the credits. The crime was simple. But it took them many repetitions to follow, with Malcolm making flowcharts on cocktail napkins, his ballpoint ripping the wet paper.

According to Ed, their operational version of the story had been wrong in several details, beginning with how Benjamin Stone was caught in the fall.

Two money-types met at a New York dinner party: the CEO of a Philadelphia brokerage house and the president of a Florida bank. This was the Miami bank where Stone had the construction loan on the basis of the forged securities. The Miami banker introduced himself to the CEO.

"What a coincidence. I'm working with one of your biggest clients." The CEO had never even heard of Stone. He launched an internal investigation, and when he suspected one of his own men (Mallory, Stone's childhood broker friend), he called the Florida banker and the FBI.

The FBI had already been watching Mallory. Mallory was buddies with Fred Gianotti, who had what are called "ties" with organized crime. Compared to Gianotti, Stone was a shoplifter. The January bust of the brokerage house did not concern Stone and the forged securities; nor did the FBI care about Stone and Mallory's sideline in cocaine. Stone's case was close to wrapped up, with the brokerage house, ironically, likely to be fined along with its employee. What the raid really concerned was approximately $1.3 million in illegal gambling money that Mallory had laundered.

Nora watched Ed Tarry as he talked. He talked with the slightly exaggerated informality of a college professor. She looked into the disconcertingly light blue eyes and tried to determine if she liked him. She also tried to determine if Julie had told him about her $30,000. She'd love to know whether Tarry thought there could be any connection between her money and Stone's, especially when she zoomed back from these thoughts to the conversation and Chris began to explain the role of Theodore Klein, executive loan officer and senior vice president at Stone's bank—and Nora's.

For a payoff, Klein had set up construction loans for Stone, using the forged securities as collateral. Each month the loans were repaid with dirty cash, again through Klein.

"The trouble is," Ed said, "we haven't been able to prove Klein's role."

"And they caught him today?" Julie asked.

Chris began to report, with some pride, how he had helped the FBI and IRS analyze the bank's bookkeeping, searching for any holes or kinks that would indicate Klein had channeled his payoffs through the bank, that any other bank officers were involved, or that Klein was linked to Gianotti as well. To explain, he and Tarry had to provide Julie, Nora, and Malcolm with a crash course in banking procedures.

"As one might expect," Tarry explained, "most foreign trade transactions are not conducted by men in bowler hats boarding airplanes, briefcases stuffed with bucks handcuffed to their wrists. Geneva's computer communicates with New York's computer, and if a Wichita burgermeister wanted to get his money to France, it probably goes to another office first."

"It's terrible," Nora said. "Nothing happens in person anymore. Remember when the king used to stroll onto the balcony to say hi? The president on radio shows?"

"You know how in old movies," Chris said, "the millionaire on his deathbed would ask for the phone book and choose five people at random to inherit his fortune? What do you think he'd do if he got an answering machine?"

"Hang up," Julie said sternly, giving Chris the don't-stray look that Nora remembered from the mental institution. "So? We're on bank acceptances."

As in a game of Telephone or Hot Potato, Ed continued, there were many places along the bank route for money to get scrambled. That made sense, but Malcolm was unsteady on the details (Nora just gave up): how bank acceptances can be sold at a discount on New York's short-term money market, or how message transmission systems could be tampered with in internal record-keeping to transfer large sums of money from one bank to another.

"This is ridiculous," Nora complained. "Cocaine, illegal betting, bank transfers. I was expecting . . . I don't know. Something more imaginative."

"You think computer fraud isn't imaginative?" Ed asked. "Think again."

"So what did you find in the end?" Julie asked.

"Nothing conclusive," Chris said. "But what I found was enough to get him. He ran a little mortgage insurance scam, illegally collecting premiums from borrowers whose policies had been terminated."

"Small potatoes," Ed said. "It's kind of sad."

"Tragic," Julie said, and Nora could tell, from the look Julie and Ed exchanged, that they'd had this discussion before: some kind of disagreement about the morality of his work, or the relative merit of his work and hers.

"I feel sorry for Stone too," Malcolm said. "I keep imagining him trading in the Jag for a Pinto. No more favorite tables at four-star restaurants but greasy spoons with health code violations."

"Not necessarily," Chris said. "We'll see. Stone and Mallory could spend half a year writing 'Crime Doesn't Pay' books in jail. Then they might be back in business, depending on how much they manage to keep from the Feds."

Ed said, "It'll probably be over a year before the indictment on Klein, and even then we may not know what happened."

"And ultimately," Julie said, "you don't care. Whoever you catch, no matter how big, you only use to catch the next guy, on the next rung."

Ed patted her hand. At the end of the pat their joined hands disappeared under the table. Soon thereafter, Ed's beeper sounded. When he left to make his phone call, Chris turned to Nora and asked, "Hear anything about your money yet?"

"Why?" she said lightly. "Think I will, now that this Klein guy is caught?"

"What do you mean?" he asked.

"Is it paranoid to imagine a connection?" Nora asked. "Like: what if once Stone was busted, Klein slipped the money into my account—and other customers' accounts—planning to draw it out when the coast is clear?"

Chris shook his head.

"Why not? He doesn't have to know about my connection to Malcolm. Maybe he just picked accounts at random, or he picked a name starting with a *W* because he knew the IRS was auditing and he wanted someone far down the line."

Chris laughed. "You think audits are alphabetical? Anyway, if Klein were collaborating with someone at the bank, it'd be more likely be someone higher up, who could help him get the money out of the country. Think about it. Why would he put it in his own bank? Why wouldn't he just get his cash into a foreign account, or even just a safe-deposit box?"

"I guess," Nora said.

Julie was looking at her sternly, Malcolm uneasily.

"Don't worry," Chris said, "I didn't say anything."

Nora asked, "Why not?"

He thought about that for a minute, replied, "I don't know. Friend of the Little Guy. An old habit—older than my hacker days. I guess it's left over from Vietnam."

"You were there?" Malcolm asked.

"No," Chris said. "Out on mental disability."

"Me too," Malcolm said.

"Yeah? What was your number?"

"Twenty-one," Malcolm said, and Chris laughed—his number had been thirty-six.

Malcolm and Chris swapped stories about their inductions. What their psychiatric letters had said and where they were when Nixon's resignation speech was broadcast. Chris had watched it from the patient lounge of the mental institution, his first adult visit there. Malcolm confessed that it took him years to recover from his mental exemption, that he wasn't sure if he'd *ever* recovered.

By the time Ed Tarry returned, the conversation had strayed far from Nora's money. It never did circle back.

They were on their third round without food, and Nora, at least, was growing fuzzy. Anxiety was catching up with her. She couldn't wait to get Malcolm alone and tell him what had happened. The bar crowd—a young and energetic group, half artists, half stockbrokers—seemed to be closing in, and all the conversation she overheard from the neighboring tables (she was a dedicated eavesdropper) was investments and careers, investments and careers. The bartendress, an aspiring actress, had just had her head shots redone; she reported this to a gigantic, muscular black man, maybe a professional athlete. It you were a first-draft pick, you could just dunk those hoops and feel good about yourself. A lawyer at the next table wanted to buy a beach property as a tax shelter; his companion was an assistant professor, worried about publications and tenure. Didn't anyone talk about orgasm anymore?

Chris withdrew a portfolio from somewhere and turned his winning eye contact on Nora. "Would you mind too much," he asked, "looking at this stuff while I have it with me, telling me what you think? What I could do to improve, who I might contact to show?"

Nora said she'd be delighted. "I was just thinking about you the other day, in fact. Have you ever played with computer-generated art?"

Chris looked hurt. "Why? Something wrong with the old-fashioned way?"

"Just wondering. I liked what I saw before," Nora encouraged him. Luckily, this was true. She'd hate to have to be the one to tell Chris to stick to computer programming.

Nora safe from the bank, Benjamin Stone getting his due: this might have been climactic, cathartic. But it wasn't. As Ed Tarry had predicted, no article about Theodore Klein's bust made the paper, so they had only Ed's word that the case had been resolved. Meanwhile, their own case hadn't changed at all. Wasn't there a story about how, when American soldiers liberated Auschwitz, they fell to the ground in tears, then offered a feast that killed most of the survivors? Bodily shock.

"Do me a favor," Malcolm said, when Nora suggested this analogy. "Don't repeat that. We have few enough friends left as it is."

Still, they were hardly flooded with relief.

Days later—the day that Malcolm's lawyer called with the next in the series of continuances on the common-pleas date against Stone—Rymer provided more bad news. Despite his best efforts, the College of Physicians deal had fallen through. Yet another historic structure would go the way of the Bulletin Building, which despite all possible restraining orders and appeals would be demolished within the month.

"I feel bad about it," Rymer said, "but we tried. Maybe we can work on something in the future. And of course you'll be compensated for your effort."

Lucky thing, for in a month, when Rymer's wine cellar was done, Malcolm would once again be unemployed.

If he took this badly, Nora took it even worse. The jubilance of the screening party felt like an event remembered from a past lifetime (the actress, Nora remembered with irrational disappointment, had never called), and her spirits were not lifted by the pressure of planning their wedding, now only a little over three months away.

Sylvia Worth called to explain, in a patient tone, that she needed to attend to things. Caterers got booked years in advance; so did bands and photographers. She needed to book the minister.

"No minister," Nora said. "Justice of the peace, and in private."

They argued about who would attend a ceremony deemed private. "Certainly," Mrs. Worth said, "you've got to include me and your father, and Malcolm's mother, and your grandparents who will be in town, your brothers and their wives and kids—"

"No kids," Nora said.

"You have to invite the kids. When are we going to meet Malcolm's mother and sister, by the way? I need to know who she's planning to invite to the rehearsal dinner—"

"No rehearsal dinner," Nora said.

Mrs. Worth sighed. "Have you done anything about your dress?"

"Not yet."

"Your rings?"

"No rings," Nora said.

"What do you mean?"

"I don't want a ring, and neither does Malcolm. I don't wear rings. I wear earrings."

"Don't give me this shit!" Mrs. Worth said. "I don't care if you buy a Cracker Jack ring for fifty-nine cents and wear it that night only and then dump it in the trash, but you must have a ring for the ceremony! What's the minister going to say—"

"Mother, *no minister*. We're both atheists."

"Do not say such a thing, even in jest!"

Indifferent as Nora was to the wedding details, she was obsessed with them compared to Malcolm. The thought of his upcoming poverty made him far too depressed to think about looking for work. As he struggled to garner his energy, he dissipated what little he had by explaining to Nora why he didn't have more.

All his life, Malcolm had tried to work in a middle zone—low-budget films, nicely detailed small buildings—that seemed more and more impossible to nestle into. That was his problem, the *nation's* problem. You were either rich or poor, successful or a flop, unemployed or a slave to work. It got harder and harder to devote yourself to any reasonably sized efforts. Everything grew and grew and grew. Look at their wedding:

what had begun as "small and simple" was now dinner for 130 people, at $70 a plate when all costs were factored in, the flowers and china rental—and that was for chicken. In the end their wedding would be a dull fiasco, like all weddings.

Malcolm tried to explain to Nora how disgusted he felt by a $70-a-plate party, when in a month or two he wasn't even going to be able to afford his mortgage.

"Don't think you're going to spend our wedding booty on utility bills," Nora warned.

"Try to listen to me."

"What do you want me to do? Cancel because you're unemployed? If we wait until you're solvent, we'll never do it."

"Bitch."

"Well, what do you want from me?"

"I want you to get your mother to heel."

"How?" Nora asked. "It'd be easier if you'd just be a little more involved in the planning."

"Well, I'm not going to be," Malcolm retorted. "I told you. You can see I'm busy, and *I'm really depressed*. I'll go through with this because it's important to you, but I feel like slitting my wrists—"

"How dramatic."

"Yes it is, and all I keep hearing is china patterns. I don't *want* any china!"

"James Dean here. The rebel without a cause, too cool to fool with a wedding."

"Fuck you," Malcolm said. "And fuck your mother."

"When *are* you planning to tell your mother, by the way? The day before the ceremony?"

By the beginning of May, their marriage was off.

Just as they had sort of gotten engaged, and sort of planned a wedding, they sort of reneged on those plans. After a ferocious argument about some wedding minutiae, Nora called her mother and told her to hold off on the invitations for a week or two. "We need to go back and think about this for a while," Nora said, and Sylvia Worth, choking back tears, said that was fine, Nora and Malcolm should take their time. She just wanted Nora to be happy.

Since Malcolm had never told his mother he was getting married, he wouldn't have to tell her he was not.

"I called my mother," Nora told Malcolm, "and told her it was off. Happy now?"

"Did I ask you to do that?"

"No. You just said I was a bloodsucking cunt and you'd rather die than marry me. 'Bloodsucking'! Me! When you owe me—"

"If you called your mother, *you* don't want to get married. Don't pin it on *me*."

"So you're not even going to admit to having said—"

"No. You're projecting."

"Ha! *I'm* projecting?"

It was Nora, he said, who had cried wolf, offering tales of domestic discord to her parents before she and Malcolm had even had a chance to reconcile. To call her mother that very night had been worse than impatient. It was deranged. If only she didn't feel it necessary, each time she was confronted with a little ambiguity, to leap wildly between options without thinking.

"'A little ambiguity'?" Nora retorted. "Is that what you call this?"

"Is what what I call what?"

"That. This."

Whenever things between them got really bad, they argued fiercely about vague pronoun references.

Their relationship, they agreed, had grown to resemble the FBI investigation: ongoing, *there*, but never resolved. Why prolong the agony? They were like the survivors of spouses missing in action. Without confronting the corpse, they would never be able to truly mourn. They just sat in the silent house, waiting for the telegram.

RATHER THAN PLUNGE into a fugue, Nora stalked to her studio, filled a favorite old fountain pen with ink, and started to doodle.

She drew with ink rather than charcoal, on a lined yellow legal pad rather than a sketchbook. Not trying to draw was an old trick. Even though it hadn't been particularly effective for sneaking up on inspiration in the past, she hadn't fondled that pen for so long that just its shape against her palm might elicit a response, instinctual as breaststroke. Drawing was a talismanic self, pre-Malcolm, to which she returned with a vengeance.

What could he do to her, anyway? Just not love her. If that's how he felt, she was better off. Jerk. But behind the posture of strength lurked the shadow, B movie–style, of her fear and sadness. She was frayed, Ellis Islanded, sitting on her suitcase like an abandoned child.

She drew a cartoonishly nasty car, a car like a pit bull. Cars had been on her mind. The more hers got on her nerves, the more her unconscious champed at the bit as the car commercials panned the glinting hoods, the drivers' hair blowing in the wind. Wanting a new car, she thought, was like tiring of a marriage. Her car was over seven years old now, and she had an itch.

She drew a series of cars in raggedy boxes, as on a story board, and tried to impart to the cars the sense of fascinated repulsion you feel when scratching around, but not directly on, the raised white welt of a mosquito bite. When her superego accused, *Cars or cows, what's the difference with you and your dumb, derivative series?* she forced herself to change the brain channel.

Except that she and Malcolm had never even married. None of it had been real. She'd had Malcolm like she'd had $27,900 in extra cash.

Any art responsive to our time, the pompous art critic continued, on a roll now, *would reflect the speed of 'remote,' the sense—*

Aw, shut up, Nora thought.

She gave one of the cars a "Just Married" sign. Bride at the wheel, veil still in place. No groom in sight—he's smashed like a possum on the road behind her. Next frame: Abdul-Jabbar executing a perfect skyhook (basketball was on her mind too, what with the NBA playoffs), but the ball is a VW beetle. And the rounded line at the head of the key, shown 3-D, is the jagged side of a cliff.

In the water below the cliff, a scuba diver gazes up. A bride in the falling car.

Nora Worth sat there for long enough to lose track of the time, which is, after all, the point.

Malcolm, meanwhile, had stormed to his own office, taken out the plans for Stone's building and the College of Physicians and Ivy Street from the pile of plans for projects he had never actualized, and felt completely defeated. How was he supposed to evolve into a decent, let alone inspired, designer if he never got to *do* anything? He opened the book of photographs of finished projects he showed to perspective clients and flipped the pages. His defeat turned into revulsion. In five years he'd completed, what, four projects? And none reflecting his current ideas, which weren't even his *own* current ideas but amalgams of ideas that had charmed him in the current journals.

Why was he doing this?

He took an old *Progressive Architecture* from the shelf, opened it at random. The Lloyd's of London building, which he loathed, sort of. On a yellow pad, with a felt-tip pen, he began to redesign it, stripping away the layers of Pompidou pomposity until the building made some kind of quieter sense in its surroundings. After that he traced an 1890s photograph of a Frank Furness building, putting a modern car before it. Then he put a horse-drawn buggy, traced from the Furness photograph, in front of the Lloyd's. *I am having fun*, he told himself grimly; it was almost true.

For three or four days Malcolm and Nora barely spoke. They were mostly out, but when they were home they stayed on separate floors, hating, beyond all measure, each others' guts.

Nora took Malcolm's advice, a little late, and withheld the announcement of the canceled nuptials. Timely, since Julie was finally ready to talk about Ed, her feelings for him. For Nora to interrupt would seem selfish, competitive.

The only person Malcolm wanted to tell was Ann Marie Lewis, but she wasn't home. She was among the last people in America without an answering machine, so Malcolm couldn't even leave a message. When he called her at the IRS, he was told that she was on vacation for ten days. He assumed she was in Boston. He didn't even know her boyfriend's last name. As Nora stormed off to a shoot, he tried to imagine how he'd proceed if he flew to Boston to find her. How hard could it be to locate a pale green Pacer with Philadelphia plates and an IRS parking sticker?

He went to Tobias Maxwell's office, as he'd done before Thanksgiving, and confessed to his friend that he might be in love with someone else. Now that his wedding was called off, maybe he should really pursue Ann Marie, before it ws too late.

"Wait," Tobias said. "You're getting married?"

"Was."

"And you didn't tell me?"

"I didn't tell anyone except Ann Marie."

"That's sick! So secretive! Don't you trust me?"

Malcolm thought it best to let that one go.

Tobias took him to lunch and extracted the whole story. He managed to repress most of his mirth at the idea of Malcolm dating his IRS agent. Malcolm, unused to drinking during the day, was expansive in extolling Ann Marie's virtues. Her wedding was planned for late June. If he wanted a chance with her, he had to move fast.

"What would that entail?" Tobias asked. "Even assuming she's touched by your barging in on her with this guy in Boston, what are you going to say? Down on your knees—'I had a fight with my fiancée, so I thought I'd drop by'?"

"She knows about Nora."

"What kind of timetable? You'll kick Nora out tomorrow—why not, she doesn't have a lease, just put all her stuff on the street until she finds a place, let her pay for the storage—so you and Ann Marie can date? Are you ready to marry Ann Marie?"

"Maybe I should be," Malcolm said.

"She's been with this guy, what, four years? And you've been with Nora six? You know this doesn't make sense."

"Maybe it's not supposed to."

"Wrong," Tobias said.

"Wrong?"

"Isn't that what you want me to say?" Tobias asked. "If you wanted her, you wouldn't ask me. You'd just do it."

"How do you know?"

"Your heart isn't in it, Mal."

"So what if Nora's right and my heart can't be in anything?"

"Then you're sunk. Why tear your life apart?"

Tobias's plan: Malcolm would go home and lift weights until he dropped. Then he would take a very hot bath and a nap and try to collect his senses, and in a week or two he'd probably remember why he'd been with Nora this long.

"Comfort isn't good enough," Malcolm said. "It only gets harder and harder to get out. It's like playing hooky, or falling behind on bills."

"Do me a favor," Tobias said. "Don't tell Nora about Ann Marie. Or at least promise that before you do, no matter what hour of the day or night, you'll call me first. Old AA trick—the buddy system."

"Maybe I *should* tell her."

"Just promise you'll give it a week."

The next night Nora climbed into their joint bed, claiming that the spare bedroom, closer to the street, was too noisy. Then, as Tobias had predicted, by the day of Ann Marie's return Nora and Malcolm had begun to sneak back into each other's good graces.

Their reunion had to do with art, and with basketball. Since they only had one television, they had to sit together to root for their team during the NBA championships. Since they were sleeping together again, they found they might as well bump butts, for warmth. Then Nora came to Malcolm's study one night, late, while he was working on his drawings.

"What are you doing?" she asked.

"I'm redesigning a Robert A. M. Stern house."

"Yeah?" she asked. "What's wrong with it?"

"If I knew that, I'd be great."

"Oh." She bent closer, looked hard. "The drawing's good," she said.

"It's pretty crude."

"Part of its charm. What a funny car."

"There are cars in all of them."

"Really? I've been drawing cars too."

He showed her the rest of the sketches, which he had now collected in a folder. He waited for her to criticize him for doodling instead of sending out résumés, making phone calls. Instead she said, "These are terrific. I can really see these as illustrations in the *New Yorker*."

"Get serious."

"Really. They're good. And when you get enough of them, you'll have a book—"

"No goal," he said sternly. "No point. Pointless. I'm just doing it, okay?"

She looked at him and shrugged.

Then they visited her studio. He liked "Autobride," recently completed.

That evening they had their first friendly dinner since the dissolution of their marriage plans.

They didn't speak about the wedding for over a week. They just tentatively interacted in their house. They didn't discuss the canceled wedding until, several weeks later, Nora finally asked, "Can we get married now?"

"No."

"When can we?"

"When I can trust you again."

"When will that be?"

"When you don't ask questions like 'When will that be.' Obviously, when we can talk."

For Malcolm, "talking" entailed Nora submitting to his assertion that, in "placing her family before him," she had undermined his confidence in her; that, especially given his work situation, she should have been more accommodating, exerted less pressure. In the interests of conciliation, Nora bartered. She would agree to agree to this if Malcolm agreed that in his own passive fashion he had forced her to be aggressive; that in not having firm opinions of his own about the wedding, he'd been complicit in forcing her to make arrangements that displeased him. He contended that he'd made his feelings crystal clear, only to be brushed aside by Nora and her barracuda mother. "I hate that 'poor nervous groom' shit," he said. "It's such reverse sexist trash. You treated me like a fucking cypher."

To which Nora could not resist shooting back, "Then try not acting like a cypher." She even tied his method of "self-expression" vis-à-vis the wedding to his ineffective behavior with prospective clients, a repulsively low not to mention untrue blow that set them back to vicious arguments about their methods of argument. From there, it would be a slow crawl back to discussing the wedding again. So they just fell into vaudeville routines. After sex, Nora would sometimes ask, panting, "Trust me yet?"

Maybe, they agreed, they'd just seen too many movies. No matter how many times they bitterly argued, it was hard not to imagine that, like Cary Grant and Katharine Hepburn in *A Philadelphia Story*, they would be united at the end. Of course, that was what Nora used to think about David, but in a forties' film, Martella would be the jilted social bounder. Grant and Hepburn are made for each other because they are, after all, the stars, and because they have names like Lord and Dexter-Haven. If Malcolm and Nora had learned nothing else from Stone and the bank windfall, it was to stifle the strife. Some time, they knew, would pass—and it passed faster and faster.

They were either foolishly evading their problems or brilliantly bypassing them. Either their relationship was so solid that they could transcend their daily woes, or they were both so weak and afraid of change that they were ignoring the fact that they had no core at all, just a mass of trivial compatibilities. Either or neither or both. They didn't know, and they agreed that they weren't going to know. Not yet, anyway.

"What are you waiting for?" Sylvia Worth asked her daughter, when Nora tried to explain why she hadn't packed and left after being abandoned at the altar. "A plane to write it in the sky?"

"I'm trying not to watch the kettle boil."

"Malcolm isn't boiling. He isn't even hot. The stove, I'm sorry to say, is off."

Sylvia would not have dared to say this to Nora's brothers.

"It's more complicated than that," Nora said.

"Why?" Sylvia Worth demanded, and launched into the lecture that usually begins with walking miles to school in the snow and ends with goosebumps across a crowded room.

The only thing that came to any real closure that spring was the Bulletin Building.

Malcolm spent the week before the demolition taking pictures. He shot from every angle, with every lens, in every light, as if the building were Monet's cathedral. He searched through the rubble, throwing out his back to put into his car trunk a chunk of stone that said IN B—the center of the "Bulletin Building" sign.

On what promised to be the building's last day, he brought Nora.

She'd expected dynamite, nuclear fireworks, the structure collapsing inward on itself like a body's final breath. In fact the building's death was slow, as slow as Malcolm's financial ruin. All week, over and over, the wrecking ball hit, then traffic was engineered so the trucks could pull up to clear away the debris, then traffic rearranged so the truck could be moved, the wrecker moved back in. The Bulletin Building died like an innocent man being kicked to death—in the balls, in the head. A man getting kicked to death publicly, the crowds eddying around him. What could they do? Throw themselves in front of the building and shriek, *Take me first*?

Malcolm and Nora stood behind the barricades, bearing witness. They watched for hours, until the last ragged, blackened wall, like the stump of a rotten tooth, was excised. Then they walked silently to their car. From a distance they could see the meter maid. Malcolm began to sprint, reaching the uniformed woman like a cartoon of someone sliding into home plate, just as she brought her pen down to write the first number of his license plate.

Four

MANY EVENTS OF note occurred in June, many of them weddings.

Julie Peszko's pregnancy was unplanned, but less surprising than the discovery that both Julie and Ed Tarry wanted the child. Julie still believed in Fate, which she cloaked in psychological determinism. She believed, for instance, that some people were simply destined to get parking tickets: their bad luck was bad insight, failure to know when a "No Parking" sign meant business. So the fact that Julie had, without consciously dieting, lost enough weight to make her diaphragm a poor fit must have meant she *wanted* to be pregnant. She claimed she knew on some level that she had conceived, at the moment of climax. Nora was dubious, but had known Julie long enough to allow her—even to expect—this corny mysticism.

29

"I'm so happy for you," Nora said, over the dinner where Julie sprang the news. "But that diaphragm business sounds fishy. You probably just didn't use enough goop. You have to remember to really slather the stuff on."

"The gynecologist said any gain or loss, even as little as five pounds, can change the size."

"But if you lose weight, wouldn't the diaphragm be snugger?"

Julie laughed. "Nora, you are such a goof. Focus. I'm going to be a married woman in a week."

"A *week*? You're not serious."

She was. Reporting her plans, Julie wore a double glow, from impending bridehood and pregnancy. Her angular face and sharp shoulders seemed to have filled out imperceptibly, from joy or water weight, and there was a new softness in her voice. Her satisfaction wasn't holier-than-thou. She didn't act as if she'd invented love or procreation. She was glad on the simplest level—profoundly, personally—and Nora was glad for her.

Nora and Malcolm were not invited to the ceremony at the Justice of the Peace. Julie and Ed both had parents and siblings more appropriate for that role. Their several recent foursome dinners had been as wary as double dates; to Nora, the friendship felt as nerve-wracking as a pregnancy, as if the group were being genetically recombined. Nora couldn't help but feel a little sad, even though she liked Ed. She'd have to have a child herself before she and Julie were really close again.

The local wedding announcement pages were like a yearbook that month. Behind every dreamy smile was a name or face they knew.

Nathaniel Rymer's daughter married into a family as old as her own. John Singer Sargent's portraits of her new husband's ancestors hung in the Philadelphia Museum of Art. Frayed nerves had gotten the basement renovation finished on time, and almost on budget. Now Malcolm hoped to receive some phone calls from some law-abiding people who could afford his services.

Tobias Maxwell's break-dancing cousin Donald married a model. This was a refined, white model with Rumpelstiltskin hair—the kind of woman Tobias himself always fell for. At the wedding Tobias met a college friend of the bride's and asked for her phone number. They went on a date, then another. After a while Tobias asked Malcolm to cook them dinner. Forget love at first sight: the truth about negotiating a relationship is that eventually you have to introduce your prospective mate to the old buddies who claim they only want the best for you but secretly want you alone, available, with the same familiar, forgivable flaws. Nora and Malcolm caught themselves in this trap before they met Janice.

Nora had always claimed that Tobias would eventually marry a Jewish girl. He'd be perfect for someone who hoped to cause her daddy grief with a shocking mate but still wanted safe emotional territory. Malcolm thought Tobias would stay single—there was too big a rift between his expectations and the women who were likely to respond to him.

Given this theorizing, they didn't expect Janice.

A hospital administrator and health care activist, she was the first black woman Tobias had dated since high school. If she was "torn," it wasn't on the basis of race. Her parents were both physicians; she was the baby of the family, the one who couldn't pull it together to be a hard-core professional. She was slumming it with Tobias! And yet she seemed to genuinely like him, the same Tobias that Nora and Malcolm liked most—a clown and a somber, loyal man, clinging to political conscience.

On the subject of their own canceled wedding, Nora still thought Malcolm had been a stubborn jerk, and he still thought she had. When they attempted to discuss their rocky year, they still could descend into argument. But they seemed to be registering each other in a new, more gentle way, so that often, as they fought for space on the cutting board in their tiny kitchen or to spread out the morning paper at the table, Nora would feel a waft of good feeling that cut like a draft across their routines.

Loving Nora again, Malcolm thought, was like seeing your own face in the mirror after shaving off your beard. The chin underneath raw, fragile. What he feared was that an admission about Ann Marie Lewis and his near-occasion of sin would be a requisite component of their reunion—and it almost happened, the morning that Ann Marie's wedding announcement appeared in the newspaper.

Nora didn't recognize her. She merely held the newspaper up, pointed, and said, "She's pretty, isn't she?"

One of their routines: she had a fairly good success rate in identifying women Malcolm would like.

From across the table, Malcolm squinted, focused, and said, "Oh."

His surprise should have made Nora suspect at once. But she merely asked, "Know her?"

"Look again," Malcolm advised.

Nora read the announcement. When she got to the "Internal Revenue Service" part, she laughed.

He sat stiffly, at attention, as if he'd just been pulled over by a policeman who now held a flashlight to his license and registration. But Nora just flipped the page to the movie section, where an ad for David Martella's film appeared daily. The film had opened locally, to good reviews;

a flurry of features on David had appeared, and each had given Nora a little twinge of the excitement she was missing, but she scolded herself: *Who are you fooling? It's not as if you're Jane Wyman.*

"I don't think I told you," she said. "I spoke with David. Rita got the job in California, but she didn't take it, and I don't think she'd stay here unless they were about to get married."

Malcolm found himself resentful, rather than relieved, about the change in subject.

"Of course," Nora continued, "David seems to believe that she'll tolerate him sleeping with other women. He still actually tries to pass off serial sex as a vigorous, experimental philosophical position. Remember 'open marriage'? Why does the phrase remind me of Robert Culp?"

She felt a twinge of guilt. Not for failing to confess—she'd long ago decided to refrain, since it would only relieve her conscience at Malcolm's expense. She felt guilty for betraying David's confidence. She felt the twitching gut that always accompanies a moral trespass: failing to correct the checkout girl when you know very well that the total is low, or speeding past a line of stagnant traffic when you know your lane is closed up ahead.

"I'm so lucky," Nora added, "that you're not like that. That you're a non-lech and a faithful type."

"Well," Malcolm said, "don't get *too* confident."

"Aren't you more likely to fall in love?"

"You think that's preferable?"

"I think it has more integrity, don't you?"

Malcolm thought about how Nora had revealed her affair with David years ago. He'd allowed her to play out the attraction—a favor she would never return. Apparently they were pursuing parallel tracks. "You were so good about David," she said. "I learned so much from the way you behaved. I hope that if you ever *did* fall in love with someone else, I'd be able to do as well."

She said this earnestly, without double meaning. Then she mounted him—the way she climbed into his lap, knees first, always made him feel like the Lincoln Monument—to seal the compliment with a noisy kiss.

The next wedding Nora and Malcolm didn't even learn about until after the fact. Nora's mother received a telegram from Rome: Alan and Jane had married at the American embassy there.

By this marriage Nora felt more threatened. Not only did this leave her the last single member of her family, but Alan and Jane had stolen the idea of eloping to Italy from her. That was precisely what Malcolm and Nora had told Alan and Jane they wished they'd done—married in Venice, in winter. But it turns out there is, surprisingly, no American embassy in Venice. Besides, they would have had to get the American papers and blood tests here and bring them abroad along with their passports, which would cut into the spontaneity.

When Alan and Jane returned, there would be another party in Pittsburgh with presents and envelopes containing cash. Ken and Annie would attend with their adorable daughter and new son, whom Nora had spent a fair amount of time with, even through her crisis with Malcolm, and who was changing much more dramatically than anything in the Worth-DeWitt future. Mark would be show-stoppingly solicitous to his pregnant wife (whose newborn Nora would soon travel to another New York hospital to exult about). Her love for Alan aside, Nora did not relish confronting her mother's disappointment with her, her mother's friends' questions about how her relationship with Malcolm was "progressing."

"Aren't you sorry, though," Nora asked Malcolm, "not to get the presents?"

"Not at all."

"Just think of all the new pots and knives and vases."

"We'd get candelabras and cut-glass crap."

"So we exchange it. Anyway, my parents' friends give cash."

"How mercenary."

"Why? It makes them feel good. They owe my mother. We could have gotten an Alessi teapot, and Tuxedo plates—"

"How about a new roof? A new mattress?"

"We do need a bed," Nora agreed.

Not a time, however, for major purchases. Their finances were just where they'd been at the onset of the Stone crisis. Worse. The time Nora had devoted to searching for costume jobs had eroded some of her steady food-styling work. As for Malcolm, however wary he'd been about his opportunities last winter, there had been some; now he answered ads in the paper for architects and got no response. Once more they were two months away from disaster. Maybe they would *always* be two months away from disaster.

"What percentage of the American population," Nora asked, "do you think lives like this?"

"You mean who aren't migrant farm workers?"

Malcolm guessed that they were not alone. But they felt alone. Because it was hard to answer an innocent, conversational "What's up?" they kept to themselves.

"I feel," Nora said, "like one of those cartoons of the ragged old couple with the shitty little television and the millions of dogs and cats, without even the dogs and cats."

"It's not just the money," Malcolm said. "Yesterday, coming home, the Expressway jammed—only Philadelphia would close all major routes into the city for construction at the same time, I swear it must be a conspiracy, Goode's way of punishing everyone who didn't vote for him—I took the back way, through the 'slums.' All those perfectly fine city houses! And I hated everyone who fled the city when the blacks moved in. That's when it ended. I mean, city life. Yesterday, it felt like the only thing that'd change the course of things is a nuclear disaster. Just blow it all up."

"Maybe. Or maybe a couple of thousand bucks in the bank would make you feel sunnier."

Malcolm confessed his hope: that Stone would soon be out of his life in the same cathartic way that the taxes were. After the third continuance, they finally had a date for their case.

Malcolm hadn't seen Benjamin Stone for almost a year. He could barely recall what Stone looked like, aside from an uneasy impression of speed in an expensive suit. And Nora had never met him.

Malcolm and Nora were the first to arrive on the eighth floor, courtroom C, for pre-trial arbitration. They chose a back row. Soon they were joined by Malcolm's lawyer, Preston, who shook Nora's hand and said,

"Stone not here yet"—more statement than question. "Things'll get going about a half-hour late," Preston added. "I'll go check things out." Leaving his briefcase, he approached the bench to bend over a printout.

Of course Stone and his lawyer would enter the room when Preston wasn't there to act as a buffer. Nora picked out the small, chubby, imperious man immediately. Stone's lawyer scanned the room, saw Preston, and went to greet his colleague, leaving the opponents only feet from each other.

"Ben," Malcolm said.

Stone acknowledged Malcolm by nodding once deeply, eyes to the floor.

"I don't think you've met," Malcolm said. "Ben, this is Nora Worth, my wife. Nora, Ben Stone."

They always said "husband" and "wife" in such introductions; they always had. It was easier.

"Nice to meet you," Nora said.

Stone nodded agreement. "Sorry we're not meeting under happier circumstances," he said to Malcolm.

"Me too."

"Why, exactly," Stone asked, "are you doing this to me?"

"Pardon?"

Stone repeated, slowly.

"I'm sorry," Malcolm said, puzzled. "No hard feelings. Nothing personal. I needed the money, and I just thought I should get in line."

"No one else has sued," Stone accused.

"Really?"

"No. Only you."

"What is everyone else doing, just writing you off as a loss?"

Malcolm meant that to sound factual, not nasty. "I mean—" he began to clarify, but the lawyers had returned.

"Gentlemen?" Preston said, gesturing toward the door.

Like everything else in Philadelphia, the hallway was under construction, so the waiting area was a makeshift grouping of chairs near a water fountain and a wall that had been punched out (to reveal, no doubt, asbestos). Even if there had been enough chairs, they would have had to speak over an obese woman in a nurse's uniform and her chain-smoking escort. They moved some yards away and huddled near the wall to negotiate.

"Mr. Stone," Preston told Malcolm, "is still willing to offer you two thousand dollars."

"Plus," Stone's lawyer said, "we will offer four hundred dollars to cover your lawyer's fee."

"Not enough," Malcolm said softly.

"You understand," Stone's lawyer scolded, "that my client has no way to pay you. I'm sure Tom has explained that we'll appeal any judgment you win, so it's in your best interest—"

"If he can't pay," Malcolm asked, "how's he going to give me $2,400?"

"Mr. Stone's father is willing to write you a cashier's check for that amount."

Stone seemed to cringe on the word "father." Malcolm had to smile, wondering if Poppa Stone had to pay all of his son's legal bills as well. "Can't he just pay the whole $6,800, then?"

"Impossible," the lawyer said.

Malcolm shrugged. The two lawyers caught each other's eyes wearily, and Malcolm caught Nora's. They had agreed that much as he needed the money—*any* money—he wouldn't surrender too easily.

Soon they were joined by a young man, long-haired and not very cleanly shaven, who wore jeans and a sweatshirt sawed off at the sleeves. "Stone?" he said, looking at Malcolm; then, at Stone, "DeWitt?" He carried nothing; he rubbed his hands together merrily, like a camp counselor proposing volleyball.

"Law clerk," Preston whispered to Malcolm when he saw his client's uncertain expression.

Around a table (Nora sat rearward primly, like Mrs. Dean at Watergate), the lawyers explained the case. Stone's lawyer pointed out that Stone had lost his business, his house, and about two million dollars in assets. 'Furthermore, he wasn't that happy with the work Mr. DeWitt was doing."

Stone looked away.

"Now, Jack," Preston scolded, "you know that isn't relevant here."

From Malcolm's twitching upper lip in profile, Nora could see that the last had hurt. But low blows tended to make him more stubborn, so when the clerk advised him to accept the offer, he said quietly but firmly, "No. Four."

How ludicrous, Nora and Malcolm would later agree, that Malcolm had been shafted and still got treated here—even by his own lawyer—like a difficult child. How repairmen treat you when you try to fix an appliance that's under warranty, or how doctors treat a hospitalized patient who dares to ask questions about his own condition. All across America, as they spoke, people were getting framed for crimes they didn't commit or waging hopeless battles against the pharmaceutical companies that polluted their waters and destroyed their health; people did check in for gall bladder removals and get brain surgery instead. *It's the principle of the thing*, Malcolm actually said at one point, but fifteen minutes down the line they'd somehow settled on $3,000 and shaken hands.

Nine months of complete financial panic came down to this: an exchange of numbers, as at the antique auction, and a friendly agreement about what amounted to pocket change, enough to keep Malcolm afloat for another month and a half. Stone's Dad bailing him out as Malcolm's couldn't, even if he were alive—and they'd probably never know what Stone had done, how his crime fit with the general scheme of drug dealers and Mafia and shady bank transactions. They would never know how Stone felt about his fate or if—as Malcolm somehow did know, even without the lawyer's dig—Malcolm could have tolerated the monomonaical, drug-dazed little capo if everything had gone as planned.

"Sorry," Malcolm said, standing.

"Yes," Stone said coldly. "Well."

Stone met Malcolm's eyes. Hardly a soulful look but Malcolm saw a host of emotions there: guilt, anger, shame, and also a trace of the old cockiness, the old condescension.

Nora must have been feeling it too. Under her breath she said, "Bastard." But Stone didn't hear her and didn't respond, to Malcolm's comment or to hers. Malcolm put his hand on the small of Nora's back as everyone said good-bye.

There was no point. They'd have to wait for the same elevator and exchange farewells all over again on the ground floor. It was hard to determine which would be more embarrassing: for the group to ride down together, or to manufacture whatever excuses would allow them to leave the floor at staggered times. The lawyers, evidently more experienced, averted the decision. Stone and his lawyer headed the opposite way, and Preston said he had to make a call from the pay phone, would see Malcolm the next day when he came for his check. So Malcolm and Nora walked to the exit alone, holding hands.

BENJAMIN STONE WAS sentenced to eighteen months in Al-
lenwood, the Pennsylvania institution that housed all the senators and
congressmen, federal district judges, city councilmembers and union
leaders, blackmailers and bribe takers who were deemed to be minimal
security threats.

Malcolm and Nora would learn of the prison sentence from a most unlikely source: not from Ed Tarry or
their friend Lucy, but from Malcolm's mother. They
were paying one of their too rare visits to her when she
told Malcolm, "That man you worked for. He's in jail."

30

She knew this by a route that, Malcolm and Nora would later concur,
just about summed up Philadelphia. She repeated for Nora the story that
Malcolm had told Ann Marie Lewis, about the rich old woman who had
owned the house on Mortimer Street before Benjamin Stone. For fifty or
sixty years, Mrs. DeWitt had religiously read the "Real Estate Transactions" column in the Sunday paper. Since she knew Stone's name and
address, knew the prior owner, and knew that Stone had been Malcolm's client, she had taken note when the house on Mortimer Street
changed hands. Coincidentally, the buyer was the son of a friend of hers,
and at the beauty parlor where both women had their hair done she'd
heard that this son had gotten a deal on the house because the previous
owner was in jail.

"Isn't that something?" Mrs. DeWitt remarked. "What did he do
wrong, do you think?"

Amazingly to Nora, who called her mother immediately with news of
any kind, Malcolm had not mentioned that he was in trouble, had sat
through Christmas dinner at his sister's saying everything was fine. "Oh
dear," Mrs. DeWitt said, shaking her head to indicate that such corrup-
tion was beyond her grasp.

"I almost forgot!" Mrs. DeWitt said. "Your letter!"

He had received official mail at his ancestral address: notice of selection for jury duty.

For a week his mother had been begging him to pick up the letter. Maybe there are two kinds of people in the world—those who can ignore a parking ticket summons or a jury duty notification, and those who can't. Malcolm had told his mother that he wasn't at all eager for the city to have a listing of his current address and encouraged her to just throw the letter out, or write across the front *Dead—Return to Sender*.

If Benjamin Stone's year made for the worst kind of hard-luck story, Chris Mann's year was a blazing success of the kind that newspapers like for features on the triumph-of-the-will-over-adversity.

Just as in forties films, where the understudy's brilliant career begins when she steps in at the last minute for the peevish starlet, Chris got to participate in a show when the slated artist defected without notice to a New York gallery. Nora had introduced Chris to the gallery owner. The despair that previously had consumed Chris's life was now tidily contained in his frantic animal sketches.

"He's such a brilliant guy," Ed Tarry told Nora and Julie when they met at the opening. "I don't think I've ever met anyone as smart, or as funny."

Julie, pregnant, was beginning to look angelic.

Malcolm hadn't arrived yet. He had appointments in the afternoon and was supposed to meet Nora here.

Philadelphia was small enough that she knew many people at the opening. While some of Malcolm and Nora's avant-garde pals had also gone into different fields, some, like the photographer with whom Nora sometimes worked on commercial shoots, had remained artists. Those people treated Nora as if she had been voted Most Likely to Succeed in high school and wound up a shoe salesman.

The artists' disdain hurt her less now that she'd made some progress in getting work outside of food styling. The art director for whom she'd done the mouthwash dragon had finally called to ask her to bid on another project. The film art director who had taken her card at David Martella's screening had called as well, inviting her to submit slides of her art to be considered for a film-gallery-opening scene: the stars would stand

against her work, holding drinks and considering a love affair. In re-
viewing the slides she mailed, Nora had felt so nostalgic that she had begun to make art again in earnest—not necessarily with delusions of
fame and fortune, but just to entertain herself.

As Nora's luck promised to improve, so did Malcolm's. One of Rymer's wedding guests actually looked likely to hire him for an addition.
It was a small job, and the clients didn't seem as ideal as Rymer, but Malcolm might avoid starving. Over dinners, Nora and Malcolm discussed
whether they could hang on long enough to achieve some balance of
hope and realism in their work, a tough-mindedness that still allowed
for serendipity. Difficult, they agreed, but maybe not impossible.

Nora should not have been surprised to see David Martella at this opening. He sometimes attended openings, if he was in town and had nothing else to do.

Maybe he could act after all. He managed to project his lingering disappointment from a distance of fifty feet or so as they caught each other's
attention. From the same distance he forgave her—made her feel as if
she were exuding twinkly light while he maneuvered through the
crowd. Nora had always liked his boyish, go-get-'em walk, a kind of
schlumpy strut. She found herself focusing warmly, almost proprietarily, on the fabric of his pants around his thighs, then thought, *What is
wrong with me?* Then at his mouth. Immediately, it was talking.

"What kind of shoes are those, anyhow?" he asked, pointing to her
feet.

They were her favorites, an eccentric pair in mint green and violet,
shaped like high-performance sports cars. "Italian," she said.

"Well, I suppose you have to get *some* color into your life, in your
wardrobe if nowhere else."

"Why how nice to see you too, dear."

David smiled.

So why *was* it nice to see him, when he demanded a recitation of
professional developments only to look bored as she complied? His eyes
glazed as she meditated on how amusing it would be if, after having not
shown art in years, she now had a faux-show in a Hollywood film. He
then told her about the parts he'd auditioned for, the megastars he'd in-

terviewed, the villas and penthouses where he'd partied. No question, his life was more exciting than hers. Nora wasn't wearing heels, so she and David were iris to iris. By the champagne bowl, Nora put her hand out quickly to stroke David's arm. "I'll always care about you, you know," she said.

"Yeah," David said. "Sure. Loyal to the death. You haven't met Rita, have you? Rita, Nora."

Without warning, at David's side, there appeared an assured, radiantly intelligent looking woman: Rita, her hand out. Nora shook it, her heart doing a stupidly happy beat. For some reason Nora liked the woman strongly and immediately.

"Congratulations on the California job," Nora said. "Any regrets about not taking it?"

As Rita answered, Nora could hear herself reacting like a salacious male buddy of David's at a bachelor party: *Why you sly old dog! Where you been hiding her?* What if, after Rita soothed David's ego—allowing him to fantasize about an eternity of cheerful sex and adventure—he turned out to be a faithful husband, a devoted father? It was possible.

Soon after, Rita saw someone she knew and excused herself, then David swam off to be a big fish in a small pond, telling the locals about his friendships with stars from "his" film. Nora shouldn't mock him. The truth is that people lit when he approached, displaying an office-party, gossipy eagerness. Throughout their chat acquaintances and old lovers had steered toward them, greeted him, waved. It had always been like this with him, since before the film, even back at the party where they'd met, when he didn't even have his film column yet. That sense that David had singled her out, like Cinderella at the ball, or like the colorfully plumed male pheasant that she and Malcolm had recently watched at the zoo with Ken and Annie and their children. The poor dull female pheasant danced around in dizzying circles until she deigned to hop across his tail. "In human mating," Ken told his daughter, "where females are more plentiful, the gals get the plumage and do most of the dancing." True—or maybe the male plumage was Accomplishment.

Nora realized with no bitterness—even with pride—that someday David might well be minor-league famous. He'd have his own sitcom or public-broadcast movie review show. She would not lose touch with David. If nothing else, he'd need to call her up to say *I told you so*.

Nora knew that after tonight she might again think of him with the old shiver. But she also knew that she was not going to be able to extend the shiver to a tidal wave. How she admired the energy and persistence of schizophrenics, the people in Julie's wards who repeated the same line over and over for years, obsessed forever about lost loves! After a hard day's work, Nora barely had the energy to keep up an ordinary neurosis.

Malcolm arrived at the opening late and uncomfortable. He hated to lie. He'd told Nora that he had to meet with his new client, but in fact he had been saying good-bye to Ann Marie Lewis.

She was getting married in a week. It was hardly the ideal time for packing and moving—Ted couldn't even get off work to help her—but her lease was up. She'd decided to shift her belongings from her Old City one-bedroom to an efficiency in Malcolm's neighborhood, walking distance from Wharton Business School, where she'd be taking classes several days a week in the fall. The new apartment was almost as cheap as storage, and she thought it was best to have all this over with, since after the wedding she and Ted planned to take a month in Europe.

Malcolm had not longed for her. When he thought of her it was as a dull ache, like the perpetual pain in his back from bending over his desk late at night by weak light. But he'd expected a cleaner break. He hadn't anticipated her living half a mile away in September.

"I just can't get out of Philadelphia," Ann Marie told him. "Why didn't I just apply to Harvard Business School? Ted and I will be married, and we're *still* going to be living in different cities."

"Why rush into anything?"

Malcolm met her at her old apartment, now almost empty, and helped her load boxes of books into her car. What remained were the items that are always the last to be packed at the old address and the first to be unpacked at the new: the dregs from the bottom of drawers, the back of closets. They sat on the floor to finish off the last beers from her refrigerator, and for some reason found themselves sharing unanchored anecdotes from their pasts. Crying themselves to sleep at summer camp and the demise of their childhood pets. How Malcolm's mother had called him one night to say his father was not well; Malcolm had gulped down a sandwich, rinsed the plate, driven to his parents' house, and arrived to find his father dead.

"Why am I telling you this?" Malcolm asked.

"Because it's sad," Ann Marie said. "And we're trying to catch up, fast. How have things been with Nora, anyway?"

He told her about the wedding cancellation. He talked about the day he'd wanted to track Ann Marie down; but he told her the context as well—it didn't make sense to lie now. It felt strange to discuss Nora, but she discussed Ted too, and their feelings about their respective mates seemed to be the same: while they had reservations, they also both felt they had to proceed.

"I don't know," Malcolm said. "The question is still if we're settling. Why we're not more certain. But then, why should we be certain? Nora has never bought a single item without worrying that she should return it the minute she leaves the store. And I ponder each article so long it's gone by the time I make up my mind."

"A perfect couple," Ann Marie said. "Maybe you'll balance each other out."

"Either that or make each other even more extreme."

It was difficult to explain, especially to someone he barely knew, but he tried. He told her how, lifting weights in the heat, he would find himself stopped short by a thought so strange he'd share it with Nora, who would be across the room drinking wine, eating corn chips, and looking up from her magazine occasionally with mild disdain for what he was inflicting on himself. *You know*, he'd say, *I was just reading how in ancient Rome they'd torture people by hammering on their temples, slashing their throats, and disemboweling them all at once*. To which she'd respond, *You are depressed, aren't you?*

"She kind of reminds me of a dog," Malcolm told Ann Marie. "She jumps up to look out the window, or stares at me. Sometimes it seems that trading her in would be like donating your pet to the SPCA just because it sheds or, high-strung breed that it is, occasionally turns on its master."

"Flattering," Ann Marie said. "I hope you haven't told her that."

"I have. She thinks it's funny. That's the thing about Nora. She thinks everything's funny, and everything depresses her."

"That's how I think of you," Ann Marie observed. "You get this grin every time you tell me about something awful."

She had to leave if she wanted daylight driving, and Malcolm was late for the opening. As they said good-bye, promising to keep in touch, there was a great deal of motion between their joined hands, a great deal of emotion expressed thereby. Malcolm felt as if he were trying to communicate an urgent message in a language he didn't know, in a foreign country, as sometimes happens in dreams, with that dreamlike double sense of danger and security.

If Malcolm had lost a possible lover in Ann Marie, he had gained friends in Chris Mann and Ed Tarry. He liked both men a great deal and was happy to see them at the opening. He didn't see Nora at first. When she finally emerged from a different room, caught his eye, and waved, he was gratified to see how good she looked.

When Nora, more champagne in hand, approached Chris and Malcolm, they were discussing their favorite childhood TV shows. Malcolm was recalling a network show broadcast from a local archaeological museum, "What in the World," in which haunting music played as a spotlight drifted across a strange object on a chair, and a panel of experts would try to identify the object's use: *That's a weed-chopping tool from the Bonga-Bonga tribe. No, it's an Egyptian pottery scraper, circa B.C. whatever.* The buzzer would sound, and the object's true identity would be revealed. Television, Malcolm said, was not what it used to be.

Before they left the show, Malcolm and Nora toured the exhibition together. Their discussion of the paintings would not have impressed David Martella, who had left before Malcolm arrived, but they enjoyed it.

By the time they got home they were hungry and not quite hungry, the way you are after hor d'oeuvres. The almost-summer twilight glimmered suggestively. It was the kind of light that often made them say, in unison, *I wish we were in Paris*, which is to say strolling through their lives, alive to impressions. The nice thing about knowing someone for a long time is that you can say *Paris* and conjure up the yearning without extraneous words. You can say, *Are you hungry?* and read from the shrug or squint you get in response to your lover's metabolical state. Before dinner, if they chose to eat, Malcolm and Nora might be ambitious enough to fall into bed, and though their moves were as familiar now as their repertoire of dinner menus, they could work on this closure, at least, as if their lives depended on it.

MALCOLM DEWITT AND Nora Worth married on a Friday in November, almost a year after Benjamin Stone's bust.

The wedding wasn't exactly planned, but neither was it spontaneous. They staged the kind of formalized improvisation they had decided made sense for them, the right amount of sense—enough so that Nora felt secure, and not so much that Malcolm felt op- **31** pressed.

Through summer and early fall, time had moved for them as it's supposed to but rarely does: not too fast, not too slow. They'd been busy but not too busy and had encouraged each other about work without getting in each other's way. This wouldn't last. They were in feast-or-famine, do-or-die businesses and had to ex- pect new rough periods, new disappointments. Still, it was hard not to enjoy the bower of peace and ease.

If they had been good Marxists, they would have admitted that their feelings for each other had always pulsed to the beat of their finances. They had needed to learn to sing some version of "I Got Plenty of Nothin'," which, for them, involved making art without expectation of reward. Malcolm liked Nora's madcap collage-sculptures. She liked his architectural drawings as well (which she'd nicknamed "Reinventing the Wheel"), but she thought he should have a whole collection of them by now, and he was still designing and redesigning the same Robert A. M. Stern house.

"What do you expect?" he demanded. "I can barely do perspective yet."

"But that's what makes the drawings nice," Nora argued. While Mal- colm was flattered, that wasn't the point: he was trying to educate him- self, in both drawing and design.

He got the addition in the suburbs. The work would keep him alive, if not pay Nora back. Luckily, her own work was going well (she'd won another New York costume project bid), so she hadn't given him any grief.

For the first time since his police photographer job, Malcolm had actually done the paperwork in April for an extension on his taxes. Then, in August, he *actually filed*, for the very year in question. He was shocked to learn that, when you added up everything he'd taken in that year— from Rymer's basement, from the Stone settlement, from his tax refund—he'd earned over $10,000. An extraordinarily frugal person could live on that, as long as he had a solvent mate to help on shutoff days.

Some of Nora's friends, she knew, thought that her willingness to keep bailing him out was neurotic. David had tried this theory years ago: she wanted control. How sexist. Women could mouth the present wisdom about how, if you wanted a "sensitive" male, you had to be willing to relax some of the old standards of monetary support, but few seemed willing to do it. So what if Nora still harbored a fantasy of Malcolm as something like a frog prince, someone about whom she could eventually say, *I knew him when*?

For his birthday in July, as well as the more personal presents, Nora fixed the roof. Malcolm bought himself a present too: Ann Marie Lewis's Pacer. She needed a less picturesque car for the commute to Boston. She'd tried to give it to him, but he insisted on paying. Good timing, since his own car soon died on a highway in New Jersey, on a run for contraband liquor (the only thing about Philadelphia he hated more than the Parking Authority was the Liquor Control Board). He took his license plates from the dead old car and had them transferred to the Pacer. The last thing he hid from Nora—the last thing, he told himself, that he would need to hide—was the vehicle's previous owner. He told her he passed the car on the street and saw a sign in the window.

She thought he was crazy.

They had been talking about marriage again for months, since the spate of weddings in June—playfully, cautiously.

"I really don't see the point of it," Malcolm said once, "unless we're going to have children."

"I'll make a deal with you," Nora said. "Let's not get married. Let's just have children instead."

Malcolm made his children-face: a gray-green, nauseous wince. "How could you not want to have children? Nora asked.

"It's 'children' now," Malcolm said, "and not just 'child'?"

"Do I detect a statement here that you would like just one?"

"Did I say 'like'?"

"Accept, then."

"One seems more than sufficient."

"But are you *agreeing* to one?"

"I can't say I like the idea right now. Maybe sometime in the future—"

"Will you put that in writing?" Nora asked.

On another occasion they discussed what their child might look like. There were combinations of their features that could be surreal. Furthermore, they had a fifty percent chance of having a boy, and neither of them much liked boy-children, especially the twelve-year-old boy-children who passed their house scratching car hoods with sticks. At the very least, Malcolm said, with him setting a bad example of male bonding and Nora's nagging, any male child they spawned would be homosexual.

If it was a boy, Nora suggested, they could give it up for adoption.

Malcolm did not think that Nora would make a good mother. He feared she'd be overprotective, bossy. Nora disagreed. She'd certainly been adequate with her brothers. Anyway, from everything she'd heard, the dominant factor was heredity, not environment: all of her friends and relatives claimed that the buggers were howlers or sweethearts from the second their heads emerged, if not before.

"Then we're sunk," Malcolm said. Both of them had been awful babies, screamers and sulkers, hard to wean, impossible to toilet train. And Nora was not the kind of woman you'd trust to create a tranquil environment in the womb.

"I don't think it's that direct a correlation," Nora said. "I think it's luck of the draw."

"Just what I'm afraid of," Malcolm said.

On yet another occasion, while watching a woman scream and grunt in a TV documentary on natural childbirth, Nora said, "I'll tell you one thing. I don't want to do it natural. I don't even want an anesthetic. I want to be flat knocked out. They can wake me when it's over."

"Good," Malcolm said, "because I wouldn't watch either. I'd wait outside with the cigars."

After several more conversations of this sort, they agreed, in a more serious tone, that neither of them appeared to be ready to have children. But what about marriage? Wasn't it getting around time that they ought to be able to decide whether they were going to stay together?

"We *are* together," Malcolm said.

"But every time we argue, we're both afraid the whole house of cards will collapse. I don't like the idea of our relationship being outside our control. We've weathered our sundry crises fairly well, but if—*when*, I guess—we have problems again, I'd like us both to know we're in them together. If we made some kind of statement—"

"I hate statements," Malcolm said. "I don't trust them. I trust acts."

"I didn't suggest we promise to love, honor, and obey, so we can mistreat each other. If your argument is that we're essentially married anyway, why not?"

"Because," Malcolm said, "I haven't liked a single wedding ceremony I've ever seen."

"I think they're all sweet. They all make me cry."

"Yeah. Well, you cried at *E.T.*"

They discussed whether there was any kind of wedding that might be meaningful. What can the ritual signify, when you fear neither God nor State? They seemed to be drawn to something unconventional, like a double ceremony with Tobias and Janice (who might beat them to the punch at this rate) performed by a ship's captain—except that the ship should be docked. The wedding processional could be Bernard Hermann's score for *Vertigo*, or Morton Feldman's ecstatically nonclimactic "False Relationships and the Extended Ending." But finally, such ideas had the manic self-consciousness of old Beatles movies and didn't promise to wear very well.

They didn't need to be married for legal purposes, Malcolm pointed out. They already had joint wills all properly signed and witnessed naming each other their beneficiaries, wills they'd made out (retyped, actually, from Malcolm's old will bequeathing everything he owned to Beth) before a European vacation. Furthermore, if they waited a mere ten months, they'd be officially married by common law in the eyes of the state.

"I think you have to have lived together for seven years, not just dated," Nora observed.

In one of these conversations, Malcolm remembered that Pennsylvania was one of two or three states in the country that still recognized common-law marriage for legal purposes. A holdover from the Quaker days: all it took to prove you were married by common law was to *say* you were married, and to have that statement overheard by witnesses. Under those terms, they had in fact already been married for years, since they always called themselves husband and wife when booking airplane tickets or calling roofers. They were married for purposes of their car insurance rate. What would they gain by making it more official than that?

"Common law's a dumb idea," Nora said. "I mean, it's legal here, but what if we skip town? Will we be married here, single in L.A.?"

"Have you forgotten what happened last time we tried a wedding?"

"That was my fault," Nora said.

"Oh yeah?"

"I've thought about it a lot. Actually, something snapped for me when Alan and Jane got married. At first I just felt bittersweet-sad, like I always do at the brother-weddings, but then I felt weirdly free. Like, 'Okay, I've done the dishes. Now can I go outside and play?' Does that make sense?"

"No."

"Remember my Aunt Patty? Doesn't it seem odd to you that my mother should be such a breeder and my mother's sister should never marry? She was always so tied in with all my uncles and their families too. I just got this glint, over Alan, that there was some warped generational thing at work, something conspiring to turn me into a bitter, wiseass maiden aunt—that's the very phrase Julie used, in fact, when you and I were fighting last winter and I got snowed in with her—and I didn't want to play. Like Oedipus, you know? 'Hey, count me out!'"

"I don't get it."

"What if I *chose* you way back when—knowing your reservations about marriage and children, knowing that you weren't very tied in with your own family—then set out to 'reform' you, when, in fact, your stubbornness was cozy, because I didn't *really* want to get married, but since you were you I didn't have to confront that, I could just pin it on you?"

"Oh," Malcolm said. "That's exactly what I told you."

"I know."

"I've been telling you that for years."

"Better late than never."

Maybe later, Malcolm thought, she would understand him better too. In their most recent arguments she'd still tried to characterize him as a strong silent type who found it safer not to make his feelings known. The fact is, he *had* made his feelings known, at high volume, since 1984 when they met: his reservations about her and marriage, his anger at his parents (who had given up on him when he gave up the church and his government job), his disappointment about work, his various voluminous feelings of failure. Nora simply hadn't found it convenient to hear him. She listened only in spurts. But at least she was trying to think of him less as a cartoon, and at least now—when she "discovered" something about herself that they'd discussed more than once, at length—she'd admit her selective amnesia.

They attended Alan and Jane's postnuptial bash in Pittsburgh. Nora's family was cool to Malcolm. Her parents hadn't seen him, after all, since the wedding cancellation. During the boisterous, slightly hysterical family breakfasts, Malcolm was silent except for the foghorn of his nose-blowing (allergic to cats). Even Nora's brothers eyed him with deep fatigue as he snuck off with his black notebook to study buildings and investigate the local record and wine shops.

Nora found that she didn't want to defend him anymore. He would never act like a Worth. If that was the only model they could accept, tough luck.

Thereafter, Nora found herself thinking about the idea of a common-law ceremony more and more. "You know," she told Malcolm one night, after the kind of sex that they called a nap, "I think I could be satisfied with that. And it probably wouldn't scare you as much. Let's do it."

"Fine with me," Malcolm said, patting her stomach. "I now pronounce us man and wife."

"No," she said to his neck. "I want it to be serious and thoughtful. I'd like to pick a date, think about it, and say some things we can remember with a full and fond heart, lest one of us gets hit by a truck."

"You know," Malcolm observed, "I was just reading somewhere that in Pennsylvania you don't need any kind of officiator for a wedding. You can just do it yourself, get it signed by witnesses, and turn it in. A Quaker license—that might be the only single decent thing about this state."

"You mean a real wedding, without a minister or judge?"

Nora would always remember that this was Malcolm's idea, as it had been the past winter. It was Malcolm who proposed the damning legal paperwork, with the vial of blood backing it up.

"Who would you want as witnesses?" Nora asked.

"If you're serious about this," Malcolm said, "I'd feel a lot better if we didn't invite anybody, or even tell anybody until afterward. Certainly not here, with your whole clan assembled. Then we can have a party if you like, but if you want the ceremony to be 'meaningful,' I think it should be private. Really private."

"I don't know," Nora said. "Everyone I know who has gotten married like that says afterward they regretted it."

"I wouldn't."

"You don't even want Lucy and Jack? Tobias and Janice?"

"Not really."

"Okay," Nora said. "But you have to promise to be good. No smarmy jokes. Just straight and solemn and deep in love."

They married in the afternoon. Neither was a morning person. They'd agreed that Malcolm could have his usual amount of time to drink coffee and read the paper in his pajamas. But he wouldn't work. No drawing or phone calls. Nora had scheduled no shoots. They turned down the sound on the answering machine and meditated on their impending bond in separate rooms, as was the custom; they would convene at the appointed time dressed for the occasion.

As a compromise, they had decided to host a nice dinner out after the ceremony, their private vows summarized for spectators (Lucy and Jack, Tobias and Janice, Julie Peszko and Ed Tarry) who would sign the license. None of Nora's brothers had been invited: they simply could not invite Nora's brothers and their wives without inviting Nora's parents, Malcolm's mother and sister and her husband, and then it was a gang event, with some people like Laurie, whom Nora didn't feel close to, tagging along. So they'd decided to keep it out of the family. Nora didn't feel totally comfortable with that choice—somewhat childish, it seemed to her, with Malcolm, at forty, too old to elope—but she had to admit that of all her brothers' weddings, she'd thought Alan's had made the most sense. And odd as it was to have this small a party attended by Janice and Ed, two spouse-types they barely knew, this was also, they believed, fitting, given their recent alienation from everyone and everything.

The weather for their wedding was perfect. The car started right up. No flat tire, and there was gas in the tank. But they hit their first hitch when Malcolm headed in the wrong direction.

"Where are you going?" Nora asked.

"To the bank."

"The *bank*?" she cried.

"It's Friday," he said. "I don't have any cash."

"*Cash*? It's our *wedding day*!"

"No big deal. It'll only take a second."

"My bank or yours?"

Nora's was closer. It had recently been the victim of a takeover—same address but different name and, no doubt, somewhat different staff, though the teller with the curly fingernails was still there, and still cordial to Nora.

Ever since she'd been caught, Nora entered this bank with an irrational jubilance. It was like the silly rush of warmth she always felt, despite the sixties, about policemen: she'd never been able to shake her childhood sense of security at the sight of the blue uniform. As if she had some kind of insider's view of the bank, its façade of good taste and efficiency. Sometimes she'd feel a tickle of pride in her guts and luck, in not having been forced to return the $4,000. Then that feeling would be shattered by a jolt of the old panic, as if she were still running from the law. But most times she didn't think about the money at all. Ultimately, she and Malcolm didn't care much about money. They were getting by—living, granted, a marginal life, teetering on the edge of the middle class in a country that might at any moment drown in acid rain or smother itself in its deficit, but for now, at least, living well-ish was a good enough revenge.

In line at the bank they held hands, and soon enough they were out, with a goodly number of clean new bills.

They walked to the car—Nora's, not the Pacer. She'd bought a new car herself in August, shocking Malcolm. Hers had been acting up again, and she'd marched right to the Honda dealership to trade it in. She so loved the blue-gray of the car she test-drove, the wheel felt so crisp turning corners, and the end-of-summer deal was so good that she'd just withdrawn her money market checkbook from her purse and asked the salesman, "What can you do for me?" It took about three seconds to get her credit rating approved. How free she'd felt buying the car, how American! Julie Peszko was right: this could *never* happen in the Soviet Union.

As they got in the car, Nora chanced to peer over at the speedometer. "Look!" she exclaimed. "1666!"

"Almost the devil's number," Malcolm said. "Maybe we should turn back."

"It's amazing how many numbers on the speedometer are meaningful. It's always saying 1492 or 1776 or someone's birthday."

"Maybe in the first year or two," Malcolm said. "When you get up to sixty, seventy thousand, out of the date range, the numbers tend to be less exciting."

"True."

They drove in silence, watching the world out the windows.

Several sites had been considered for the ceremony.

Malcolm had proposed the zoo: the zoo was quite nice, with many endearingly eccentric Victorian buildings, and both of them were fond of wild animals, if not housepets, but Nora had pointed out that the connotations of a Monkey House wedding were too facile, and anyhow, the rental fee (she'd checked) was over $1,000, a tad extravagant for six guests. They had dismissed all public buildings as being not quite in the spirit of things. The city offered parks, some with secluded paths near babbling brooks, but a natural setting didn't seem right for diehard city people; though they wanted some greenery and privacy, they didn't want anything *too* pastoral.

So they'd settled on a spot that, once they thought of it, seemed perfect: a wonderful gazebo in a park that wasn't used because it was in a slummy neighborhood, or actually not in a neighborhood at all—it was just an island in a park that had been desiccated by the construction of a major highway. To get to the park, you had to pass rows and rows of stately old houses now decaying, deserted, and condemned, their doors and windows boarded up.

Nora and Malcolm often drove out-of-town visitors past these streets. The houses were heartbreaking, the clearest indication of Philadelphia's failure. Once these houses had been the city's finest, but by the time the blacks moved in the rich had long since fled and no one wanted these places—far too mammoth to heat and, even by that point, too far gone to renovate. They were never torn down.

They slowed to look at the houses.

"Magnificent," Malcolm whispered.

Then he got mad.

He'd been on a rabid antimodernism kick since the Bulletin Building was destroyed. The idea was old hat, and that was the problem. Why *don't* they make 'em like they used to? Because everyone wanted to be *new* hat, but every sixteenth-century Parisian house, with its stucco slathered over stone, was preferable to a modern tract house. Aluminum siding was invented to look like overlapping wood shingles, which could be gorgeous, simple, even cheap. What was *wrong* with people?

"See that door?" Malcolm said, pointing. "See that cornice? A lousy $3,000 on a $300,000 construction job could give you that. Why don't—"

Nora made a megaphone with cupped hands, adding Taste Police siren noises. Malcolm put his hand on her knee.

She wasn't cutting him off. She knew his argument for creative re-use of existing architecture—the theory she called (because she was wedding-obsessed) "Old, New, Borrowed, Blue." Their dinner conversations had been filled with the economics and aesthetics of cities. It was as if they had finally attended to each other—that scrawny patch of roof-deck garden called a relationship—and could attend to the world.

Both of them were a little shaken, as always, by the sight of the decaying houses. They'd anticipated that, and even thought it might help a bit, to get them into the frame of mind that would push the ceremony past comical, provide a metaphorical backdrop for the notion of eternity.

After a while of staring, their windows rolled up and doors locked, they drove on, parked, and walked to the gazebo. Malcolm was carrying his camera: they needed *some* kind of evidence, Nora insisted, that their marriage had really happened, and Nora wanted a good picture, not one from the Polaroid she used to set up for food shoots.

They were the only people in the park. They sat down on a bench in the gazebo. Nora was shivering. Malcolm put his arm around her. The gazebo had a pleasant mossy smell, at least for a second, until they saw the empty beer bottles collecting in one corner and detected the scent of urine.

"Yuck," Nora said.

Malcolm assured her, "I looked before we sat down."

You could see the rows of houses from the gazebo. From this distance, if you squinted, you could almost manage to fuzz out the boarded-up windows, the collapsing fronts, and imagine the houses as they used to be.

"Well," Malcolm said, taking Nora's hand. "How do we do this?"

"I think we say some tender things."

"You first," Malcolm said.

"I love you," Nora said. "It took me a while to be sure of that, but I'm very sure of it now. I want to stay with you. Or should I say 'thee,' now that we've converted to Quakerism?"

"Thou too," Malcolm said.

Nora squeezed his hand, encouraging him to go on.

"I love you too," he added.

Nora told Malcolm that she thought he was a good person. She couldn't think of a single person in the world she'd rather grow old with—except maybe Sam Shepard.

"I thought this was supposed to be serious," Malcolm said.

"Right," Nora said. "Sorry. I really respect you, Mal, aesthetically and morally, not necessarily in that order."

He told her that she was a good person too, and he liked her mind and body and sense of humor, and he was very happy they had managed to stick everything out, and he hoped they continued to do so.

"You can't say 'hope,'" Nora said. "You have to say you're going to. That's the whole point."

"Okay. I'm going to. I want to."

"Me too," Nora said. "Well, can either of us think of anything we should say now or forever hold our peace?"

They thought about it. They couldn't.

From his black notebook, Malcolm withdrew the certificate they had obtained from the marriage bureau of City Hall, from one of the most depressing rooms in civilization: an ornate, high-ceilinged, beautifully proportioned room now stupidly partitioned and smelling like a men's room, with scuff marks on the walls, ancient plastic chairs, and brown shag carpeting studded with cigarette butts. "We hereby certify that on the _____ day of _____, one thousand nine hundred and _____, we united ourselves in marriage." They filled in the blanks, then took turns signing, each leaning carefully on the notebook.

Malcolm replaced the certificate in his notebook and took Nora's hand as he stared at the buildings, his deep-set eyes clicking off details. Nora loved his profile, the sharp angle his jaw made meeting his ear, the faintly receding line of his fine blond hair. His smell was familiar as her own, a sweet and dusty smell the color of rust, of exposed brick.

"This is ludicrous, I realize," Nora said, "but I feel all weepy inside. I think I'm going to cry."

"You don't want to lose a contact lens here."

"Do you have a tissue?"

He did. He handed it to her. She began to cry. "I guess you have to be the sobbing relatives too," he smiled. "Play all the parts," but then he just stroked her hair for a while, until she calmed down, until they both did—his own pulse was bonging like crazy.

"Well now," Malcolm said. "May I kiss the bride?"

They didn't stay in the park long. The gazebo stank, and it wasn't safe. Several cars full of threatening-looking people had slowed to stare. It was cold enough that they could see their breath. Malcolm was carrying a lot of cash, and he had the camera.

Not that it was much to steal. The camera was over twenty years old, inherited from his ex-girlfriend Beth, whose first husband had bought it for something like $15 on a hunting trip in Nairobi. The camera still had the address and telephone number of a Kenyan camera shop stuck to its base. Malcolm was exceedingly fond of the camera and his antiquated light meter, which had to be shaken several times hard upside down, like a thermometer, before it would operate. He was dreading the inevitable day when the camera would break and he'd have to adjust to one of those automatic numbers with endless bells and whistles. That day came sooner than he thought. In fact, the camera was already broken. The picture they took that afternoon would not come out.

The ruined picture was a pose they struck fairly often—something of an inside joke from their trip to Paris, when Nora had pointed out that they didn't have a single shot of the two of them together. She'd suggested they hand the camera to a tourist, but Malcolm had said that no human on earth besides him would ever be able to figure out how to use it. So he had just pressed his head against hers, held the camera at arm's length, and clicked the shutter. They were always laughing in these pictures, their too-close faces distorted, their blurred teeth long as fangs.

It would be months before they'd know the camera hadn't fired. In truth, both of them forgot all about the picture until Malcolm developed the roll. It also contained several shots from the Bulletin shooting session. All the pictures were overexposed. The lens wasn't shutting right. The Bulletin Building looked like a mythical tower swimming in sun. Their wedding picture was dimmer than the Shroud of Turin, but they kept it anyway. What was interesting was that they hadn't laughed, as they usually did, despite the familiar silliness of the pose. They'd just smiled, completely still.